THE
STONEHENGE
GATE

BOOKS BY JACK WILLIAMSON

The Legion of Space
*Darker Than You Think
The Green Girl
The Cometeers
One Against the Legion
Seetee Shock
Seetee Ship
Dragon's Island
The Legion of Time

The Undersea Trilogy (with Frederik Pohl)
Undersea Quest
Undersea Fleet
Undersea City

The Starchild Trilogy (with Frederik Pohl)
The Reefs of Space
Starchild

Rogue Star
Golden Blood
People Machines
The Trial of Terra
Dome Around America
The Reign of Wizardry
Bright New Universe
Trapped in Space
The Pandora Effect

Star Bridge (with James Gunn)
The Alien Intelligence
The Moon Children

H. G. Wells: Critic of Progress (nonfiction)

The Farthest Star (with Frederik Pohl)
The Early Williamson
The Power of Blackness
The Best of Jack Williamson
Brother to Demons, Brother to Gods
The Humanoids

The Birth of a New Republic (with Miles J. Breuer)
Manseed

Wall Around a Star (with Frederik Pohl)
The Queen of the Legion

Wonder's Child: My Life in Science Fiction (memoir)
Lifeburst
*Firechild

*Land's End (with Frederik Pohl)
Mazeway

The Singers of Time (with Frederik Pohl)
*Beachhead
*Demon Moon
*The Black Sun
*The Silicon Dagger
*Terraforming Earth
*The Stonehenge Gate

* A Tor Book

THE STONEHENGE GATE

JACK WILLIAMSON

TOR®

A TOM DOHERTY ASSOCIATES BOOK

New York

This is a work of fiction. All the characters and events portrayed in this novel are either fictitious or are used fictitiously.

THE STONEHENGE GATE

Copyright © 2005 by Jack Williamson

Edited by James Frenkel

A Tor Book
Published by Tom Doherty Associates, LLC
175 Fifth Avenue
New York, NY 10010

Tor® is a registered trademark of Tom Doherty Associates, LLC.

ISBN 0-765-30897-5

Printed in the United States of America

To
Mike Resnick, Fred Pohl, Connie Willis, Larry Niven,
David Hartwell, Stanley Schmidt, Melinda Snodgrass,
Eleanor Wood, Jack Chalker, Jim Frenkel,
Scott Edelman, Jack Speer, Michael Swanwick

My friends on that wonderful panel
at the 2004 Worldcon in Boston

And to Bob Faw, who taped it

THE
STONEHENGE
GATE

CHAPTER 1

We called ourselves the Four Horsemen, though Lupe was a woman and none of us owned a horse. We were friends and good companions. After classes on Friday we used to gather at my place for a potluck dinner and a few hands of low-limit poker.

Derek Ironcraft taught physics and astronomy. A wiry little man with keen gray eyes and sandy hair he kept too short to comb, he wore rumpled khakis to his classes and called himself an apprentice cosmologist. He spent his summer vacations as a NASA research intern and liked to surprise us with the wonders of space. Our weekly game was over that night, early in the fall semester, but we still sat around the table sipping the last of our bourbon and water. He opened his briefcase to show us his latest enigma.

"We were scanning the Sahara with ground penetration radar." He spread his papers and a satellite atlas on the table. "Dry sand is pretty transparent to it, and the sand there's as dry as it gets. We got good images of old river beds and an impact crater where something big hit the Earth a few million years ago."

He pointed to a hazy blot.

"Looking for another crater, I found this: a circle of huge stones under a dozen meters of sand. It looks like an older Stonehenge, larger than the one on the Salisbury plain." He looked at Lupe. "I think it must be artificial."

"Man-made?" Her black eyebrows arched. "I don't know what the Sahara was like when your meteor fell, but I know it now. Your ring of rocks may look odd, but nothing intelligent ever set them up and no hominid ever saw them."

She likes to puncture false assumptions, but that time she was wrong.

That was how it all began. Eastern New Mexico University is a small college in a quiet little town. We were still at home there, enjoying one another, finding adventure enough in our work and the campus feuds and those poker dinners.

Lupe used to come with *chili verdi* stew or a pot of *posole* or *menuda*. Derek brought good Kentucky bourbon. Ram brought Indian curry, the kind his father had peddled from a cart on the street in Mombasa. A shrewd player, he sent most of his winnings back to hungry relatives in Kenya.

Lupe had come to Portales to search for bones of the first Americans at the Blackwater site, where the first Clovis points were found. She and I were most of a generation older than Ram and Derek, but she was still a lively little woman, restless as a sparrow.

She must have been a beauty once. Her fine-boned face still has a lean grace, but years of field work in Yucatan and along the Great Rift of East Africa had turned her skin to tawny leather. She wore faded blue denims and a floppy field hat and spoke with a free vocabulary.

"I can do most things better than most men can," I heard her say, "except screw another woman."

I'm Will Stone. I teach English lit.

Ram was the stranger among us. A fine physical specimen, he was six feet tall and black as night, except for an odd little birthmark on his forehead. Eclectic in attire, he wore Western hats and boots, with colorful African shirts. He carried the genes of a half-dozen races. He called himself Kikuyu, but he was named for a grandfather who had left the Punjab to avoid religious strife. He said he had a drop of Portuguese blood, and a drop of Dutch. One great-grandmother was a mystery he had never solved.

Lupe had found him shoveling sand at her Koobi Fora dig and brought him to the university on an athletic scholarship. He went on for a linguistics degree at Yale and came back to teach linguistics and African history. Derek and I had never been to Africa.

That poker night seems an age ago when I look back now, but it's still as real as today in my memory. We all leaned over the radar image. To me it was only a hazy blur, but Derek and Lupe were lost in a hot debate.

"You think it's artificial? You think a human culture existed there before the Sahara was a desert? A culture that early, high enough to anticipate Stonehenge? I don't think so."

"Climates change," he told her. "The Sahara has been wet as well as dry. Haven't you heard of Farouk El-Baz? He did the pioneer research. Using penetration radar, he traced the beds of rivers that ran maybe five or six thousand years ago. People could have lived there."

"Maybe." She shrugged. "But five thousand years ago? The

Neolithic hunter-gatherers had begun to settle down and farm
along the Nile. In the Middle East. Maybe in China. But they
weren't hauling big rocks out of nowhere."

Ram leaned to frown at the radar map. After a moment, he
looked at Derek with a baffled shrug.

"Look at this." Derek pointed. "See this half circle of stones?
They're in a hollow where the prevailing wind has scoured the
sand out to build this dune. See how they dim toward the end
of the arc? That's because they're deeper down. I think the circle is complete, the rest of it buried too deep to see. Maybe half
a mile across."

He looked up at Lupe.

"Dr. Vargas, what is your opinion?"

She blinked at him.

"Dr. Ironcraft, you've already heard it." She mocked his formal tone. "I think you're suddenly *poco loco.* If you've really
found anything like Stonehenge, you'd be rewriting prehistory
and wrecking a hundred careers. Archeology from space is a
field I know nothing about, but I've seen coincidence play a lot
of tricks. I'm afraid you're trying to make a very long leap from
pretty flimsy evidence. Your rock formation does look remarkable, but I'd want to know who put it there. And when."

His elation dimmed, but only for a moment.

"How could it be natural? The stones are big. They all look
about the same size. They're spaced the same distance apart.
Radar's not as sharp as visible light, but I got a better image of
these." He pointed again. "Two taller megaliths, standing at
what would be the center of the circle. It's all too symmetric to
be any sort of natural formation."

She bent to squint at the image and shook her head.

"I've been over most of Africa, looking at the traces of early
man. Hominids did evolve there, and spread into Asia. We've

found traces over most of the continent, but none I've heard of there under the sand. The Phoenicians and Greeks never got far from the coast. Even Alexander never got beyond the temple of Amon, where he got himself made a god." She shook her head. "The Sahara has been forbidden territory."

"I'd love to see the spot, if I knew how to get there."

"I like you, Derek." Her tone was very serious. "You're a great teacher. You can run a wicked bluff when you don't hold the cards. But please don't go public with the hand you've showed us tonight. Not if you want any respect in your field. Science is a cutthroat game. It's too easy to play the fool."

"Could be I am."

He sighed and folded the map, but Ram wanted to study the image again.

"Why not take a look?"

"Here's why I can't." He opened the satellite atlas and jabbed his finger at a wide white spot that reached into three nations on a map of North Africa. "The Great Erg Oriental. The greatest sand desert on earth. Probably the most hostile spot outside of Antarctica. I doubt if that site has ever been visited, not since the sand covered it up."

Ram reached for the atlas and found the map again.

"My great-grandmother came from somewhere close to there."

His lean dark forefinger traced a path on the map, out of the desert and west along the coast from near the site of ancient Carthage, past Gibraltar, down around the Sahara, and back east through the Sahel to Kenya. He had never said much about himself, and we pushed the books aside to listen.

"My father called her Little Mama." His eyes had lit as he remembered. "A strange little woman, with no name I ever knew. She lived with us in Mombasa and took care of me after my mother died. Later, when I was only seven or eight, I tried to care for her."

Old emotion warmed his voice.

"My mother's aunt accused her of *uchawi*, witchcraft. My father thought she was crazy. Maybe she was, but I loved her. And she—she loved me."

His voice quivered and he wiped at a tear.

"I knew she was dying. Of old age, I guess. She was toothless and nearly blind, wasting away to nothing. All she could eat was a little thin mealy gruel. She didn't talk much, even to me. We spoke Swahili, but she said it wasn't her language. It had no words, she said, for what she wanted to say.

"Close as we were, I never really knew her. I know there were things she never said. Something had hurt her while she was young. Hurt her so terribly that she couldn't bear to talk or even think about it. I don't think she was African."

He paused to study Lupe.

"She had a nose like yours. Her hair was just as straight, though thin and very white by then. She had this birthmark."

He touched his forehead and turned his head for us to see the mark. A tiny thing, it was a sort of negative freckle, a pale spot in the dark pigmentation. It was a neat little rectangle with seven white dots in an arc above it.

"My father had it, and it came down to me."

"A hereditary birthmark?" Lupe frowned. "That's odd."

"Little Mama was as odd as they come. I never knew what to make of her story. She wanted nothing to do with Christian missionaries, but she was terrified of metal devils. She said they snatched her out of her village and tortured her in a white metal cage. She said she stole the key to hell and got away through a gate in the temple of bones."

He shrugged at Lupe and turned to Derek.

"The temple of bones?" He shook his head. "What she meant I can't imagine, but it could put her somewhere near your buried Stonehenge. She said she was still a girl when the Tauregs had caught her in the desert. I don't know when, but she'd seen the Lebel rifles they took from the French army soldiers they slaughtered at Ain Yacoub in 1928.

"They traded her to the Bela, who sold her to the Dogon, down in Mali at the edge of the Sahel. Somehow she got to Kenya. She was one tough little cookie, but there were things she wouldn't speak about. She was afraid to sleep alone. Toward the end she wanted me with her in the room day and night.

"My father tried to tell her that the Tauregs and the Dogons were a lifetime behind her and thousands of miles away. That didn't help. She'd spent her life in terror, but she never really said what she feared. Maybe she thought we'd laugh at her. Maybe because she thought we wouldn't believe or understand. My father kept at her till she told him about the metal devils and the temple of bones. He thought she was crazy, but at the end she gave me what she said was the key to hell.

"That was all she ever said, except once when she had a malaria fever. I heard her raving about *adui*, 'the enemy.' About *mababa*, 'our ancestors.' Something about *mfalme*, 'the king.' About 'god-folk' and the 'god-mark' and the 'god-blood.' Nothing that made any sense. I asked her about it when she got better. She shivered and said she must have been dreaming, but she gave me this the night she died."

He snapped a thin silver chain off his neck.

"She was light as a feather when I held her in my arms. Too weak to tell me much about it."

He gulped and wiped his eyes again, and passed the chain around to let us see the pendant on it. About the size of an American quarter-dollar, it had the look of polished emerald.

Derek laid it on the table and set a pocket lens over it to let us see it clearly. One face had the image of a gate in a wall, two square pillars with a lintel block across the top. The chain ran through the gate.

Lupe took her turn at the lens and looked a little dazed.

"Ancient," she said. "Anything recent would have an arch instead of the lintel stone."

Derek turned it over. The other face had a line of sharply cut characters below the hole. Above it was the image of a crown with seven points above the band, each point tipped with a tiny circle. Lupe bent close to study it through the lens and looked up to squint at Ram's face.

"Your birthmark!" she whispered. "What does that mean?"

"You tell me." He shrugged. "Little Mama said we were marked. She said it was why she had to get away, before the demons killed her. She couldn't read the inscriptions. She called the mark 'the crown of worlds.' My father thought her whole story was a *uchawi* hoax she'd invented. I'd like to know."

He shook his head and hung the chain back around his neck.

"She told me to keep it, because the road to heaven runs through the gate to hell. I don't know what she meant. It stumped a jeweler when I showed it to him. He said it isn't emerald, but something he'd never seen. Hard as diamond. He wanted to send it off for evaluation, but he seemed so eager that I thought I'd never get it back."

"If she came through that gate—"

With a new enthusiasm, Derek opened his folder and spread the radar image on the table.

"If you look, you can make out a shadow beside those two taller pillars." He set the lens over them. "So deep under the sand that it's hardly visible, but it has a rectangular outline. Could it have been the lintel stone before a quake knocked it off?"

Eagerly, Ram bent over the lens.

"I see it!" he whispered. "It really was a gate!"

"I'd like to know." Derek looked around at us. "If we could look. I've located that dune on a Landsat visual image. There's a faint black fleck in the hollow. It could be the top of those columns, sticking out of the sand."

"If there's a chance—" Ram caught his breath. "I want to get there, for Little Mama's sake!"

We met every Friday evening through that fall semester, poring over Derek's maps and images, searching the Internet for facts about the Sahara, talking to travel agents, and playing very little poker. Still unconvinced, Lupe brought monographs on hominid evolution.

"They were growing bigger brains and learning to chip flints," she said, "but I don't think they were hiding megaliths under the Sahara."

Ram and Derek longed for a look.

"I'd go in half a minute," Ram said, "if I had the money."

Derek got Ram to let him micrograph the pendant and make spectrographic tests. Not emerald at all, it was nearly pure silicon, with traces of nickel, platinum, and copper. With no trace of iron, it was still strongly magnetic. The chain looked silver, but it was something stronger than steel.

Lupe sent the micrographs to scholars who knew cuneiform, Egyptian and Mayan hieroglyphs, and a dozen other early forms of writing. Nobody could read them.

"You're barking up the wrong tree." She lectured us as if she had us in the classroom. "I know of just one stray australo-pithecine fossil found in the Sahara. If they were building anything, it was certainly no Stonehenge. Homo sapiens did appear in Africa something over a hundred thousand years ago. By the last ice age, the Cro-Magnon artists were painting their sacred caves in Spain and France, but I can't imagine any high culture buried under the erg."

The travel agents found pilots who had flown over the Sahara, but nobody wanted to take us to Derek's site or anywhere near it. The caravan routes had always avoided the ergs. Any motor vehicle able to negotiate the dunes would cost more than we could raise. No plane could land us in the erg or take us out again. Any accident that didn't kill us would leave us stranded beyond hope of rescue.

Yet we kept on dreaming. One evening Lupe came early with enchiladas and a pitcher of margaritas. When the enchiladas were gone and the table cleared, she made Derek get out his maps and find his satellite images of the Oriental.

"If you're still determined, I'm no dog in the manger." She offered to refill the margaritas. "Radar research is out of my field, but Derek's half-circle of stones could be worth a look. Ram's pendant is still a riddle. The odds look terrible, but if we don't take chances we'll never win a pot."

"So you'll go?"

"Just for a quick look." She shrugged. "If we can get there. If we do find something worth a dig, which would amaze me, we can try to get back next summer with a bigger grant and a larger crew."

Before Thanksgiving, we'd agreed to spend the Christmas break in the Sahara. Lupe had grant funds she could tap. Derek sold his car. I got a loan on the house to stake Ram and myself.

The day after fall commencement we took off for Tunis by

way of Dallas, Heathrow, and Rome. Groggy from too many hours in the air, we landed at the Djerba international airport. Ram was fluent in Arabic and good enough in French.

We spent three days with travel agents eager to show us everything. The medina, which was a cultural heritage of great historic interest. The gold souk, built in the seventeenth century. The Great Mosque Ez-Zitouna, begun by the Umayyad rulers in 732 and finished by the Aghlabites in 864. The Souk el Attarine, which specialized in perfumes.

Some guests wished to see the site of ancient Carthage. If we were really anxious to rough it, a safari might be arranged to take us south as far as the Roman ruins at the edge of the desert, but not to the erg. It held nothing of interest. No ruins of any antiquity. Nothing alive. Nothing to film. Prudent men avoided it. Dust storms could be sudden, blinding, suffocating. Reckless adventurers had died there.

On the third day Ram found a helicopter for charter. The pilot was an Algerian who had learned to fly in the French air force. He had a global positioning satellite system that could guide us anywhere we wanted. Ram bargained for a charter, paying a fortune in advance, with another left in escrow till he got us back to Tunis.

Rain delayed us another day, but at last we got off with our gear aboard and flew south over the mountains. We stopped for fuel at Gabès, an oasis town near the coast. Beyond it, green vegetation gave way to an endless sea of bare brown dunes, empty of everything, as strange and lifeless as the moon.

Derek watched the GPS and studied his satellite images until at last he stopped the pilot over the giant dune that he said was our destination. To me it looked exactly like a thousand others. He kept us a long time over it, fussing with the GPS locator.

At last the pilot set us down with our gear and a dozen big

cans of water on the floor of the wind-carved cup in the lee of the dune. Even through dark glasses, the sun on the sand was blinding, the heat suffocating. The pilot took off at once, leaving us standing alone in the wind of his blades.

Squinting into the sun and rubbing the dust out of my eyes, I watched him climb. My colleagues seemed elated. Ignoring the parching heat, they pitched a little tent and stretched the fly to make a tiny scrap of shade. Sweating under that merciless sun, I felt suddenly lost, too far from the old brown brick my grandfather built on First Street, the house where my mother was born and I grew up. I said nothing, but I couldn't help a pang of regret, a moment of sick longing for the quiet security of college life and all the activities of the new semester, soon to begin.

We had a radio. The pilot had promised to return and pick us up three days later, unless we called earlier, yet I felt a stab of cold unease. What if he forgot? The others were more confident. Squatting there, they opened the box lunches we had brought from the hotel.

Derek unrolled one of his images. He said his circle of buried stones should be just north of us, under the edge of the dune. Winds had blown away the sand where we landed down to hard brown clay. Lupe walked out across it, kicked at something, and went back to our gear for a spade and a trowel. Ram helped her dig, till she stood up to show us an odd brown stick.

"Bones!" she cried. "We're down in a dry lake bed or an old water hole. Something I never expected. Maybe worth the trip itself, if we happen on a trace of any hominid."

Derek wanted to get to his radar site, but the bones came first for her. She gave us a quick lesson in fieldwork and we spent the rest of the afternoon there. She identified an antelope horn, the skull of a giraffe, and what she thought was a warthog's jaw.

"But not a shard of pottery." She shrugged an apology at Derek. "Not a stone that might have been a tool."

Derek was fretting to move on, but suddenly she was prying out something else. A slender sliver of some glassy stuff that had a pale yellow color under the flakes of clay. She scraped them off and dug again. We were there another hour. She found another sliver, and another, till she had a dozen. We helped her clean them and fit some of them together.

"Another horn?" Ram asked her. "Or what sort of thing would have bones like that?"

"No horn." She wiped at the dust on her forehead. "But these were really bones." She lifted two yellow fragments. "The ball and socket of a joint. See how they fit. But the odd thing—" She bent to frown at them. "They're brittle, but something harder than calcium. Maybe silicon. They aren't the bones of anything I know. And these."

She picked up one of those yellow splinters and raised her dark glasses to squint at it.

"They look like shells. Too badly shattered for any reconstruction. They look like the exoskeleton of an insect, but too big to come from any insect I know. It looks worth another dig, if we can get a grant for it."

We carried the little pile of fragments back to the tent, gulped precious water, and plodded out again across the sandbank north of us. Derek kept peering at his radar image. He stopped us where he said his arc of buried stones must be. All we saw was the wind-rippled sand, but suddenly he was shading his eyes to look farther on.

"Those rocks! Let's see what they are."

They were huge, jutting five or six feet out of the sand. He had us stop for photos, and rushed us on to see them close.

They were identical: two square columns of smooth black stone, some ten feet square and spaced twice as far apart.

"They're the center stones I found on the visual image." Derek squinted again at his radar map. "They stand on bedrock, under the sand. See that shadow? I think it's the lintel stone that lay across the top to frame the gate."

"Gate to where?" Lupe asked.

"To hell." Ram shrugged. "If you remember my Little Mama. My father never believed her tales, but I did when I heard them. What kind of hell I don't think she knew. She was certainly terrified of whatever she thought might follow her through the gate."

"No matter what she meant," Lupe said, "I've never seen any prehistoric stonework to match it. It should certainly get us a grant."

Derek was already tramping on to study the nearest stone. It was an odd black granite, veined with thin green streaks, perfectly squared, polished slick. He rubbed it with his finger and blinked at Lupe.

"What do you think?"

"It's impossible." She looked dazed. "I'm no geologist, but I never saw stone like this. It certainly wasn't quarried anywhere near. No culture so old ever worked stone so well."

Derek started on around the column, searching for inscriptions. Ram followed. Only a step or two behind him, I stopped to look at an odd green mark that might have been a character in some unfamiliar script. I heard him gasp. When I turned back, he was gone.

"Ram!" Lupe was calling. "Ram?"

We heard no answer. We ran on around the column, then around the other. We scattered out to search the sand around us and found no footprints, no sign of him or where he had gone. We were gathering again in the shadow of the column when he came staggering back out of nowhere and fell on his face right beside me.

We dropped to our knees around him. He wasn't breathing. His skin was blue, that tiny birthmark starkly white. His hand felt limp and lifeless when I caught it. We turned him over. I'd brought a canteen. Lupe wet her bandana and wiped the sand off his mouth and nostrils. His eyes looked glassy when she opened them. She took his pulse.

"He's alive," she whispered. "Just barely."

His chest moved. He gasped for air, coughed, and tried to sit up. We lifted him to sit against the pillar. Lupe put the canteen to his lips. He gulped, strangled, and sat there breathing hard, his eyes closed again. It must have been an hour before he roused himself to look at us.

"Something—something happened. I don't know what."

His voice was a labored wheeze, and he had another fit of coughing before he found the breath to go on.

"The sand crumbled under me. I slid down into a dark place—I don't know where. The fall knocked my breath out. I couldn't get it back. The air—the air hurt my lungs like burning sulfur. I had to climb back up the rubble slope. Nearly—nearly passed out before I made it."

He wanted water. Lupe offered the canteen. It shook in his hands till she took it and held it to his mouth. He took a few swallows, coughed, and gave her a feeble smile.

"What was the place?" she asked him. "What did you see?"

"Not—not much." He had another fit of coughing. "It was too dark. The fumes burned my eyes. The sky—a dim red sky. Like low clouds with fire behind them. I remember great square columns standing all around me. Every pair had a lintel block across the top."

"Trilithons?" she whispered. "Like Stonehenge?"

"Like gates." He nodded and stopped for another long breath. "Like this one." He touched the pendant under his thin tee shirt. "I never saw Stonehenge, but I think this circle was bigger. A lot bigger. Seven gates, all of them open. Nothing but red sky and dark rock behind them."

He wheezed and had to cough again.

"These two stones—" He lifted his hand toward the other column and looked up at Derek. "I saw the lintel stone you found under the sand." He was gasping again. "It was back— back across them at the top."

His eyes were inflamed and tearing. He wiped at them and lay back against the column. Lupe gave him a few minutes to rest.

"Was that all?" she asked. "Can't you recall anything else?"

"Not really." He caught a long breath and blinked at her. "It took forever to get back here. That was all I thought about. I do remember a pop in my ears, like you get when a plane makes a quick change of altitude. And something like the feel you get when a fast elevator starts up. But nothing about it makes any sense."

"Or maybe it does." Eyes narrowed, Derek gazed out across the dune. "If what you felt was real—"

"It was real. Too real! It nearly killed me."

"I wonder," Derek whispered. "Could you have been some- where off the Earth? I never believed any possible spacecraft could ever cross the distances between the stars, but that change in air pressure and gravity—"

Awe hushed his voice.

"Maybe somebody found another way across space."

"What way?" Lupe stared at him. "What way is possible?"

"The math of space and time has been a sort of quicksand since Einstein and the others found limits to Newton's laws. There are theories of wormholes between the stars, but no proof they are possible. Maybe, just maybe, we're on the brink of finding out."

"He was gone." Lupe nodded slowly. "He was almost asphyxiated. But what does that have to do with the stars?"

"I want to know." Derek stopped to peer at the two great stones and the dunes beyond them. "I want to know what this is. Who was here. What they did. Why they went away."

"I don't care." Ram shivered. "It's an ugly place. I've had nightmares, but nothing like it. We've got no business here."

CHAPTER
3

I felt a sudden chill in the air when the sun went down. Ram felt able to walk with us back to the tent, refusing any help. Lupe wanted a campfire, but there was nothing to burn. In the pale glow of an electric lantern, we ate a cold meal out of cartons and cans, and debated what to do next.

"We'd better keep quiet about what happened to Ram," Lupe said. "What with the bones and photos of the megaliths themselves, there's enough we can carry back to get another grant. We can be back next summer with an expedition to write ourselves into history."

"Next summer?" Derek shook his head. "I don't want to wait. This thing's too big to leave alone."

"There is more we can do right now." She nodded. "Dig for more bones. And those silicon splinters. I wonder what they are."

She stared off into the dark.

"Whatever you find, don't publish too much." Ram shook his head at her. "Not if you want to come back. You could lose the site."

"Huh?" Derek blinked.

"Jealous bureaucrats. Frontiers here aren't marked on the sand. If the site's anything important, two or three nations will be clamoring to claim it as a national treasure. You'll be frozen out of the game."

"Which means we've got to learn more while we can." He turned to stare at Ram. "I've been thinking. You were somewhere. You felt that different gravity and air pressure. I think you were off the Earth. I don't know why this place was built, but there had to be a reason."

Lupe frowned at him.

"If those pillars framed some sort of gate, I want to get through it."

"Through it?" She looked blank. "How? I've walked all around both stones. So did you. Where's any gate?"

"I wonder." Derek looked toward the megaliths, lost now in the dark. "Ram was wearing his pendant. His Little Mama called it a key. We found magnetism in it. Could be it trips some kind of lock."

"The key to hell." Ram shook his head. "That's what she called it. I didn't see Satan or anything alive, but that place did have the look and sulfur stink of hell." He shivered. "You can't breathe there."

"You know—" Derek sat straighter. "We'd have to get oxygen equipment, but we can try to find out if it really is a key to anywhere. Let's call the chopper back."

"Oxygen equipment?" Ram shook his head, his dark features grim. "If you'd been there, you wouldn't be so keen about it."

I'd tried to smooth the sand under my sleeping bag, but I never found a good fit for my body. With too much to think about, I hardly slept. Up before the sun, Ram made coffee and pancakes on a propane stove while Lupe labeled her collected bones and sealed them in plastic bags. When we called the chopper pilot, Ram wanted to get out with him.

"It's a place where we don't belong." He stared across the sand at the two great megaliths, still dark in the shadow of the dune and ominous even to me. "I don't like it here."

"It's your chance to learn who your Little Mama was," Lupe told him. "If she really got here through some kind of gate." She peered at his birthmark. "Maybe your chance to learn who you are."

He rubbed at the mark and shook his head.

"It might be better if I never know."

Yet he agreed to stay and help her at the dig while Derek and I went out to Tunis. I'd spent a year in Paris, writing a novel that never sold, before I came back home to teach English lit. With my little French and his little English, the pilot and I got on well enough. Content to assume that the megaliths were Greek or Roman, he was baffled by our interest in them. I don't think he liked the erg any better than Ram did, but the tourist season had been slow. He wanted our money.

We left Lupe and Ram at work at the dig, dwindling figures beside our tiny tent, soon lost in the sand's blinding glare. The infinite sea of star dunes caught me again with an uneasy fascination. I felt relieved to escape it, even for a day.

The engine noise made conversation difficult, but we had time to think.

"Beautiful, isn't it?" Derek raised his voice and gestured at the intricate pattern of waves on the tawny ocean of sand below, wind-carved cup and wind-piled point, wind-carved cup and wind-piled point, repeated forever. Empty of life or motion, the erg seemed as strange to me as the alien landscape Ram had glimpsed beyond the megaliths.

"Just wind and sand." He was silent for a time, gazing through the window, and turned slowly back to me, smiling with what must have been a sort of rapture. "But look at the shape of the dunes. An infinite order born out of chaos. It's a kind of natural art, if you can see it. A harmony of nature, as unexpected but yet as complete as the movements of a symphony."

He paused to peer at me.

"Don't you get it? The grand enigma of our universe. The joy of science, the power of math, the elation of discovery." He looked out again, speaking half to himself, yet eager to share what he felt. "That's the mystery of the natural creation. Galaxies and planets, life and mind grown from the fire and dust of the big bang. That's the enchantment of science. New vistas of wonder exploding out of every advance."

I tried to get it, but the dunes seemed more cruel than beautiful. I felt stunned by too much wonder, glad to get out of the erg and back across the mountains, cheered to see roads again and a freight train crawling around a curve, the green circles and squares of irrigated farms. Here were things men had made, things I thought I understood.

The pilot stopped at Gabès to have a mechanic check something about the engine. Dusk had fallen before we got back to our hotel. Washed free of sweat and sand, we went out for dinner. Derek found an Internet café and spent an hour on a computer.

Standing behind him, I watched math symbols flicker across the screen and glimpsed articles about dark matter and dark energy, about negative mass and negative time, about a false vacuum that might generate an infinite foam of universes. None of it meant anything to me or seemed to satisfy him.

"Nothing." At last he shrugged and quit. "If what happened

to Ram is what I think it might be, most of what we think we know will all have to be rewritten."

Next morning we met the pilot at an Italian bank. Derek released the escrow to give him the balance of his fee and bargained to renew our charter. We found a supply house and I used my own credit card to buy oxygen systems. Four thirty-five-liter units, complete with masks, cylinders, regulators, gauges, tubing, and smoke hoods.

Noon had passed before we got back across the dunes to the camp. We found Ram waiting alone beside the tent. In haste to get out before dark, the pilot dumped our crates and took off at once. I saw nothing of Lupe. When Derek asked where she was, Ram shook his head in a dazed way.

"I don't know." He stared blankly across the sand at the black megaliths, his features drawn tight. "I don't know."

Derek led him out of the sun, back into the shadow of the tent flap. I gave him a cold beer we'd brought from Gabès. Squatting on the sand, he gulped a few swallows, set the bottle down, and rubbed absently at that odd little birthmark on his forehead.

"It itches," he muttered, "since I went through."

"Tell us," Derek urged him, "what became of her."

"This morning." Peering anxiously back at the megaliths, he spoke in abrupt and disjointed phrases. "Early. We'd had breakfast. She was already down at the dig. I walked out of sight over the ridge to relieve myself. I heard her yell. Pulled my pants up. Ran back. Saw them coming."

His head jerked toward the megaliths. His hoarse voice stopped and he stared toward them till Derek asked him to go on.

"Three." He was almost whispering. "Three monsters. Gigantic. Jumping. She tried to run. They jumped too fast."

"Monsters? What were they like?"

"Nothing on earth." He shivered and stared at the megaliths, his lean forefinger on the birthmark. "Maybe like insects. Maybe like grasshoppers, if grasshoppers could be as big as airplanes. Not much like anything. They were hideous. Splotched yellow and green. Shiny like glass. Great red eyes that blazed like fire. Long hind legs. Short front limbs with claws."

He shuddered again.

"Terrible claws. All bright metal the color of silver. Great metal jaws. And the things had wings. Stubby little wings that seemed too short. Spread when they glided. They came too fast for me. Nothing I could do."

His shoulders sagged in helpless regret.

"One of them took her. Snatched her up with those bright claws. It was gone with her before I got back to the tent. It carried her back to the monuments. Crawled between them. Never came out. Took her back to the hell where I was."

He wiped at his eyes.

"No air there. No air she can breathe. I'm afraid she's dead."

"Maybe not." Derek caught his arm. "We brought the oxygen gear. We can go after her. Try to find where she is and help her if we can. If your key can take us through."

He cringed again.

"Of course." He picked up the beer and got stiffly to his feet. "If we can."

He stood a moment staring blankly down at the old water hole.

"If we can," he muttered again, and shook his head. "If she's alive." He shivered. "I—I loved her. She found me shoveling

dirt at Koobi Fora. She helped get me to college on the track
scholarship. She brought me back to Africa to work with her
on two more summer digs. She—well, she gave me a life."

He turned his head to hide his tears.

The western sun was already low, and the day had been ex-
hausting. We could have rested and prepared for an early morning start, but nobody spoke of that. We uncrated three of the
oxygen units and found the manuals. Printed in French and
Arabic, they were brief and cryptic, but Ram deciphered them.
We got the units assembled and tried them on. The smoke
hoods had a sharp plastic stink and made vision difficult.

"No matter." Derek's muffled voice was hard to hear. "Not if
they keep us alive."

Ram asked how long the oxygen would last.

"Depends on demand," Derek told him. "I hope it's long
enough."

"To overtake those hopping things?" Ram took off the hood,
wiped sweat off his forehead, shook his head. "We'll never find
Lupe alive. Not in the place where I was."

"We can look," Derek said. "If those trilithons are terminal
gates—" His voice trailed off, but he caught his breath and
went on. "We'll go where we can. Learn what we can. Help
Lupe if we can. Let's get on with it."

I longed for the comfort of a weapon, but airport security
had forbidden knives or guns. We went empty-handed, but the
oxygen cylinders themselves made heavy burdens. We wore
canteens of water clipped to our belts. I had a light backpack
stuffed with a flashlight, spare batteries, a jacket, and not
much else.

We ate a quick meal and set out for the megaliths. Ram led

the way, grimly silent under the smoke hood. I plodded after him, sweating, half sick from the stink of the smoke hood, thinking wistfully of spring registration, only two weeks away.

Derek was exuberant.

"Don't count the odds. Win or lose, this is the greatest game men ever played."

Ram went ahead, eyes on the hoppers' footprints. They looked like the tracks of gigantic two-toed birds, pressed deep into the sand and spaced perhaps forty yards apart. He stopped us near the megaliths, pushed ahead to inspect the sand around them.

"The things came out on the west side," he said. "Went back on the east. No tracks go anywhere else. They did take her through."

He stood between us at the end of the hopper trail, the setting sun a blinding glare on our goggles. My heart was pounding. He seized my arm.

"*Moja.*" He'd been giving us Swahili lessons. Huskily, he whispered the numbers. "*Mbili. Tatu.*"

He gripped my arm so hard it hurt.

"*Nenda!* Go!"

We stepped forward together. The sun was gone. My ears clicked. The sand crumbled under me. The sudden surge of gravity dragged me down into darkness.

CHAPTER 4

For a few seconds the darkness was total. Feet first, I slid down a rubble slope that melted under me. Light came back, a dull red gloom. I came down hard on flat stone. Ram let go my arm. Under the weight of the oxygen cylinders I staggered for balance and tried to get my breath. I felt nauseated with the smoke hood's plastic reek.

"*Wapi?*" Ram gasped. "Where are we?"

I turned to look back. The two great megaliths stood where they had been. Or were they really still the same? Giddy for a moment, I wondered. They were far taller, the sand gone from around them. The fallen lintel stone lay back in place. Beyond them, sand dunes and sunlight had vanished. Instead, I saw a dark creation of fire and violence. Flame red clouds hung low over dead black lavas.

We three huddled close together, shut in by the seven great trilithons. Towering all around us, they felt like the walls of a nightmare prison. The lavas beyond were a black-fanged desert, flows of it frozen on older flows, twisted into monstrous gouts, cut with bottomless crevasses. Great boulders were scattered across it, and shattered ejecta from volcanic explosions. Jagged mountains in the distance rose into a roof of fire-colored cloud.

I felt wrenched with a sick distress for Lupe when I tried to imagine what she must have felt when that nightmare thing snatched her out of the dig. Dazed by the shock of it, I longed for the campus, the classroom—for anything familiar. All I saw was Little Mama's hell. Derek stood a long time scanning it, and finally raised the little camera slung from his neck.

"It's not the Sahara." Cooler than I was, he spoke as if dictating research notes. "A waterless world. No river channels. No sign of water erosion." He snapped a picture and looked at Ram. "A wonder you got out. The atmosphere is likely nitrogen, maybe mixed with carbon dioxide and sulfur gases. Can't guess what the clouds are, but they don't make rain."

He frowned again at that dark wilderness and turned to me.

"Without water there's no green life. No photosynthesis to liberate free oxygen. If this is really the sort of interworld terminal I think it must be, the site may have been selected to make a trap for trespassers. Nobody gets through without the right gear."

"A lot have failed."

Ram was pointing across the thick dark dust on the floor inside the trilithons. I saw the white gleam of a human skull. He kicked at a ridge and stooped to pick up the long horn of an oryx. Stirring the dust with that, he uncovered bones. An impala's skull with the graceful horns still attached, the skeleton of what he said had been a dog or wolf, the remains of something larger, perhaps a lion.

"We need Lupe with us."

He picked up the human skull.

"She would know, but this must be Cro-Magnon. An unlucky guy that fell into the trap maybe thirty thousand years ago."

Careful with it, he laid it back in the dust. Derek pushed ahead to find another skull that Ram said was Neanderthal, and then a third that looked more modern. Ram dug into the dust around it and uncovered a bit of flint that he studied under the lenses of his smoke hood.

"A Clovis point!" His head shook under the smoke hood. "Like those from our own Blackwater dig. It's the right length for a spear point. Double-edged. Fluted from the base to hold the haft. Beautiful work!"

He held it for us to see.

"Clovis?" Derek was incredulous. "How did it get here?"

"Lupe would die to know. She'd wonder if the first Americans came through here."

"That's hard to believe." Derek peered at it. "It's a far hop from here to Alaska."

"A farther hop back to New Mexico." Ram stood a moment gazing around us at the great trilithons and the dark desolation beyond them. His voice fell. "If we do get back."

We walked on, till Ram stopped to look at a long pile of older, stranger bones, buried under a thicker blanket of dust. Rib cages, backbones, leg bones, most of them puzzling even to him. Empty eye sockets mocked us from a sharp-crested skull the size of a car. A white thighbone was four feet long.

I felt chilled with a sense of the trilithons as a vast temple of death, dead and abandoned for many millennia. Could Lupe's kidnappers be its custodians, somehow here to haunt it? Shivering from too many of those cold unknowns, I longed for the little riddles of Shakespeare's life, for Christopher Marlowe, Boswell and Dr. Johnson, even the dull toil of freshman comp.

"Look there!" His voice suddenly sharp, Derek pointed and called to Ram. "This was your Little Mama's temple of bones. She came through here."

I saw a line of footprints in the dust, prints of small bare human feet. Left a lifetime ago, on this lifeless world they looked fresh as yesterday. They led toward the trilithon behind us. We followed them back the way they had come across that strange boneyard. I jumped when Ram grabbed my arm, pointing silently. I saw a deep depression in the dust that blotted out Little Mama's footprints. It might have been made by the foot of a gigantic two-toed chicken.

"The thing!" He shouted at my ear, his voice muffled in the hood. "The thing what took Lupe!"

Farther on, we found another great two-toed track, and then a third. Following the same line as Little Mama's footprints, they led straight toward the opposite trilithon. I saw Lupe's wide-brimmed field hat and then her sandals, dropped yards apart.

"She was alive." Ram's hoarse whisper was hard to hear. "Struggling to get away."

We followed that double trail, Little Mama's coming in and those great two-toed feet departing, to its end between the immense black columns of the trilithon. Beyond them, all I saw was that jungle of frozen lava where nothing could ever walk.

"The gate." Something in Ram's tone sent ice down my spine. "The thing carried her through to Little Mama's hell."

We huddled there. Derek found his camera and leaned for a shot of that last gigantic footprint. Ram seized his arm.

"Lupe's alive. Somewhere." He gestured at the black lava flow beneath those lurid red-lit clouds. "We've got to follow. If we can."

Once more we stood close together, side by side at the end of the trail. I gripped Ram's muscular arm. He counted again, this time in ringing American English. I caught my breath, stepped forward with them, felt nothing at all. No change in air pressure. No tug or lift from another planet's gravity.

Ahead of us the tortured lavas were still frozen into the same grotesque monsters. The bleak landscape beyond sloped down into the same dark canyon. I saw no possible path ahead. Behind us the trilithons stood where they had been forever, enormous against the low red sky, the only evidence that anything alive had ever been here.

What sort of life had the builders' been? I felt almost afraid to know.

"If that's another gate, that's the wrong key." Derek made a dismal shrug. "We'll never find her."

We stumbled back inside the trilithons, as if they could offer any shelter from that dark hostility. Derek stopped to peer at us through the smoke mask.

"What now? What do you think?"

"Let's get out." Ram crouched away from the empty gateway where the trail had ended. "While we can."

"Not yet." Derek glanced at his oxygen gauge. "We have time left. What we've found is a fabulous pot if we get back with it."

I was looking back the way we had come. He frowned at me anxiously.

"Can't you get what it means? Not just for us. Not just for Lupe. It's new science. It's a new universe I don't understand. We've got to get back with every fact we can."

"We could lose it all." Muffled in the smoke mask, Ram's voice was grim. "In half a minute, if those monsters come back."

"Or even if they don't." Derek had sobered. "We need Lupe's expertise to interpret what we've found. Her reputation to land another grant. If we get back without her—" His head shook. "We could be accused of inventing the whole story to cover something up."

Ram shrugged. "I see no way to go on."

"Okay." Derek turned back to the bones. "But we've got to take what we can to convince people."

"Get at it quick," Ram muttered. "Something else could be collecting our own bones ten thousand years from now."

Watching the oxygen gauges, we got at it. Derek photographed us standing in the trilithons to prove their size. He photographed the red-lit lava-scape around us. He photographed the long pile of skeletons. He made us pose beside that monstrous skull and that huge leg bone.

Ram tried to hurry him.

Scratching in the dust around the human skeletons, we found an odd-shaped stone Ram said was a hand axe, and shards of a pottery vessel that could have been a water jar. He brushed the dust off the Neanderthal human skull and then an egg-shaped shell about the same size. A pale yellow color, it had two short horns and two empty hollows that could have been eye sockets.

"Nothing human or even kin to human." He turned it in his hands and shook his head. "Silicon, I think. Like what Lupe called an exoskeleton. Maybe from one of the things that built the place?"

He grinned and handed it to me.

"Can you carry it? It ought to start a real debate if we get it out."

He stowed the hand axe and the flint point in his backpack. With nothing else to contain the bones, I dug the jacket out of my backpack and we wrapped what we had collected in that. Derek was still not done. He found a steel tape in his backpack and measured the base of one of the columns. He had me walk straight across the circle and count my paces to get dimensions for his notes. He drew diagrams of the site.

Finally, he wanted photos from outside. We left his collection piled near where we had entered and followed him back along that double trail and let him lead us out again, back through the passage where it ended. The trilithons stood on a flat stone shelf. We walked out across it to the edge of that dead lava ocean. Derek took several careful shots, and made us stop twice on the way back to pose with the trilithons in the background.

"Let's go!" Ram squinted into the thickening gloom. "It's getting dark."

"It is." Derek nodded at the crimson sky. "I'd guess we have a red giant star for a sun, setting now. I wish we had time to estimate the planet's rate of rotation."

"We don't."

Ram caught his arm to hurry him but froze between the columns, his hand raised to stop us. Ahead of him I saw a thing out of a nightmare. Its body was narrow and long, splotched with pale green and orange. Bright metal covered most of its great head, but I saw a yellow crest, like the saw-toothed crest on that huge skull. Lean lever-like legs held it tall as some ancient saurian. It was following our footprints, its whole body tipping and tipping again to bring its huge red-glowing eyes closer to the floor. It stopped in the middle of the circle.

"Freeze!"

Ram gripped my arm. I thought the thing had seen us, but Ram was pointing at something sliding out of its armored belly: a strange chain of odd silver-bright objects clinging together. Large and tiny, they were balls and cubes, disks and cylinders, star-shape crystals transparent as glass, and shapeless gray lumps.

It dangled there, twisting back and forth. A thin ray of red light shone from a crystal star at its tip. Searching the dust, it found the trail and followed it toward us. I shivered from a cold certainty that it would find us, but it stopped on Lupe's field hat.

Detaching itself from the monster, it sank down into snake-like coils, glittering in the dust. After a moment it rose again, its bright metal bits flowing into a fantastic parody of something human. Bits bunched themselves into a head, two stars glowing like alien eyes. Forming arms and hands, it bent to pick up Lupe's hat. It came on toward us, and stopped for her sandals. Stalking closer, it found our little pile of relics and formed two more arms to gather them again in my jacket.

Derek raised his camera.

"Don't!" Ram whispered. "Please!"

The thing lumbered back to the monster. The knobby head dissolved itself into a rope that climbed back to the opening in the great body. It anchored itself there, contracted, and pulled itself and its burden out of sight. The opening closed. The monster bent its great legs, sank close to the dust, and sprang. I heard Derek's camera click, but the thing was already high, spreading stubby crimson wings. It dived straight at us, red eyes blazing.

I stood fixed with dread till Ram caught my arm.

"Hide! Let's hide!"

We darted out of its path and ducked into the next trilithon. Blackness flashed. The ground rocked under me.

CHAPTER
5

Something shoved me. My ears clicked. The ground slid under my feet. I staggered for my balance till Ram caught my arm. Bright sun blinded me. I rubbed my eyes and staggered again. Around us, that black jungle of frozen lavas was gone, but the Sahara dunes had not returned.

We stood on a wide pavement that ran straight into infinite distance.

The whole circle of trilithons had vanished. A solid stone wall towered behind us now. I saw no opening at all. Still swaying for my balance, overwhelmed with the shock of too much that made no sense, I was confused, uncertain of anything.

I was giddy, my stomach uneasy. Where was this? How had I gotten here? Was I sick? Had I had an accident? Groping for anything real, anything I knew, anything sane, again I felt a homesick yearning for the easy security of the old brick house back in Portales, where I'd lived with my mother till she died. I longed for her patient smile and her gentle voice when she used to read the plays of Shakespeare to me before I was old enough for school. I needed the comfortable permanence of my father's law library, which she'd kept as he left it as long as she lived.

"Will?" Ram's voice was hollow and strange in the smoke hood, but it was real. "Are you okay?"

It took a moment to get enough breath to speak.

"I—I don't know."

The smoke hood had a hot plastic stink. I felt weak, my orientation gone. Yet a wave of gratitude came over me. Gratitude for Ram and Derek, standing close beside me, staring down that road that ran forever into hazy distance. They were fellow Horsemen, old friends and loyal companions. Reality returned, the radar image, the erg and the old water hole, the megaliths under the sand. I caught a long breath and heard Ram's startled yell.

"Hey!" He turned to point. "That wall! It's moving!"

It had been close behind us. It was now a dozen yards away, moving steadily.

"Let's get back."

He went back to it. I saw no doorway, but he snatched the emerald pendant off his neck and tapped it frantically against the spot where we had come out. Nothing opened. He kept trying for half a minute, running to stay there as the pavement flowed out of the wall.

Still groping for anything sane, I studied the pavement. Perhaps thirty yards wide, it was striped with the pale colors of a double rainbow, red down the center and fading through all the hues of the spectrum toward dark stripes along the sides. I felt no vibration, heard no sound of anything, but the wall pulled steadily away.

Derek lifted the side of his smoke mask, sniffed, and slipped it off, breathing deep. I took mine off. The air was fresh and cool, with a sweet scent of life. With better vision, I looked around again. The wall behind us was the side of a mountain, cut as smooth as if a giant's knife had sliced the rest away. It rose sheer for many hundreds of feet. Rugged mountain slopes above it climbed still higher.

Sliding silently, the pavement swept us steadily into what I felt was the east, through an empty landscape. Tall green grass rippled in a gentle breeze. I saw a flight of birds, black specks wheeling far away, and a white thundercloud building over distant mountains.

"Another world." Derek caught my arm. "Let's wait for Ram."

He had fallen far behind. We ran for the edge, staggering for balance as the road slowed toward the edge, strip by strip. On the black strip along the side the motion stopped. We stood there until Ram came down the red center strip to overtake us.

"Crazy world!" He was trembling, breathing hard. "My Little Mama called it hell." He shivered. "Maybe it is."

"With a warm sun shining?" Derek grinned at him. "Air we can breathe? You want gravy on your bread?"

"You feel good about it?"

"Fortunate." Derek seemed curiously elated. "We're the luckiest men alive!"

"Lucky?" Ram shook his head at the black mountain behind us. "I don't see how."

"Let's keep cool and think about it." Derek sat down on the curb and slipped off his backpack. "Did you ever hear of serendipity?"

Ram looked blank.

"We've just defined it. We came here looking for rocks under the sand and stumbled into what has the look of a high-tech interstellar empire. Think of Cortés when he got to Mexico. Galileo when he saw the moons of Jupiter. I think we're luckier." Soberly, he added, "I hope we can leave a better legacy."

"I don't get it." Ram crouched away from that topless wall. "Where do you think we are?"

"Somewhere off the Earth." Derek paused to scan the green landscape before us. "It has to be, though a lot looks familiar. I've seen grass like this on my uncle's West Texas ranch. But how we got here—" He shook his head. "If we can't turn back, we've got to go on. The story of the trilithons could change the world, if we get back with it."

"And how do you hope to do that?"

"I have no idea." Derek shrugged. "Let's leave that till later. Right now we've dealt ourselves a royal flush. Let's play it out. If we win the pot, it can outweigh all the gold old Pizarro found in Peru."

"If we play it like a game, what's our next move?"

"Ride the road." Derek shaded his eyes to stare along it into blue-hazed distance. "See where it takes us. Learn what we can. Look for Lupe if we ever find a clue. Get back home with proof of where we've been. Do the best we can. The pot's too big to lose."

"Lupe?" Ram blinked at him. "Is there a chance?"

"We can hope." Derek shook his head. "I don't know what else. Hope, and do what we can." He opened his backpack. "Let's look at the cards we hold."

He laid his notebook, the camera, and a little pack of memory cards on the flat curb of the road. His canteen. A chocolate bar he'd bought when we stopped for fuel at Gabès. Finally, the stone hand axe and the Clovis point.

"And there's a sweater, a change of underwear, and two pair of socks." He grinned. "I used to be a Scout."

All I could lay out was a bag of dried dates from Gabès.

Ram spread empty hands.

"Never mind." Derek shrugged. "We'll share what we have. Live off the land if we can."

He glanced up at the mountain wall, suddenly pointed.

"See those green streaks!"

He went back to study a fallen boulder with his pocket lens and found his camera to take a close-up shot. Back with us, he opened his notebook to make an entry in rapid shorthand.

"One puzzle solved." He nodded in satisfaction. "The source of those Saharan megaliths. This mountain has the same fine grain and the same green veins. They must have been quarried here and carried out to Earth."

"If we're really off the Earth—" Ram squinted at him. "Where could we possibly be?"

"That's the big question." Derek nodded. "But there are things we know. Or things I think we know."

"Tell me what."

"First of all, the trilithons."

Frowning in speculation, he opened the notebook to write again. I saw the words *Day One* lettered above his rapid shorthand.

"I think they are, or were, a sort of terminal." He spoke the words as he wrote, as if dictating. "They seem to connect seven planets. An interstellar empire with no space rockets. The terminal world, under that red sun, has to be somewhere out of our solar system. The severe location is a puzzle."

"A death trap!" Ram muttered.

"We got through." He grinned. "If it was selected to limit access, we passed the test. So did your Little Mama. The men carrying stone axes and Clovis points weren't so lucky." He shook his head. "I'd like to know what happened to the builders."

"The Salisbury Stonehenge?" I asked him. "Was it another gate?"

"Too crude." He closed the notebook. "But that's another problem for Lupe. She spoke about cultural diffusion and similar megalithic sites scattered across Western Europe. Whoever the builders were, they must have left influences. Memories, myths, maybe religions."

Ram shouted, "Lupe's hat!"

He pointed across the crawling pavement. I saw her field hat moving down that red central strip. Her sandals came behind it, one by one, and then the skulls and bones we had collected, still wrapped in my nylon jacket. Ram ran out to recover the jacket and brought it back to me. Squatting by the curb, he shivered and watched the hat and sandals and skulls carried on down the road and finally out of sight.

"Could she be still alive?" he whispered.

"Could be." Derek shrugged. "We'll learn what we can and do what we can."

"Learn what we can?" Ram was bitterly mocking. "And never get back to tell anybody?"

"Trust our poker luck! It's running high."

"Poker luck?" The phrase hit me wrong. "This ain't no game!"

I knew better, but *ain't* said how I felt.

Ram was not so bitter. He sat for a time in moody silence, and abruptly spoke again. "I can't help thinking of home." He paused to sigh. "Last summer I went back to see my kin in Mombasa and Nairobi. They're in a bad way. Bad government, poverty, sickness. Not much I could do for them, but I met a woman."

I saw the shadow of a smile.

"At the Leakey Museum. We got to talking. She was white,

but color didn't bother her. She let me buy her a beer. She was born in South Africa, trained in biology at Cambridge, now employed by a big pharmaceutical outfit in Switzerland.

"She was there with a tour group, anxious to learn more than the guides could tell her. Her company was testing an AIDS vaccine and she wanted to see more of the need for it. She let me show her around the city and translate for her. We got on well. She left her group and we spent two weeks together."

His smile grew wider.

"Weeks I won't forget. We took a camera safari through the Masai Mara. We climbed Kilimanjaro. We rode a hot air balloon over the Serengeti. Two wonderful weeks, over in a minute." Wryly, he shrugged. "I hated to let her go, but she had to get back to her job and the new vaccine. I had to get home and finish my doctorate. We promised to get together when we could. Maybe try to do something for Africa.

"But now—" The wistful smile evaporated. "I'll never see her again."

"You might." Derek grinned and clapped his shoulder. "Look on the bright side. If we do get back with all I hope we might, who knows what we can do? For Africa. For all the world." He nodded at the road. "Let's get moving."

"Not so fast." Ram shook his head. "You're a dreamer, but let's get real. The things that built the trilithons and the road may have been great engineers, but they have to be dead. I don't want to meet what killed them. Before we get too far off, I want to look for tickets back home."

We looked.

On either side of the road, the sliced-off mountain rose sheer from the grass. We took off the oxygen gear and left the heavy cylinders on the sidewalk, piled against the curb and covered with the smoke hoods. We went north. Ram tramped ahead along the wall, searching for any opening. Derek studied rocks and plants and the whole landscape. We found no break in the slick black stone.

Two or three miles out, we came to the end of the wall, our path blocked by great piles of fallen scree, with rough boulder slopes above. The grass gave way to thorny thickets, with no hint of any opening. The sun was down behind the mountain before we got back to the road.

I felt hungry and tired, but Ram led us stubbornly across the road to search in the other direction. All we found was that top-less barrier of dark, emerald-veined stone, its seamless surface hardly marred by all the ages it must have been exposed.

"Ten thousand years?" Derek narrowed his eyes, speculating. "Or a hundred thousand? I'd like to know."

Night had fallen. We picked our way back to the road by flashlight and tried to sleep on the grass beside it. For me it was a night of misery that seemed to last forever. I shivered with cold and ached in every joint. My shins itched where brush had scratched them. Insects crawled on me and sometimes bit.

I felt ashamed to complain.

Derek lay on his back, happy with what he saw in the sky. The stars seemed brighter than I remembered, the constella-tions strange. He found something he thought might be the Pleiades, though smaller and far to the south.

"We're many thousands of light-years from Earth." That seemed to elate him. "Farther than any conceivable spacecraft could go."

"Too far." Ram's voice was a croak in the dark. "With no way back."

A strange half moon hung at the zenith, far brighter and three or four times larger than any moon on Earth. Never mov-ing, it grew. By midnight it was an enormous disk, so bright that Derek could see to find his notebook and set his observations down. It was ice-white at the poles, most of it blue, patched here and there with brown and green, scattered with wisps of hazy white he said were clouds.

"It's no actual moon at all!" He was excited with discovery. "I think we're on a double planet, both members Earth-like. You see the ice caps. The blue would be water, the green vegetation. That big brown spot could be another Sahara."

"If it's a planet," Ram asked, "why doesn't it move?"

"The rotations of both are caught in a tidal lock, the way our own moon is. They rotate as a unit, the same faces always together. Now at midnight here, the sun is shining past us to make it noon on the sister planet. If I'm right, we'll see it eclipsed when the shadow of ours moves across it."

We saw the eclipse. The shadow bit into that enormous disk and slowly swallowed it. Derek jotted another observation as its light grew dim, and stowed the little book in his backpack. I shivered and tried to find a fit for my body in the rough ground under me.

"I'm freezing," Ram muttered in the dark. "I wish we'd never seen the damned trilithons."

"The sun will rise and warm us up," Derek promised him. "We're alive, with a royal flush to play. I feel like Marco Polo did, when he got to China."

"Okay," he muttered. "We'll ride the road. It's the only chance I see."

CHAPTER
6

Ram and Derek stood over me when I woke, their backpacks on.

"Ready for the road?" Derek was calling.

A cup of hot coffee was all I felt ready for, after the long night on that hard bed, but we had no coffee. I slung my pack on and stumbled after them to the wide red strip at the middle of the pavement. It swept us steadily toward the rising sun, into the unknown east.

The road was moving faster, maybe twenty or thirty miles an hour. I shivered in the wind of it. The mountain shrank behind us to a thick black stump. The core of a long-extinct volcano, Derek called it. It gave no hint of the trilithons somehow hidden inside or beyond it.

I stared back at it, wistful for any way back to Eastern, back to my old brown brick on First Street and the library of English literature I had spent so many years collecting. Ram squatted on the pavement, rubbing at the birthmark on his forehead. Uneasily, he pulled the emerald pendant out of his shirt and squinted at the crown of worlds above the hieroglyphic script.

"Strange!" he muttered. "The mark has been itching ever since we came through." He frowned at Derek. "What could that mean?"

Derek shrugged. "*Quién sabe,* Lupe would say."

He shaded his eyes, scanning the landscape ahead. Tall grass covered the flats. Green trees were clumped on the hills and along the streams. It might have been somewhere in Eastern Kansas before the settlers arrived with axe and plow.

"Don't let the unexpected get you down." He turned to grin at Ram. "Think of Marco Polo on the Silk Road into China, nine hundred years ago. He discovered a vast and ancient empire, unknown to Europe. The Chinese had invented paper, printing, the magnetic compass, gunpowder. He learned a lot and came back rich."

"How long was he gone?"

"Twenty-four years." Derek looked back at the mountain. "But we're moving faster than his ships and horses did."

He raised his camera for a shot of the mountain behind us and turned to get another of a water hole we were passing. Stilt-legged flamingos were feeding in it, and animals were filing in to drink. I recognized warthogs, impalas, and zebras. Half a dozen elephants ambled toward it behind a long-tusked bull. A dark-maned lion lay watching from a little hillock. Far off, a giraffe was grazing the top of a tree. Derek opened his notebook and asked Ram to identify a few animals he didn't know: high-shouldered wildebeest, eland, a long-horned Thomson's gazelle.

"That could be Kenya, if I saw Kilimanjaro." He shivered and blinked at Derek. "Are we crazy?"

"Not quite," Derek said. "We're explorers. With wonders to explore."

Ram turned to stare at a strange tree standing alone on a

rocky hill. Its trunk was enormously thick, the branches gnarled and bare, a vulture perching in them.

"A baobab," he muttered. "Like those at home. How did it get here?"

"I want to know." Derek took a shot of the tree. "We've simply hit a mother lode of problems, with a grand chance to look for answers."

Ram waved at the water hole and the tree. "If this isn't Earth, how do you answer those?"

"We're still looking." Derek shrugged and reached for his notebook. "Evolution does create similar forms to fill similar niches, but it doesn't repeat itself. Not so exactly as this. Could be—" He shrugged. "Could be they got here from Earth the way we did."

Ram blinked at him. "Brought by men from Earth?"

"Not likely." He shook his head. "Nobody on the early Earth was skipping around the galaxy or building roads like this."

Derek opened the notebook and made a quick entry. Ram stood frowning at the baobab and the animals around the water hole till they were gone behind it.

"*Angalia!*"

He gasped and pointed. Looking, I found one of those giant hoppers in the sky above the mountain, red wings spread, gliding down toward us. Sunlight flashed on its great silver head. It landed on the pavement a mile behind us, crouched, and jumped again. In panic to hide, I started toward the curb. Derek raised his camera. On the center strip, they pulled ahead of me.

"Come on," Ram called back. "It has us if it wants us."

I stepped back on the red strip and ran to overtake them. We stood watching. The hopper jumped and jumped again. Landing a few hundred yards behind us, it sank to the pavement and crouched there watching us.

Derek walked a little toward it to take another shot.

"Come back," Ram whispered. "Please!"

He took the shot and came back to us.

"We need a record." He grinned at Ram. "It hasn't hurt us yet."

It sat there, never moving. The road swept us on through flat green plains and deep cuts in wooded hills. Overhead the moon was a long silver blade that shrank and disappeared.

"An eclipse on the other planet." Derek frowned at his watch and nodded in satisfaction. "Lost in the shadow of ours. The crescent should come back reversed."

He watched the sky until it did.

"A useful observation." He scribbled some quick calculation. "The shadow shows that the two planets are nearly the same size. We know from the gravity that they're about the size of Earth. The trilithon builders must have looked a long time to find this system."

Saving food and water, we fasted till sunset. The hopper did better for itself. It soared off the strip, vanished over a wooded ridge, and came back with a full-grown wildebeest kicking in its claws. Back near us, it ripped its prey apart with metal jaws and devoured it, skin, bones, and guts. I heard a deep humming from it, which rose and fell and finally ceased.

"It looks half machine," Derek said. "And acts half alive."

"Alive or not," Ram muttered, "I don't like it watching us."

"We're watching it, too." Derek dug into his pack for a tiny tube that was both microscope and telescope. He focused it on the creature for half a minute. "Nature never made that thing." He shook his head. "I want to know what it is, how it got created, and what it did with Lupe."

He studied the creature again, while a thin chain of glittering geometric bits came out of its underbelly to clean the blood from its bright metal face and crawled back again. Nervous under its fixed stare, we drank a few swallows from what was left in our canteens. Cooler than I was, Derek broke three equal pieces off his chocolate bar. I counted out five dried dates for each of us, but ate with little appetite, my mouth so dry I had to drink again.

Darkness fell. The hopper shuffled closer, but stopped again. Its huge black eyes became red headlamps, fixed on us. In spite of that merciless glare, Derek said we must take turns sleeping, with one man awake to watch. The pavement seemed smoother and warmer than the bare ground had been. I dozed and woke from nightmares of the hopper ripping off our limbs.

Derek stayed awake most of the night, watching sunlight creep across the seas and land masses of our sister world and longing for the binoculars we had left in our tent in the erg. The great moon grew so bright that the hopper dimmed its headlamps. They blazed again when the shadow of our world eclipsed it. Derek looked at his watch and announced that the double planet's day, measured from eclipse to eclipse, was a little less than twenty hours.

The last time I woke, the sun had risen and the hopper was gone. Derek stood with his pocket telescope, scanning the road ahead.

"Something odd." He gave Ram the telescope. "See what you think."

Ram stared. "It looks like the tops of two big black marbles, one of them half buried on each side of the road." He shrugged and gave me the glass. "A crazy world."

It took me a moment to focus the little instrument. The road ran straight toward a mountain ridge ahead. I saw eroded cliffs and steep boulder slopes scattered with pine-like evergreens, but no black marbles.

"Lower," Derek said. "Look at the gap."

I found two brown domes, each streaked with a narrow black mark from the ground to the top. They were identical and huge, the road a thin line between them. I shook my head and handed back the telescope. He put it in his pocket and reached for his camera.

As we glided on the objects grew as tall as the hills beyond them. Their sheer dark walls closed in on us, blotting out the morning sun. The road swept us through the gloomy canyon between them. Derek picked up his pack when we were back in sunlight.

"Let's get off. We've got to look."

Ram and I grabbed our packs and followed him off the road to a rocky slope beside it and stood there with him craning up at the dark masses of the domes. They still blocked out half the sky. A rocky bank of detritus had washed down against them from the hills beyond.

"There!" Ram pointed. "Is that some kind of tunnel?"

The wall had the look of long-eroded iron. We climbed to what he had seen, a narrow archway banked high with rubble. I saw no pathway through the weeds and dust that clogged it. The hoppers had seemed half alive and the road still moved, but the domes hit me with a sense of death and desolation.

"Let's get on," Ram said. "I've seen enough."

But Derek clambered over the rocks and through the brush. He stood a moment peering through the archway, found his flashlight, and climbed inside. He was gone so long that Ram finally looked at his watch.

"Give him another thirty minutes. If he doesn't get back, we'll have to go after him."

But he came back at last, bleak-faced and breathing hard.

"It's a fortress." Blinking at the sunlight, he wiped at his dust-grimed face and sat down on a rock to get his breath. "Most of it's underground. I followed a sort of gallery that runs all the way around the dome. There's a dark pit under it, so deep I couldn't see the bottom. I heard water running somewhere below, and far echoes when I yelled.

"There's a weapon in the pit. My light didn't reach to show much, but it's enormous. A cannon or laser gun or, more likely, something we never heard of. The domes are turrets. They fired through the ports we saw on the other side. The thing was built, I guess, to defend the road or guard the gate we came though. Or maybe to launch missiles at the sister planet? I'd like to know."

"Let's go on," Ram urged again. "I don't like the place. A dead place. Dead too long. Something makes my birthmark burn. Let's get out."

"I know how you feel." Derek hunched his shoulders and sat where he was. "The mystery of it gets me. The builders of the trilithons and the road were high-tech wizards, but their skills didn't save them. I've been wondering how they died. Maybe they got too good at the science of war."

He shrugged and opened his notebook.

———

Back on the pavement, I felt relieved to be escaping the haunting spell of those dead machines. Derek stood with his camera, shooting the black domes as they fell behind. I saw Ram blinking at them, shaking his head and rubbing at the pale mark on his forehead.

The hills ahead climbed higher. We came into a valley between them. An evergreen forest closed in upon us and gave way to a rocky gorge and then a narrow cut with walls so high they hid the sun. Derek was standing with his camera, shooting the strata of white limestone and dark volcanic lavas that lined the walls.

"Get off!" Ram yelled. "Now!"

We were suddenly back in bright sunlight. The gorge had opened wider. Stony hill slopes rose beside us. The pavement was rushing us toward the lip of a vast abyss. I saw gray haze ahead, and a mountain rim miles away. The road had reached an end.

We ran for the curb. I lost my balance on the slowing strips and staggered till Ram caught my arm and helped me off the road only a few yards short of that sudden brink. Suddenly weak and gasping for my breath, I was trembling with the shock of acrophobia. High places had always turned me giddy.

In my student years back on Earth, I'd once hiked down Bright Angel Trail to the bottom of the Grand Canyon, taken a swim in the river, and hiked back to the top, all in a single day, but that was long ago. The hazy gulf before us was not so wide, not so deep, but we had come too close. I shrank back and had to look away.

We had come out on a flat shelf of something like concrete. It ran for a quarter mile along the canyon rim. Derek turned to look back. In spite of the break, the pavement still flowed toward us out of rocky hills that rose behind it, sparsely grown with tufts of brush and grass. He picked up a rock, tossed it to the red center stripe, and watched until it fell off the broken end. I heard it crash and rattle down the slope below.

"Magic engineering!" He shook his head. "I wish I knew what keeps it moving."

"Magic, maybe." Ram shrugged. "But this pit was too wide for it."

He and Derek walked on to survey the canyon. I caught a deep breath and edged cautiously closer. It was grand enough. Sheer cliffs dropped from the rim to shelf after shelf, to rubble slope after rubble slope. Streaks of white and rust and brown told the geologic history of the planet.

The river was a thin silver ribbon winding through a narrow black-walled gorge so far below that it turned me giddy again. Derek walked along the jagged lip, closer than I dared. He leaned over it, and found his pocket telescope to search the slopes below and the canyon's farther rim.

"I can see the abutments on the far side." His voice was awed. "They're maybe three or four miles away, but it wasn't too wide for whoever built the bridge."

"Or tried to," Ram said. "If it fell before they got it finished."

"I don't think it fell." Derek leaned again to scan the canyon floor. "I think it was pushed."

"Huh?"

"If it had simply fallen, we ought to see a lot of it left on the slopes. Most of it's gone. I do see a few sections, scattered far up and down the canyon. Blown there, I imagine, by some powerful explosion." He frowned and rubbed the stubble on his chin. "I think there was a war. I think that fortress failed to save the bridge."

Ram turned to look back into the gap between hills behind us, the broken pavement still somehow moving toward us. His shoulders hunched as if from a chill.

"So you think the builders killed themselves?" he muttered.

"You think this whole world's a graveyard? And we're trapped here to haunt it, with no way home?"

"Trapped?" Derek laughed. "We wouldn't go back, not yet, even if we could."

Ram stared at him.

"If something killed this world, I want to know what and why. If we can't go back, we've got to go on."

"How?" Ram gestured bleakly at the pit. "Call the chopper to lift us across?"

"We'll do what we can." Derek shrugged. "Get across the canyon any way we can. Get back to the road on the other side. I want to know what it carried and where it went. We'll go wherever it takes us."

"To hell?" Ram made a sour grimace. "The hell my Little Mama somehow escaped? She never wanted to return."

I saw no way across, but Derek searched along the rim till he found a recent-looking rockslide he said we had to try. Ram scowled at it doubtfully. The hazy pit below struck me with another wave of terror.

"Here we are." Derek tried to cheer us. "We've got to play the game with the hands we hold."

He'd spent half a summer climbing in the Colorado Rockies, he told us, with a student group. He checked our boots and the straps on our packs and led the way over the rim. I heard him whistling when he had breath to whistle, but the climb down became a nightmare for me.

The rockslide had poured over a bench below, with only emptiness beyond. I shrank back from it, sick and sweating with dread, but I had to follow. We got off the slide and inched along the bench to a sloping ledge that Derek called a natural stair.

An amateur geologist, he talked about the history of the planet when he let us stop to rest. His stair took us down along a wall of red sandstone, across a treacherous layer of shale, down again to a shelf of white limestone that he thought had formed on the floor of an ancient sea. He found his pocket lens to look for diatoms.

"Nothing." He put the lens away. "No sign of early life evolving. All the life we've seen looks as if it came from Earth. Another riddle I want to solve."

Halfway down to the river, we found ourselves on a hazardous dead end, with only giddy space below. We had to climb far back and take another way. That took us to a slippery perch on what Derek said had been an ancient lava flow. I clung there while Derek tried a chimney that took him nowhere, returned, tried another way and yet another.

We were trapped there till noon. I felt no wind. The sun was blinding, the heat suffocating. I dozed and jerked myself awake in dread of slipping off my narrow seat, dozed again and longed for Eastern and our poker nights, so far away and long ago. I felt grateful for the shadow of the other planet when it brought back a cooler night at noon.

The sun was soon back, the heat stifling. All afternoon we followed Derek from one dizzy brink to another. We emptied our canteens and ate the last of the dried dates and the chocolate bar. The sun was gone before the final rubble slope took us down to a bamboo thicket on the canyon floor.

We stumbled across a sandbar to the river and dropped on

our faces to drink and drink again. The water was brown with silt, but we didn't mind the grit. We lay there, resting, till the chill of dusk drove us to look for shelter in a shallow cave. I slept at last, in spite of aching joints and hunger pangs, and woke longing for food.

So did Ram.

"Remember our poker dinners?" He sighed. "Remember Lupe's *chalupas*? Her *huevos rancheros* and *sopapillas con miel*?"

As hungry as we were, Derek had found wild blackberries ripe in the brush on the rubble slope. We picked enough of them to ease the pangs and tried to take stock. The river had been a bright metal thread when we saw it from the rim. Close up, it ran so deep and fast I thought we could never get across.

The canyon floor was nearly flat but littered with enormous boulders fallen from above. The farther wall was black basalt, almost vertical. I saw no possible path to the top, but Derek seemed not to care. He photographed the canyon, above us and below. He updated his notebook. He hiked along the shore to search for traces of the fallen bridge.

"I'm no engineer," he said, "but I want to know what held it up. What knocked it down. The canyon's far too wide for any single span I can imagine, yet there couldn't have been any piers. They'd have been impossibly tall. We saw no sign on top of any towers or cables that could have suspended it."

He scanned the rubble slopes again and shook his head.

Stiff and aching from that long day on the canyon wall, I limped with him and Ram along the riverbank to search for clues. Ram picked up a scrap of bright metal.

"Stainless steel." Derek examined it and shook his head in

disappointment. "But that impossible span was held up by something better."

It had a sharp edge, with one end broken to a point. Ram said it might do when we needed a knife. He put it in his pack, and Derek pushed on to look for something better. We found what he said was an actual section of the fallen pavement. It was enormous, as long as a football field, half buried under great boulders that high water had brought down against it.

Derek frowned and pulled out his pocket lens to study it. The exposed end was massively thick, jaggedly broken off. He found slender threads of silver, glass, and something ruby red, all embedded in a hard black matrix that he could not identify.

"Magic." He shot photos and shook his head. "Pure magic, till we learn enough to understand it."

Ram shook his head at the rushing river and craned to frown at the thin strip of sky above the sheer black basalt wall beyond it.

"First of all, we've got to stay alive."

Ram kept us alive with Stone Age skills learned from his work with Lupe. He cut a stalk of dead bamboo and split the end to hold the Clovis point. He speared a dark-spotted trout, and soon had half a dozen. He gathered thistledown, struck sparks with a flint, kindled dry twigs to make a fire. Feasting on broiled fish, I found a shred of Derek's optimism.

Next day we found ripe fruit in a mango tree a few miles up the river. Ram speared more fish and dried them on sticks over a fire. He and Derek gathered driftwood and vines to make a raft big enough to float our packs and clothing. Swimming with it, we got to a rubble bank on the farther shore.

The rubble had come down a side canyon. Filled with fallen boulders, it looked impossibly narrow and steep, but Ram twisted vines for a rope to hold us together and we climbed for the rim. Thunder boomed before we reached it. The sky grew overcast. A sudden torrent came foaming down to meet us, boulders rolling in it. We had to climb out of the way and wait for it to subside. Dusk was falling before we clambered up the last slope to a stand of tall pines on the rim.

Weak with fatigue, I stumbled away from it and turned to look back. The canyon was already a bottomless chasm of purple night, and a new wave of dread sent me reeling back.

Derek was elated.

"Another hand played," he exulted. "Another pot won. Tomorrow we'll get another deal."

We crept into the pines to be out of the wind and piled fallen needles to make a sort of bed. With no cover over me, I shivered through the night. With the sun up at last, we made a breakfast on mangos and smoked fish and hiked back toward the road. Slopes were steep along the canyon rim, the forest dense. It took us all morning to reach what was left of the ancient roadway.

Most of it buried under rocks and silt, it no longer moved. Yet it still ran perfectly level as well as perfectly straight. Deep cuts took it through hills and ridges, dikes carried it across depressions. Floodwaters had run through the cuts, leaving only a few shattered scraps washed bare. We had to clamber over landslides that blocked the way, find paths through thickets of brush, climb over boulders and around tall pines.

Smoked without salt, our fish went bad. We had to throw them out. We ate mangos till they were gone. We tried oak acorns, roasted in the embers. Ram found mushrooms he said were black morels, but only a few. Nothing gave us strength. An icy rain left us miserable. We came to a mountain wall, with forbidding cliffs ahead.

"The end of the road." Ram made a wry face. "We've found Little Mama's hell."

I felt ready to quit, but Derek discovered a tunnel mouth be-hind a screen of trees. Inside, we found dry driftwood. Ram was able to kindle a fire. Grateful for shelter, we dried ourselves and slept beside it. Next morning I chewed a scrap of cold charcoal from our dead fire, which had a sweetish taste. With only our flashlights to show the way, we blundered down the tunnel, through pools of standing water, finally back into bright sunlight. Ram was tramping ahead, as if he saw a way back to Portales.

"People!" I heard him shout. "Live people!"

Looking past him, I saw a friendly landscape of small green fields and wide pastures with neat hedgerows or low stone walls between them. A row of windmills swung their vanes on a dis-tant ridge. Closer to us, white-painted cottages were scattered across the gently rolling hills. A spotted cow and yearling calf grazed the nearest pasture. A living man in the field beside it was riding a silent plow that cut a straight brown furrow through green turf.

I saw no more of the road.

"Peaches!" Ram shouted again. "Ripe peaches."

We ran down the slope into an orchard of ripening fruit. Bright red cherries tempted us from the trees, apples still green, golden peaches with their delicate fur. I could almost smell their aroma, taste their juicy sweetness. Ram tried to pick one and recoiled in dismay.

"Crazy!" His voice shook. "Am I crazy?"

I reached for a peach. My hand went through it. I tried again. The tree wasn't there. Ram walked into it, vanished, and ap-peared again on the other side.

"Are we dead?" He was hoarse and shuddering. "Really trapped in hell?"

"Listen." Derek held up his hand. "What do you hear?"

We listened. Birds were whirling around the cherries, but they made no cries. Leaves were trembling, but I heard no rustle of the wind. A dog in the road beyond was jerking its head at a bristling cat, but I heard no barking.

"Dead men don't get this hungry." He grinned at Ram. "More likely, I think we've blundered into some kind of supercomputer simulation. A virtual world. One more relic of the technology that built the trilithons and that bridge."

Ram asked, "What for?"

"Education, maybe." Derek cupped his had to his ear and shook his head again. "But without sound effects. Could be we need earphones."

Beyond the orchard, a stone-curbed gravel path led toward a red-tiled cottage and a tall wooden barn. We walked through the walls into the barn. It was neatly kept, with hay in the loft and farm implements arrayed along one wall. A brown sow lay on her side, a dozen piglets scrambling to reach her teats. White hens ran free. I saw a rooster strut and crow, but still I heard no sound of anything, caught no scent of manure or moldering hay.

"Nothing real," Ram muttered. "We're all in the same crazy dream."

"Or a dream of ideal perfection." Derek nodded at the windmills on the ridge and a yellow-painted tank behind the barn. "It looks very simple, but it's all high-tech. Everything kind to the environment. Power from the wind. A digester to generate methane gas from the waste."

"A devil's dream!" Ram's shoulders hunched against a wind I couldn't feel. "No wonder Little Mama ran away."

We went on to the cottage beyond it. A big German shepherd lay asleep on the doormat. It did not wake, not even when

Ram stepped over it. He pushed at the doorbell. His hand went into the wall. I followed him through the solid-seeming door. In the kitchen, we came on a scene that recalled my childhood in that old brown brick house back in Portales.

A freckled boy in a blue school uniform sat at the table frowning over a wooden puzzle, a bowl of uneaten cereal in front of him. A slender girl, a little older, was tying a red ribbon in her blonde ponytail. I thought she was beautiful, too fresh and lovely to be any kind of computer simulation.

The white-aproned mother, with her golden-tan skin and straight dark hair, might have been a younger Lupe. She was filling two lunch boxes, one blue and one green. My mouth watering, I could almost taste the food she was packing: two hard-boiled eggs, two fried chicken drumsticks, two brown biscuits, two red apples.

The mother set the boxes on the table, scolding silently. The boy thrust the puzzle into his pocket and wolfed the cereal down. The girl undid the ribbon and tied it again. The mother kissed them both, and gave them some soundless injunction. We followed them to school.

The silent dog went with us. The school was a neat single-story brick building with a green lawn in front and a paved playground behind. The children ran ahead to join friends on the playground. We walked through the front door, into a silent hall crowded with happy-seeming students and smiling teachers.

Two huge globes floated in the air over their heads.

"The double planet." Derek stopped to study them. "They must have had lessons on the dynamics of it when they were still alive. I wish I could listen in."

The globes were rotating slowly, with nothing visible to move them or hold them off the floor. They looked Earth-like, with more blue ocean than land. Neither had an ice cap. I saw a

tracery of colored lines that must have been roads, dots and circles for towns and cities, letter-like symbols that baffled me.

"Writing!" Ram pointed. "It looks like that script on Little
Mama's key." He sighed. "We need a dictionary for it."

Derek waited to study one of them as it swung close to our
heads, and looked up at the other.

"That's odd!" He pointed to a bright silver thread between
them. "A skywire?"

"What's that?"

"A cable way between the planets. That's possible. They're
locked in rotation, always facing each other. It takes a strong
material, but back on Earth we already have carbon nanotubes
a hundred times as strong as steel."

"If they were all that smart—" Ram squinted at the globes
and shook his head. "How come they couldn't save themselves?"

"That's the question." Derek shrugged. "We're looking for
the answer."

The more urgent question for Ram and me was how to find
something to eat. In a world of nothing we could touch, nothing we could taste, we followed Derek through worktables and
wallboards and busy kids that might have been in schools back
in Portales. Nobody saw us.

We went on to a village that almost might have been Middle
America, except for the hieroglyphic street signs. In an open
square at the center of it, farmers were offering ripe fruit and
fresh vegetables. The smoke of meat grilling on a charcoal bra-
zier looked so real that I had to turn away. Derek took a photo
and Ram hurried us on.

We left the village on a highway paved with gray concrete

never meant to move, busy with trucks and odd-looking pas-
senger vehicles that never veered to avoid us. It took us into a
fair-sized city, its streets crowded with people who never saw
us. Shop windows showed fashions strange to me. Our canteens
were dry, but the loaves and cakes in a bakeshop wet my mouth
with saliva.

"Look at that!"

Ram stopped us to point down a side street to an open
square. A circle of tall megaliths surrounded a taller trilithon at
the center. Banks of seats rose on either side, ready for the spec-
tators to some event on a raised stage between the columns.

"Could it be?" he whispered. "A way out?"

We followed him to it, walked through the trilithon together,
found ourselves still in the same soundless shadow city. His
hand went into the solid-looking stone when he pressed the
emerald pendant against it.

"If all this is just a simulation—" He shook his head at
Derek. "Why would they do it? What was it for?"

Derek frowned at the stage.

"If you want a guess, I think this whole place was meant for
education. Social engineering meant to show people what they
ought to be instead of what they were. Maybe meant to teach
ways of peace."

"Which fell flat," Ram muttered. "Flat as that bridge across
the canyon." He shrank back from the trilithon. "We're caught
in a ghost world that somehow killed itself. With no way out."

"There's got to be a way." Thinking, Derek scratched at the
new stubble on his jaw. "That pavement ran straight, all the
way we've come. If we had some sort of compass—"

"We don't need a compass." Ram nodded down the street. "I
was born with a sense of direction. I never got lost, not back on
Earth." He pointed. "If the road ran on, it went that way."

We followed the street until it became a highway that took us out of the city and through scattered country places, on beyond them across grassy prairie where sheep and cattle grazed. I saw rugged mountain slopes ahead and wondered if the road had really climbed them.

The sun grew hot. My tongue felt swollen thick, and my mouth had a taste of bitter dust. Hunger gnawed at me. I felt weak and sometimes stumbled over something I never saw. Sometimes the simulation itself shimmered into unreality. Plodding after Ram, I fixed my eyes on the flint point of his bamboo spear and tried to think of nothing else. I felt glad when noon came, and the cooler shadow of the eclipse. Carefully, Derek noted the time in his book. I wondered at his sanity, here in the midst of madness.

The sun returned, soon hidden by a dark cloud that rose in the west and rolled overhead. Lightning flashed around us, but we heard no thunder. Sudden raindrops struck us, but I felt no chill. Silent hailstones bounced around my feet. The rain ceased, but it had failed to cool the air.

The sun came back, suddenly hot. Thirst was bitter dust in my throat, hunger an ache in my belly. Reeling with fatigue, I tripped over something on the road that I hadn't seen. I got my balance back, but Ram staggered forward and yelled an alarm in his native Swahili.

"*Angalia*. Look out!"

Falling face down on what looked like solid pavement, he disappeared through it. Derek and I were left standing alone.

CHAPTER
9

Stunned and giddy, I staggered again. My stomach heaved. That untouchable world whirled around me. My faith in my own senses was gone.

"Ram?" My voice was a rusty croak, but I called again. "Ram?"

There was no answer. His spear lay near where he had vanished. The pavement around us was empty. Lightning still flickered in the storm cloud that had passed us, but I heard no thunder.

"What happened?" Still giddily swaying for my balance, I blinked at Derek. "Where is he?"

Calmer than I, he peered around us, shook his head, and picked up the spear.

"A virtual world." He began stabbing at the pavement. "Cleverly done. I'd been wondering about the solid ground under us. Nothing else is real, but we haven't fallen through."

He frowned at the hills ahead. I thought something had hazed them.

"You know what?" He nodded at me. "I think we're coming

to the end of the simulation. I think Ram walked onto ground that wasn't there."

He prodded at the pavement where Ram had fallen. The spear went through it. He stepped cautiously forward and his feet disappeared. Probing with the spear, he led our way down a rocky slope we couldn't see. I followed him gingerly.

The sunlit pavement rose around me as if I were wading into water. He was ahead. I saw the pavement reach his waist, his shoulders, his ears. He was gone. A stab of panic stopped me. Trembling, a cold knot in my stomach, I looked back through the sunlight to another lightning flash in the thundercloud.

"Will?" Derek's voice came from nowhere. "Let's get on."

I caught a deep breath and took another step. That sunlit world was gone, the sky darkly overcast. I saw a stretch of shattered pavement behind us, littered with broken rock. All around us lay lifeless ruin: crumbled walls, stumps of dead trees, wrecked tanks and cannon, broken stone, deep crater pits. We had walked off the end of the pavement, into the edge of a chasm many yards across.

Ram sat on the slope below us, rubbing at a bruise on his shoulder.

"Hello." He grinned at us. "I was afraid you'd never show up." The grin gone, he frowned at Derek. "If this isn't Little Mama's hell, I think it's close enough to do."

Down at the bottom of the pit, I saw a tank-like war machine, black with rust and rolled on its side, one caterpillar track ripped off. A long gun jutted out of it. A jagged hole yawned where the turret had been. Bones and skulls of men lay scattered about it, rusted helmets, wrinkled boots, fallen weapons half hidden in the mud. Derek climbed down to inspect it, picked up a wicked blade of some bright metal, and clambered back to us.

"Well?" Ram grimaced at him. "What do you think?"

He turned to shoot another photo and stood a moment rubbing thoughtfully at his jaw. "This was an interstellar civilization, on half a dozen planets scattered so far apart that their death is hard to understand. Warfare seems to have killed them.

"The trilithons must have been bottlenecks for armies and military hardware, but here's a theory. The people here knew about their danger in time to build the fortress we saw. They lost the war but some of them survived long enough to attempt a recovery."

He gestured at the tank and the bones around it.

"This could be some kind of memorial, built to hide a battlefield. A virtual display of the peaceful culture they remembered and hoped to rebuild. What you might call antiwar agitprop. All of it virtual."

"Could be." Ram shrugged and winced as if it hurt. "What I want is something real. Something like a rare sirloin with eggs over easy at the Roosevelt on Second Street. Remember?"

Virtual or real, the war-torn landscape looked to be the same in all directions. Hopelessly lost, I wondered if we would ever eat again, but Ram got back to his feet. With the bamboo spear for a cane, he limped ahead again, leading us around shell pits and on toward a wooded ridge with higher hills beyond. We came to a scrap of the ancient pavement. A sign on a post at the middle of it had hieroglyphs that must have read something like *Dead End.*

However, it was not quite the end. We climbed over a rock pile beyond the sign and into another tunnel, paved with colored stripes like the road we had ridden from the trilithons. I saw no movement, but the walls were tiled with something that still shone with a soft gray glow.

Ram insisted that he wasn't really hurt, but we were all tired. We lay down on the pavement and tried to sleep. Taking my turn on watch, a few hours later, I saw that the wall was slowly sliding back around us. Derek woke, walked to keep with the wall, and estimated our speed at two miles an hour. He made a note in his little book and smiled into the light ahead.

"I wonder what comes next."

"I don't much care," Ram grumbled. "It won't be Earth."

The road accelerated. I was on watch near midnight when it brought us out of the tunnel into the cold gray glare of that enormous moon. Full, it lit a dead landscape of high sand dunes and wind-carved rocks. Moving faster now, the pavement ran straight on across it into what Ram said was the east.

Miserable with thirst and hunger, I was still awake, lying flat on my back when the sun came up. I heard Ram's excited shout and sat up to see him jump off the road. I shook Derek to rouse him. We grabbed our packs and followed. He stood staring at a strange monument that towered out of the dunes.

"The rulers?" He stopped to take a photo. "Or maybe the gods?"

Two colossal human figures, male and female, sat facing the road on a throne the color of gold. They were nude, the male jet black. Ram might have been the model for it. The likeness seemed uncanny, even to the white birthmark on the black's forehead. The full-breasted female was marble white except for her own birthmark, a black crown of worlds.

"Your own great-something-grandparents." Derek grinned

at Ram. "If that mark's really hereditary. You may be a prince, destined for a throne of your own."

"A prince of hell?" Ram scowled at him. "I wish you'd never seen those rocks under the Sahara."

"Don't say that. We could be the luckiest men that ever lived."

Ram shrugged, with a dismal face.

"Look where we are." Derek nodded at the pavement. "On our own Silk Road. Old Marco Polo had a golden tablet stamped with a passport from Kublai Khan, but he had only East Asia to explore. We have your magic mark and your emerald key, with unknown planets ahead."

"And all of them dead?"

"No matter." Derek shrugged. "Marco got back to write a book. With luck enough, we'll get back to do our own."

"Not likely." Ram scowled at the black colossus. "We've come too far from Earth, with no way back."

"Your Little Mama found a way." Derek grinned and clapped his shoulder. "She came from somewhere people were alive. And didn't she say that the road to heaven runs through hell?"

"So she did." Ram shrugged and squinted at the dance of heat on the desert horizon. "And you can call this hell."

I felt almost too giddy and faint to care, but Ram shouldered his spear and led us on. The sun was larger and hotter, I thought, than the sun of Earth, but the daily eclipse brought a welcome shower. The sun came back to glisten on rain pools. We lay face down to suck mud-colored water out of the puddles. It was sweeter than wine, and we managed to fill our canteens.

Before sunset we were passing a water hole with a little herd of impalas grazing toward it. They raised their heads to look at us and ran in sudden panic from a cheetah darting from a clump of brush. Most of them were fast enough, but it overtook a laggard calf.

"There's our dinner!"

Ram jumped off the road. We followed. The cheetah was lugging its kill toward the brush. Ram yelled and waved his spear. It dropped the calf and bared its fangs. He advanced on it. Derek and I yelled and looked for stones. It stood snarling till Derek threw a rock that hit it in the head. It finally left the calf and slunk back into the brush.

We carried our prize back toward the road. Derek had hunted deer with his dad when he was a kid, and he knew how to dress the carcass. I looked for dry wood. Ram kindled a fire. We held chunks of meat on sticks to broil them, and devoured them rare. They were wonderful.

We slept there that night, with one man up to keep the fire going and guard our kill. Next morning we had a splendid breakfast before we went, carrying a hindquarter of the calf wrapped in its hide. Flowing on as if it had never been broken, the road carried us on through into scrub vegetation and finally into more fertile grassland.

After the eclipse on the third day we saw low brown hills ahead, and a row of tall megaliths standing in a gap between them. Derek studied them with his pocket telescope.

"Trilithons," he said. "They look like the terminal group that put us on the road, but I see another canyon in the way."

Another vast pit opened ahead, but it was not a canyon. The pavement took us around the rim. It was enormous, five miles across, Derek guessed, and perhaps a mile deep. A spiral road wound down the walls of it, to a blue lake at the bottom that shone like a mirror.

"An open-pit mine." He searched it with the telescope. "Abandoned."

He passed the little instrument to Ram and then to me. I saw huge machines along the spiral, metal-jawed excavators, tall cranes, heavy vehicles piled with ore. Nothing moved.

Ram frowned at Derek. "What were they mining?"

"I'd like to know." Derek shrugged. "Metals, I guess. It took a lot of something to build all they did."

Ram grunted, and we let the road take us on. The megaliths ahead towered high and higher, great stone pillars capped with massive lintels.

"One more terminal." Derek took back the telescope to study them again. "Busy in its day. I count thirteen trilithons."

The road slowed and stopped. It left us standing between two immense square columns of some dead-black stone. The lintel, forty feet above, framed it like a gate. The vast flat floor inside the circle shone white as new snow. Derek pointed across it.

"We saw the skywire," he whispered. "Here's the terminal!"

In the center of the circle I saw a thick disk-shape of some silver-bright metal. As large as a railway car, it had windows spaced around it and an oval doorway facing us. A bright cable that looked as thick as my arm rose from the top of it as far as I could see. Derek found his pocket telescope to follow it toward the zenith.

"Shall we take a skyride?" Derek grinned at Ram. "Up to your Little Mama's heaven?"

"Heaven?" Ram reached for the telescope and took a long time following the cable toward the long thin blade of the sister planet. He shook his head and I thought I saw him shudder. "Will it be heaven? Or a deeper circle of hell?"

Yet he shouldered his spear and we walked together toward the foot of the cable.

CHAPTER
10

The thirteen tall black trilithons towered like prison walls around us. Or more like the pillars of some strange temple, I thought, with the skycar for an altar at the center and the skywire a ladder to the other world above. Awe of it chilled me. Ahead of me, Ram stopped and looked back at Derek.

"What if it's another traffic control, another killer planet, like the first? Our smoke hoods are a long way behind."

"It's a chance we have to take." Derek grinned at him. "A run of the poker luck you always trusted."

"The only choice I see." Ram shrugged and led us on.

The skycar had seemed toylike, seen against those immense black pillars, but it grew as we neared it. A low wall of some white stone surrounded it, with a miniature trilithon framing a gateway. Derek fumbled for his camera and suddenly froze, staring ahead.

Something lay in the gate. A pile of tiny cubes and disks and cylinders that shone like new silver, mixed with bits of glittering crystal and little black lumps. They stirred as we came near, clumping into a snakelike shape. The head of it rose and changed into a grotesque travesty of a human head, with two gleaming crystal disks for eyes.

"What the hell?" Ram blinked and shook his head at Derek. "Is this really hell? And this the metal devil my Little Mama—"

He stopped when it spoke to him in a brittle, short-clipped voice. A greeting? A question? A command? Its tone told me nothing. It moved again, the knobby head rising higher, arms sprouting from the body, the base of it dividing into legs and feet.

Walking like a man, it stalked to block our way. Ram flinched back and raised his spear.

"Try your Little Mama's magic key," Derek called to him. "Maybe it's a ticket."

Ram fumbled under his shirt for the little emerald pendant and thrust it toward the monster. The crystal eyes flickered red. It barked at us. The strange head bent in a sort of bow. One gleaming arm waved us toward an oval door sliding open in the side of the skycar. A twin thing appeared there, turned those gleaming disks upon us, and beckoned us to enter.

Ram shrank from it.

"It's a robot," Derek told him. "Could be a flight attendant."

"What sort of robot?" Ram clutched his spear. "It's an actual metal devil, like those that tortured my Little Mama."

"I think it's a multicellular robot," Derek said. "I saw an experiment at MIT. The units were relatively simple, but designed to work together. Complementing one another, they made a whole greater than its parts. Let's go aboard."

Ram stepped back and gazed up the skywire.

"For a free ride to hell?"

But, in a moment, he shrugged and led us aboard. We came into a ring-shaped room with a circle of seats facing the windows. The robot quacked and waved us at the seats. The doorway shrank and closed. A gong pealed. I heard no sound of any mechanism, but the dark circle of trilithons fell away. We dropped into the sky.

A wave of nausea hit me.

The window was too large and too near. The floor under us was glass, or something like glass. It filled me with fear, the dread of falling off my narrow perch into yawning space. Chilled with a sudden sweat, I had to shut my eyes. Gripping the arms of the seat, I tried to remember the adventures of Marco Polo or the syllabus for my seminar on Shakespeare's history plays. Anything except that awful abyss. Ram asked if I was sick. I could only swallow hard and shake my head.

We were already high before I dared to open my eyes, so high that my panic fright was gone, though it had left me shaken and ashamed. Ram was sweeping the world below with the little telescope, Derek aiming his camera at the mine pit, which had shrunk to a dark little dimple.

"The cable took a lot of metal, if it's any kind of metal," he was saying. "I imagine most of it came from there."

The trilithons were already too small to see, the floor under them a tiny white dot. I thought I could trace the road, a thin dark line running straight toward the misty horizon in what must be the west. I found clouds, bright little puffs of cotton, already far below. The sky had darkened, fading into purple.

"*Chakula!*" Ram sniffed and came to his feet. "Food!"

I caught a scent like the fragrance of baking bread. We followed him into an inner room. Tables and chairs were spaced around a thick cylinder that I thought must be a shield for the cable. We sat at a table. The robot attendant came to stand over us, speaking again in that quick sharp voice.

"It wants our orders." Derek pointed at hieroglyphs on the table top. "The menu, maybe?"

He set his forefinger on a line of script. The robot clucked and fixed those crystal eyes on Ram. He made a stab at the symbols. So did I. The robot glided away. It came back with a glass of water for him, a slice of a ripe papaya for Ram, a cup of very good coffee for me. We tried and tried again. It brought me a bowl of something so bitter I spit it out, and then a basket of some strange green fruit, but we kept on till Ram hit the code for a platter of steak and scrambled eggs.

"Likely synthetics." Derek shrugged and speared another slice of meat. "Not that I care."

We ate half a dozen platters clean.

When Derek got up to look for a bathroom, the robot did more than show him the way. He came back looking like another man, his weeks of stubble shaved, his sandy hair neatly cut, wearing a trim jacket of something like silk with two intersecting circles woven into the breast. Ram and I followed him.

The sunward windows had been darkened when we returned to our seats. I felt that we were floating in a gulf of darkness, above and below and all around us, until my eyes adjusted and stars blazed out. They were the same constellations we had seen every night on the moving road, but turned strange with a million more stars, a universe of diamond dust and inky blackness more splendid than I had ever imagined.

I don't know how many hours we spent in space. Even Derek was too busy to watch the time. He swept the stars with his tiny telescope and longed for a lens with greater power. He scanned the powdered fire of the Milky Way, trying to guess where we were in the galaxy. When Ram wanted to know the direction of Earth, he could only shake his head.

The gong rang again. The attendant came to stand beside us. Seat restraints folded around us. Suddenly, we were falling into that blazing infinity. Vertigo put my heart in my throat. The cosmos tipped and swung around us. I shut my eyes and clutched at my seat until our weight came back. Secure again, I swallowed hard and caught a long breath.

"Midpoint of the trip," Derek said. "Halfway to our destination. It's below us now, no longer up."

Still famished from our long hungry march, we returned to the inside room and devoured another banquet. When I dozed, the attendant came silently to recline my seat and spread a blanket over me. Ram and Derek woke me with their excited voices.

"Pangaea!" We were coming down to the sister planet. Its globe was already vast, half ocean blue, half shaded with greens and browns and grays. Derek was scanning it with his little telescope. "Earth could have looked like that a million years ago."

He gave Ram the telescope while he shot a photo, and then he took it back to study the world below.

"A city." He pointed through the glass-like floor. "Green parks around it. No bomb craters or signs of devastation I can make out. All we've seen is death, but perhaps this world won the war."

"Or is it my Little Mama's hell?" Frowning uneasily, Ram touched an absent finger to the crown of worlds on his forehead. "My father never believed her, but when she was down with the fever she raved about the metal devils snatching her away from her people."

"Maybe they're here." Thoughtfully, Derek fingered his freshly shaven jaw. "She couldn't have come from anywhere we've been."

The other planet, now overhead, had dwindled to a narrow sickle, still so bright it dimmed the stars around it. Derek tipped his camera for a final shot and took the telescope to scan the city again.

"It lies along an ocean coast," he said. "There's a wooded mountain range behind it. It's maybe twenty miles long, up and down along the coast. Only three or four miles wide between the beach and the hills. I see a lot of trees along the streets. Nothing like a shanty town. It looks alive. Guessing from the location, the climate should be fine. Looks like a pleasant place to live."

Ram took the telescope to sweep it again.

"I don't know." He made an uneasy grimace. "It looks too empty. No vehicles moving on the streets. No ships off the beach. I'm afraid it's dead."

The black sky turned purple, finally blue. A white dot at the bottom of the cable swelled wider. Slowing, the skycar gave us time to survey the city. Wide avenues ran the length of it, parallel to the sea. Cross streets ran down to a wide white beach that looked like coral sand.

In the hills to the west, I saw a dam in a canyon, a long blue lake behind it, and snow-crowned mountain peaks in the distance. The top of a tall black butte behind the city had been carved into two colossal nude figures: a man and a woman, seated on a throne.

"You should have connections here." With an ironic grin at the crown of worlds, Derek handed Ram the telescope. "If this really is your Little Mama's heaven, you ought to have kinfolk here. Your birthmark may be your tag for some noble destiny."

"Destiny!" Ram snorted. "All the destiny I want is a ticket back home."

I leaned to look down the cable. A white dot at its foot swelled faster. The city streets rushed away. I was falling with nothing under me. A sudden sweat chilled me. I gripped the arms of the seat and shut my eyes till I heard Derek's voice and knew we were down.

"Seven gates!" He spoke to Ram. "Gates maybe to the seven worlds in the dead empire, if that's what the dots on your key stand for."

"Or maybe not."

Ram shrugged and peered around us. We were safely down on the white landing pad. A black shadow fell across the skycar, cast by an immense square column that hid the sun. The great circle inside the trilithons was empty of anything. Nothing stirred anywhere.

The door slid open. The robot stood beside it, silently bowing. We picked up our packs and shuffled out. Three little piles of bright metal crystal lay before us on the floor. Lazily, they stirred as we stepped down. They formed three thick coils that lifted and morphed.

In a moment they were three weird caricatures: A fantastic mockery of Ram, a tiny white crystal flashing on his forehead. Derek, with a two-fingered hand holding something like his telescope, craning to scan the cable. A smaller figure, stooped under a bulging backpack—that had to be me.

They bowed, quacked at us, and stood motionless.

"I'd bet they're waiting for orders," Derek said. "If we knew the language."

We didn't.

After half a minute, they bowed again and sank back into three glittering serpents. A hole yawned open in the floor beyond them. They crawled into it, and it shut behind them. We were left standing there on the vacant floor at the foot of the cable, the tall black trilithons towering around us.

Even with Ram and Derek beside me, I felt terribly alone.

CHAPTER 11

The skycar left us at the foot of the cable. We watched it climb, shrink to a black insect, disappear. A seagull soared past the cable, but I heard no human sound, saw no human movement.

"If this is anybody's heaven," Ram muttered, "not many got here."

"Empty or not, it's something new to see." Derek frowned at Ram's birthmark. "Your Little Mama came from somewhere. She must have left people alive. We've a chance to find them here."

"If we knew which way to go." Ram shrugged uneasily. "Or what we'll meet on the way."

We stood peering uncertainly around us. The great black trilithons stood far apart. Through the gaps between them I saw wide avenues walled with a magnificent architecture. Stately buildings several stories high, most of them stone. Slender minarets, a golden dome, a towering white obelisk, a magnificent arch.

I looked up the cable after the skycar, already wistful for the meals and the bath, wondering if we should have stayed aboard.

Derek hitched his backpack higher and nodded toward the morning sun.

"The ocean's that way. Let's see the city."

We walked around the trilithon to the broad avenue. Derek stopped to shake his head at the pavement. Color-striped like the road we had ridden, it was flowing in two directions, with a stationary strip between. We stopped at the curb, looking up and down it. As far as we could see, nobody was on it.

I tried to picture the city as it must have been, people riding the pavement, bustling about their business, living in the homes. Who had they been? What had they cared for or feared, worshiped or believed? What had they done for a living? My imagination failed. This world was too strange.

Ram had turned uneasily to Derek.

"Were they human?"

"They must have been." Derek frowned and nodded. "The people we saw in the virtual world looked as human as we are. The skulls on the battlefield were human. Your Little Mama's people were Homo sapiens, or you wouldn't be here."

"I don't get it." Ram blinked at the empty avenue. "Machines are still running. I don't see any damage from the war. What became of everybody?"

"The big question." Derek shrugged. "We're looking for the answer."

Ram gripped his spear and led us on.

We got on the moving pavement. Two blocks down, it divided to flow around an island that held a colossal monument. Nude figures of a black man and a white woman sat side by side on a golden throne, holding hands and smiling at each other. Both foreheads wore the crown of worlds.

"That's you!" Derek gave Ram a quizzical grin. "You've come home."

Ram stared again at the black giant. Something pinched his face. He caught his breath as if to speak, but only grunted and looked ahead. Farther on, we stepped off the pavement to stare at a white marble temple. It was another Acropolis, on a somewhat larger scale, the white columns perfect, the architrave and roof intact.

"Are we crazy?" Ram shook his head at Derek. "Did the old empire reach to Greece?"

Derek found his pocket telescope to scan it.

"Lupe wondered about the builders of the Sahara trilithon," he said. "About other evidences of their presence on Earth. She'd be itching to research a monograph about possible cultural influences if she was still with us."

He frowned at the temple again.

"It looks nearly identical, but architrave's different. Instead of the Greek mythology, the images could tell a very different story if we knew how to read it." He grinned at Ram. "There's your holy family at the center, with your crown of worlds above them.

"And look at that." His voice lifted. "A rocket ship in flight! A hint at their lost history. It must be amazing, if we only knew it. The builders had to be here before they installed the trilithons. They were exploring space, planting life on dead planets, building magnificent cities, until something went terribly wrong. I'd like to know—"

Ram jogged his elbow, pointing at the avenue behind us. I saw a figure gliding toward us fast. When it was close enough, I saw that it was another multicellular robot, pushing a cart loaded with broken tree branches and scraps of junk, a dead seagull on top of the pile.

"That's why." He nodded and lifted his camera. "That's the reason we find no skeletons, no trace of what became of the people. The robots are still on duty. They keep the city clean. Whatever happened, they've removed the evidence."

We wandered on into what must have been a business center. There were no skyscrapers, but massive facades rose several stories tall. They looked oddly half familiar. Polished granite, shining metal, spotless glass, they might almost have stood in New York or Hong Kong.

Wide show windows fascinated us. Handsome brown-skinned models were nude enough to appear convincingly human. They offered gems that looked precious, garments in styles that might have looked merely exotic at home, artifacts that Lupe would have been hard put to explain. Ram tried the doors, but they were locked. He tried his emerald pendant. Nothing opened. Derek shot photos and we walked on to a black-pillared trilithon that loomed above the roofs ahead.

It towered at the center of a wide green park, the grass around it neatly mowed. A moving pathway carried us toward banks of seats that rose on either side of it. The seats were empty, the floor around the pillars bare. I saw no movement till Ram pointed at a line of huge green hieroglyphs crawling across the great black lintel stone.

"What do you think?" He looked at Derek. "Was it another gate? Some kind of theater?"

"Or a temple?" Derek shrugged and grinned. "They must have gathered here. Could be to worship your ancestral gods."

Ram winced from his ironic tone, but said nothing.

"Tired?" Derek looked at me. "Let's sit down and decide what to do."

"Okay." I felt grateful. "We've walked too far."

We went on to seats that faced the vacant floor between the

vast black columns. The moment we sat, the silence was broken. Strange chords pealed from nowhere, and slowly died away. The columns and the seats beyond them flickered and vanished. On the front row, we were perched on the brink of a black and empty void. Too close. My stomach heaved. Giddy, I caught Ram's arm. He was frozen, watching bright golden hieroglyphs swimming though the darkness. They faded. Stars came out, but not the alien stars we had seen from the skycar.

"Orion!" I heard Derek gasp. "There's Rigel, Betelgeuse, Bellatrix. Our own stars. That's back close to home, in our own galactic neighborhood."

The stars swam apart to leave a single faint fleck alone in the void. It grew brighter, brighter, brighter, until it was nearly blinding. It vanished, leaving a dim white point where it had been. That swelled into a bright blue globe, patched with spiral storms.

Suddenly it was Earth, so near my stomach knotted with a sense that we were falling toward it. I saw the blue Mediterranean. North Africa below it, the Sahara more green than brown. We came down beside the twin pillars of a lone trilithon. This should have been the Great Erg, but I saw no sand.

Beyond the columns, instead, lay a landscape of grassy meadow and distant trees. Warthogs stood in a water hole near us. Impalas and zebras grazed toward it. Two tall multicellular robots came lumbering from it toward us, carrying something in a cage.

They vanished before I could see what was in the cage. Strange music rose and fell. Strange voices chirped and trilled. Glowing hieroglyphs raced through a dim blue haze that faded into blackness. When sunlight returned the landscape had changed. Sand lay piled high around the trilithon and the lintel stone had fallen.

I found our little tent in the hollow in the dune where the water hole had been. Lupe Vargas, in her wide-brimmed field hat, was on her knees in the dig, cataloging her collection of bones. His trousers down, Ram squatted beyond the ridge.

"*Angalia!*"

Beside me on the seat, he yelled and pointed. The sand around those buried columns had exploded. That gigantic hopper burst out of it and stood up on its long metal legs and peered across the dunes. A strange thing, its slender body green and yellow, its great head silver-bright, it was half alive and half machine, monstrous and somehow magnificent. It found our tent, with Lupe beside it, crouched flat, and sprang into the air.

The scene flickered, and we were seeing through the hopper's eyes as it soared high and glided down on Lupe. We saw her look up, shock and terror on her face. We saw the hopper's arms reaching for her, saw its long black claws snatch her up, saw Ram pull up his pants, wave his arms, and run back over the ridge.

The hopper jumped. Ram and the tent fell away. Lupe's struggling body jerked and sagged as the claws drew her close. The dune below her swelled and shrank as the hopper rose and glided, swelled and shrank again. Once more that alien music rolled.

Alien voices squealed. The desert faded into darkness, glowing hieroglyphs flying through it. When light came back, we were looking into a tiny, white-walled cell with close-spaced bars across the front. A folded blanket and an empty dish lay on a shelf along one wall. The toilet was a hole in the floor.

Lupe lay on the floor, naked, doing push-ups. Her hair was wild, her face gaunt and thin but set in grim determination. Abruptly she looked toward the door.

"Huh?" Beside me, Derek gasped and pointed.

The barred door was sliding open. A thick snake of bright geometric bits slithered inside. It split into glittering piles. On her feet, fists clenched, she watched them grow into two multicellular robots. I saw her lips moving, but heard no sound.

"Damn!" Ram whispered. "No way we can help her."

They stalked toward her, reaching for her with gleaming two-fingered hands, their crystal eyes blazing red. She flickered before they touched her, and then they all shimmered and vanished into that sickening pit of blackness. Before I had time to grab for the seat reality had returned. We sat staring through the empty gateway at the empty avenue beyond.

"So she's alive!" Ram mopped at sweat on his face. "I don't know where."

"Your Little Mama!" Derek gave him a startled glance. "Those robots! They're her metal devils. That cage is the white box where she said they tortured her."

CHAPTER
12

"Metal devils!" Ram scowled at the empty stage between the pillars. "Was that real?"

"It looked real enough." A shadow crept over us. The daily eclipse had begun. Frowning, Derek hunched against a gust of cold wind. "It could be some sort of news broadcast. We've met the robots and hoppers that still guard the trilithons. Perhaps they're still programmed to report incidents like Lupe's capture, even with nobody left to listen."

"Lupe?" Ram shivered. "We've got to find her."

"Fat chance." Derek made a dismal shrug at the bare stage where we had seen her. "Not with seven worlds to search."

A huge black bite was already gone from the sun. We sat waiting there while it grew. The darkness was never quite complete. The sun dwindled to a ring of fire and grew again.

"It's annular," Derek said. "The sister planet is a bit smaller than this one. Too small to cover the full disk."

The shadow left us chilled with a helpless concern for Lupe.

———

We spent the afternoon roving the city in search of hope or direction, or even food and water. Our canteens were dry again, our feasts on the skycar merely memories. We rode the moving ways, tramped sidewalks and alleys, found pavements flowing out of the city, up the coast and down, and toward the snow-capped mountains toward the west. None flowed toward us.

"Why?" Ram frowned at a hieroglyphic road sign. "Why would they all be moving out of town?"

"There are scenarios." Derek shrugged. "You can imagine some kind of lethal agent at work, and the whole population in panicked flight."

"Any chance we could get at the control system, wherever it is?" Absently Ram squinted at the great half moon rising in the east. "Maybe to reverse the roads? Get the skycar down again? Head back toward the Sahara terminal?"

"Not likely." Derek shook his head. "I imagine we'd have problems with the robots and the hoppers. Anyhow, we can't abandon Lupe."

Ram made a hopeless grunt and we wandered on.

I, too, was longing for home. We'd planned to be back from Africa in time for the spring semester. I couldn't help thinking of my empty house, unpaid utility bills and taxes, my unmet classes and graduate seminars, of all the friends who must surely be concerned for us. Ram was more stoic.

"No use fretting," he muttered when I spoke of Earth. "It won't get us back."

We found ourselves in what had been a residential district. Modest homes stood on stationary side streets that lay off the moving way. We passed through parks and white-fenced paddocks where I saw horses grazing. Streets were clean, shrubs and lawns neatly kept, houses freshly painted, all of them empty.

"They were happy people, on the evidence we can see." Derek stopped us to take photos. "They seem to have lived well. Lupe would have loved to document their culture."

We saw robots at work, mowing lawns, tending flowerbeds, sweeping streets. Three of them were busy around a big machine digging a pit in the pavement, perhaps to repair a cable or drain. Another lay near them in the street. A pile of shining bits, it rose as we came near and shaped itself into a metal travesty of Ram, lifting a silver spear when he lifted his. Its crystal eyes blazed red, and its voice rang like a signal bell.

"Hello." Derek shot a picture. "Can you help us?"

It barked like an angry dog and waved the spear to warn us away from the workers.

Riding the pavements farther down the coast, we saw what looked like prosperous farms, barns and tall round silos, green fields, and pastures with cattle grazing. I saw a robot on a tractor, another driving a sort of truck. But there was no sign of human life. Ram sank into a stolid silence, but Derek eagerly led us on.

"A magnificent adventure!" Enthusiasm rang in his voice. "Magnificent! Nobody before us ever had a chance to learn so much."

He hoped for records we could read. He wanted to know the geography and history of the dead empire, the science and technology of its builders, why they fought and how they had died. He hoped to learn the story of Ram's Little Mama, why she was marked with a crown of worlds and how she had got to Earth. He wanted to know what the crown of worlds might mean for Ram.

Ram no longer seemed to care. Bleakly silent, he seemed almost angry when Derek spoke of the birthmark.

Derek always had to see more. We followed him to the fast center strip of a road that ran west out of the city. It lifted us into the foothills. On a bend where we came to a railed lookout point, Ram led us off. We stood at the curb looking back toward the ocean.

The city spread far along the coast, white beaches curving along the south horizon as far as we could see. Still water made a blue mirror in a wide harbor north. When Derek passed his little telescope, I made out ships at a line of docks. We found the seven trilithons where the skycar had left us and the lone one where we had seen Lupe in her cell.

"Let's get on." Derek nodded at the road. "I want to see what's over the hill."

"I'm tired." Ram shook his head. "I'm sleepy. Those feasts in the sky were a long time ago. Let's go back and look for anything to eat. Maybe a place to sleep."

Derek shrugged and we turned back, plodding along a narrow walk beside the moving way. Out of the hills, we followed Ram off the pavement to a farmhouse. It looked as if the robots had it waiting for the owners to return. Cherry trees in the front yard were bright with bloom. The path to the door looked freshly swept, the white paint was bright. Red roses spread their fragrance from beds beside it. He tried his fingers on the lock plate by the door. It didn't open.

"Let's look for a garden." He led us hopefully around the

house. "There might be ripe tomatoes. Maybe carrots and turnips, or potatoes we can dig. Or chickens? If we find hens or eggs—we'll cook up a feast!"

Visions of that feast wet my mouth, but when we found a garden patch it was choked with weeds. The hen house and the barn were empty. We tried the dwelling again, but all the doors and windows had been well secured. We left the place and trudged on to a moving road that carried us back toward the city center.

We got off that in what must have been a shopping mall, a large square surrounded with scores of shops along a red-tiled gallery. The tempting scent of baking bread led us to a food shop, its window full of tempting pies and cakes. The door was locked.

The sinking sun was lost behind a storm cloud that hid the mountains to the west. Thunder crashed and a cold wind rose. An icy drizzle turned to driving rain. Drenched and shivering, we left the mall for an empty street. Ram tried his key on the lock of a vacant dwelling. When that failed, he kicked at the bricks around a flower bed and found one loose.

"If they were human," he muttered, "they must have eaten. They must have slept. They must have left us something."

He smashed a window and we crawled through into a kitchen.

"Interesting!" Everything inside looked strange to me, but Derek explored it, finding what he said was a cook stove, freezer, and, perhaps, a meal dispenser. That last failed to function when he tried to work it, but the house was at least dry and warm. We stripped our wet clothing off and drank water at the sink.

The pantry and the freezer were empty when Ram got them open, but we spent the night there, enjoying the luxury of warm beds in individual rooms. I slept and dreamed that I was back at Eastern, assigning a freshman English class to write a research paper on the history and technology of interstellar trilithons. Ignoring me, the students ordered pepperoni pizzas that they ate at their desks, never offering to share a crumb with me.

Ram and Derek were up before me, exploring the house. There was no breakfast, but Ram plundered the absent owner's closet. His boots were badly worn. He found a pair that fit well enough, and a pair of pants that was only slightly too large for me.

Derek was fascinated with a little box he discovered on the table by his bed. It was about the size and shape of a paperback. An oval black plate on the side of it glowed red when he pressed it, and lines of green hieroglyphs shone and vanished.

"I think it's a book," he said. "Maybe some sort of e-book. Could be connected to a whole library. If we knew how to open it—"

He spent half an hour tapping trial codes into the plate and squinting at the flashing symbols. He had Ram try his emerald pendant. It may have been a book, but it never opened. We left it on the table.

Ram took his brick when we left the house. The mall was empty and silent as ever, but a bell note rang from the food shop as we came near. Hieroglyphs danced over the door and the air was suddenly rich with the aroma of roasting meat. A spit was turning in the window, brown juice dripping.

Ram tried his pendant on the door. It didn't open. He knocked and yelled. When nothing happened, he swung the brick at the window. It was something tough, but his third blow shattered it. He gave me the brick, scrambled inside, jumped back.

A great robotic snake came after him, barking like a vicious dog, its glittering head changing into a metal mockery of his. Alarms squalled, so loud they hurt my ears. All around the mall, crimson glyphs flashed. Doors burst open. Robots slithered out and swarmed after us, crystal eyes burning red in strange heads shaped after Derek's and mine.

I thought we were done for, but Ram snatched the brick from me and turned back to throw it at the snake in the lead. The snake formed a many-fingered hand and extended a shining arm to field it. He waved his bamboo lance. The robot's arm became another waving lance. He waved his emerald pendant. The snake came on.

"That way!" He caught my arm. "Let's get to the pavement."

I ran with him. Derek turned back to aim his camera. The snake stopped, and its lifted lance became a mock camera. He snapped a photo. A crystal disk flashed white and green and white again. Bell tones chimed.

"Come on!" Ram shouted. "While we can."

"They haven't hurt us." Derek stood still. "They weren't made to harm anybody. Could be they're trying to signal."

"Could be," Ram muttered. "But we don't know."

He tugged at my arm. We ran on. Derek followed us. The robots swarmed after him, but terror gave us speed. We got out of the mall and jumped on the moving pavement. Ram looked ahead, pointing.

"That trilithon! The one where we saw Lupe in jail. It could be another gate. We didn't try the key."

"We can try." Derek nodded. "It could be another world to see. If it does let us through."

We got to the rapid center strip. Behind us, the robotic serpents stopped at the curb. Derek took another shot and we rode toward the trilithon, immense and black against a crimson sunrise. Green symbols shone across the columns when we came over the curb. Ram gripped my arm to urge me faster. Derek stopped to look back and I saw his jaw sag. A brazen bellow thundered out of the sky and echoed against the trilithon ahead.

"The joker." Derek's stubbled face turned grim. "They're playing the joker."

I saw a gigantic hopper gliding down toward us.

"*Epesi!*" Ram gasped. "Quick! We've still got a chance."

"The luck of the game." Derek's scowl turned to a hard bleak grin. "We're looking for Lupe. Here's a chance to join her."

He left us and walked back to meet the diving hopper.

CHAPTER
13

The hopper bellowed again. I glanced up and horror froze me. It came straight down at Derek, the sun mirrored on its huge silver head, its great legs extended to cushion its weight, its cruel black claws reaching to snatch him up. He stood still beneath it, his camera lifted for one final shot.

"Run!" Ram yelled. "While we can."

The beast was too strange, too vast, too close. Terror held me, and dread for Derek, but we had to run. Gasping for breath, we stumbled past the bank of seats below the pillars. I glanced back. Derek stood looking up into the red glare of the monster's eyes. He glanced back at us and beckoned it toward him.

"Fool!" Ram whispered as he seized my arm. "I hope it takes him to Lupe."

He snatched for his pendant and hauled me through the trilithon. The world tipped under me. My breath went out. My ears rang. The morning sun was gone. Off balance, I staggered into dead black midnight, stumbled, and kicked something that rattled in the dark. A cold wind struck me. It had a piercing burnt-sulfur edge and a faint taint of vegetable rot. It brought back recollections of the root cellar where my grandfather used to store fall crops of potatoes and squash and tomatoes on the vine till most of them decayed.

We stood there till our eyes adjusted and the stars came out. The Milky Way was still more or less the same, but I knew we had skipped again across the galaxy. I found no moon. A huge red star burned near the zenith, so bright that I saw bones on the ground around us, the skeletons of animals and men. I'd kicked a human skull.

Shivering, we crept behind one of the great pillars to get out of the wind and huddled together for warmth until the red star had set and a white sun rose. It showed us a circle of standing stones out around the great black columns of the lone trilithon and the ashes of dead campfires scattered over the rocky scrap of level ground where it stood.

We were on the rocky summit of a barren butte, maybe the core of another dead volcano. It was only a mile or so across. We walked out through the barrier stones out to the rim. A sharp and sudden drop. I crept as close as I dared. Far down below, I saw a carpet of green jungle. A wide, mud red river wound across it. I saw no mark of any human presence, and no way off the butte.

Ram nodded at another yellowed skull grinning at us out of the bones beside a pile of ashes. "An unlucky native. Or maybe crazy, if he climbed up here to get through the gate." He squinted at me. "What do you think?"

"I don't like it." I shrank from the rim. "Let's get back to the robot world and try another trilithon. If we can."

We went back inside the circle. Holding the emerald key ahead, he took my hand and walked back between the pillars. I felt no shift of gravity, heard nothing in my ears. Time-bleached bones still cluttered the bare rocks around us.

"A one-way gate." Ram shrugged. "I guess we're here to stay." He gave me a dismal grin. "Maybe in my Little Mama's hell."

Our feasts on the skycar were worlds behind. I felt light-headed with hunger. Our canteen still full, we wet our bitter mouths and walked back toward the rim. Ram had lost his bamboo spear. He kicked at a little pile of bones and shriveled leather that had been boots and clothing and picked up a rusty blade.

"Still wicked enough." He tried the edge with his thumb. "Something we could need—" He glanced ahead and his voice changed. "Maybe right now."

A man was clambering over the rim. He got to his feet, looked down behind him, and came on by us at a limping run, carrying a sort of machete. He was naked to the waist and dark as Ram. One eye was swollen shut, half his face caked with clotted blood. With only a glance at us, he ran through the trilithons, came back through, stumbled around one column and then the other.

"He's not the first." Ram made a grim little nod at the pile of bones. "They get here with no magic key."

The fugitive looked back at the rim and limped to crouch behind the trilithon. A pursuer scrambled into sight and stopped to stare at us. Just as black, he wore tall boots and a dingy red breechclout. He carried a crude leather backpack, and a long blade hung from his belt.

He shouted and came on toward us. As tall and muscular as Ram, he looked savage. Yellow tiger stripes were painted around his bare black torso and his face was a fright mask done in white and scarlet. Ram gripped his rusty blade. I shrank behind him.

"What a welcome!" he muttered. "One of Little Mama's demons?"

After a moment the man looked back at the rim. Another warrior came scrambling over the rim, then another, till I saw six. Tiger-striped like the leader, they carried long spears. With only a glance, they marched past us through the trilithon.

I looked at Ram. "What can we do?"

"Wait for a break." He shrugged. "It's all we can do."

The fugitive came limping back through the trilithon, the spearmen behind him. He had lost his machete, and fresh blood shone red on his arm. The fright-masked leader snapped a command. He squatted on the ground, head drooping in abject misery, blood still dripping from the wound.

With one spearman left to guard him, the leader brought the others to surround us and inspected me as if I were somehow remarkable. He peered into my face, lifted and turned my hand to look at the skin. He was feeling the fabric of my jacket when one of his followers shouted and pointed at Ram. The crown of worlds seemed startle them. They whispered to each other, shouted at the leader, dropped to their knees.

The leader bowed to Ram and intoned something I thought was a prayer. Ram looked startled and said something to him. He answered. They talked, Ram's words halting and slow, often repeated. The leader studied the birthmark, gestured at the trilithon, grew animated, bowed again. One of his men picked up Ram's blade and handed it back. He bowed again, called his men off their knees, and took them back to huddle around the captive.

"You know the language?"

"You'd never expect it!" Ram shook his head at me. "But I do. At least enough to get his name. He calls himself Ty Toron. He wanted to call me Ty Chenji. The Ty must be an honorific. The crown of worlds seems to daze him. He seems willing to believe we got here through the trilithon. That seems to awe or maybe frighten him."

I stared at Ram, hardly believing. "How could you know?"

"The language? It comes back." He turned to listen to the leader and his chattering men and stood for a moment staring into the hazy gulf below the rim. "It was the first one I learned. My mother died when I was born. My grandmother was busy with my father, making the curry and filling the bowls when he sold it on the street.

"My Little Mama took care of me. My father tried to scold her for it, but she used to croon songs to me in her native tongue when she was rocking me to sleep. Songs about Anak, the noble black king, and Sheko, the white witch who murdered him. I'd almost forgotten, but it's all coming back."

One of the men prodded the captive back to his feet at the point of a spear. Toron spoke to Ram and led us off the mountain. I asked where we were going.

"He tried to tell me." Ram shrugged. "Something about Blood River. Something about slaves. Nothing I understood."

We climbed down a hazardous stair the trilithon builders had carved into the cliffs. Toron led the way, with Ram and me ahead of his spearmen and the captive. The steps were no trouble for him or Ram, but I had to cling close to the wall, ashamed of my dread.

Trying to keep my eyes and my mind off the sickening gulf below, I counted the steps. One thousand steps. I couldn't help looking. My empty stomach roiled. Two thousand steps. I was trembling and wet with sweat. Two thousand, one hundred and eighty-eight before we got down into the green gloom of the rain forest, safe at last on solid ground. I pitied the captive moaning and staggering behind me.

The path into the forest had once been paved with cobblestones. Most of them had been washed away or buried under mud. Twice Toron sent men ahead to hack a better way through dense undergrowth. We stopped once to rest. The men opened their packs and found bread they shared, brown pones that looked like the corn dodgers my grandmother used to bake. They were hard and dry, but mine turned sweet as I gnawed it. We slept that night on a bed of fallen leaves beside the trail. Dusk was darkening the next day before we reached a little river and a long dugout canoe beached beside it.

A man left to guard the boat had killed a wild pig. He had it roasting on a bed of coals. I felt famished, and it was delicious. Toron let Ram and me sleep that night in the canoe, which had been carved from a single enormous log. Next morning they dragged it back into the water and paddled down the stream.

We came to shallows where the men had to wade and pull the boat, and several times we stopped to let the men forage or hunt. Toron made us stop at a ruined shrine and ordered his men to clear away the jungle that covered two great figures side by side on a throne, the black giant with the crown of worlds on his forehead, and his white woman companion, an altar before them.

"Anak," Ram murmured. "And Sheko. It comes back to me now. He was the hero who brought men to inhabit the world. She was his queen. She grew jealous when he loved a human woman. She killed them both."

The men kindled a fire on the altar. Toron had Ram stand behind it while he led his men in a chanted litany and then slashed the captive's wrist, caught blood on a slab of bread, and tossed it into the fire. Ram stood there in the smoke, his features set hard, staring off into the jungle. His uncanny likeness to the figure of Anak sent a chill down my spine.

Late that day we reached what must have been a city. The river ran through it in a stone-walled channel that was overhung with trees. I caught glimpses of great stone columns towering out of fallen masonry, but Toron made his men lean to their paddles. They didn't want to stop.

On the seventh day we reached Blood River. Dyed red-brown with upstream silt, it was an inland sea, stretching flat for a mile or more to the jungle wall beyond it. The men laid their paddles down when we came into it, bowed to Ram, dipped its dark water from their cupped hands, and drank to him.

Looking uncomfortable, he bowed in return and muttered his thanks.

"I'm happy they didn't kill us." He gave me an uneasy frown. "But I don't like to be taken for any kind of god. I don't want the consequences."

I couldn't help thinking how far we had come from our classrooms at Eastern, or wondering if we would ever get back.

The captive lay sprawled on the floor of the canoe. I think he had a fever. For a day or two he had seemed to be hallucinating, shouting, screaming, chanting in an eerie monotone, but now he was sunk into a lifeless torpor, never moving except to whimper for water. Flies buzzed around his untended wounds.

CHAPTER 14

Blood River was home to the men. They laid their paddles down, content to let the dugout drift with the current. I was shivering, hungry, scratching at swollen insect bites, wet from a drizzling rain, and not so happy with the river.

Running fast and high, it threw me into a dismal depression. It was too vast and too strange. The endless flat bends reached on forever, twisting from jungle wall to jungle wall like a monster serpent crawling. It had cut its channel ages before the trilithons were built. It would still flow on after the last life was gone. We were helpless atoms, lost in its uncaring current.

Ram was more cheerful, or at least more stoic.

He tried to help the moaning prisoner, bringing him water when he whimpered for it, offering him a crust of bread he couldn't eat. He found a handkerchief in his pack and tied it around the wounded arm to keep the flies away.

The rain ceased at last. A pale sun shone through the clouds. Yet, still, a terrible loneliness haunted me. Searching for any crumb of comfort, I saw a few birds flying high. A fish jumped now and then. Once a gaudy butterfly perched for a time on the prow. But I saw nothing human, nothing else alive.

Ram was learning more of the language and trying to teach me what he could. Staring at his birthmark, the men whispered among themselves until Toron hushed them. Ram kept an uneasy silence with them, but he shared his apprehensive uncertainties with me.

"They think I'm some kind of messiah that the priests have been predicting. A son of Anak, sent to lift the curses Sheko left upon the world and set things back to right." Gazing into a bend where high water had undercut the shore and great trees had toppled into the river, he paused for wry little shrug. "No job I ever wanted."

The river carried us past dense stands of palm and bamboo. I saw taller forests inland, but I saw no work of man until, at last, Toron pointed out a marble white pyramid, far off in the jungle. It looked as vast as those at Giza. He said it was the tomb of Anak.

Ram asked if he had ever been there.

"Who would go there?" The question seemed to alarm him. "Sheko breathed death upon it. Fools have tried to enter it, and died of fevers that rotted their bones."

He had the men paddle to keep us far across the channel from it, and they kept an uneasy silence until it was well behind. I wondered what Lupe would make of the strange ruins we had seen and this even stranger folklore and myth.

The hard bread and few scraps of dried meat had run out. My stomach growling, I rejoiced when the men threw hooks in the river and grilled their catch over charcoal on a pile of dirt in the bottom of the boat. A group went ashore and came back with bags of fruit and nuts and a straw basket filled with combs of wild honey.

We filled ourselves again and Ram huddled with Toron in the bow, learning what he could of the planet's geography and history.

"I don't get half of it," he told me. "I don't have the words or the background I need, but he's literate and intelligent. He's been to school in Periclaw. That's the capital city, down at the mouth of the river. He's not sure what to make of the birthmark—no more than I am. But he wants to know who we are and he likes to talk."

"Get all you can," I urged him. "Get us back home."

"Worlds away, but I'll do what I can." He shrugged and shook his head uneasily. "I guess we're lucky to be respected, but I didn't come here to lead any revolution. I don't like a game where I don't know the stakes."

Toron was telling him something about the planet. It had two major continents, with names he translated as Norlan and Hotlan. Norlan lay over the pole, most of it under an icecap. A white race lived on the fertile peninsulas that reached into warmer regions. Toron despised them.

"He calls them the curse that Sheko laid upon the world," Ram told me. "Calls them arrogant tyrants who think they own the world. Bloated spiders, sucking blood till they bleed it dry."

Hotlan straddled the equator, with a chain of high mountains along the west coast. The great Blood River drained most of it, flowing toward the east. Its natives were black. Their civilization had been high when Anak ruled them, but they lived like jungle animals now, Toron said, since Sheko breathed death upon the world.

Norlan claimed it, he said, and tried to rule it.

"It's too big for them to swallow, but they try with a high commission based in Periclaw and gunboats on the river." His fright-mask twisted into a horrific grin. "The slave masters may be fat, but in the end Sheko's curse will rot their guts."

Ram and I were sitting in the bow of the dugout to keep as far as we could from the captive, whose untreated wounds had begun to smell. Ram glanced back at Toron, who was taking a turn at the paddle, keeping us well out in the rapid current.

"I don't know how much truth he tells us, but he does spin a colorful tale. He says he was a slave on a cotton plantation, down on the delta. He respected his white master, or so he says, and worked hard to earn fair treatment. He rose to be a field boss and got transferred to a better job in the cotton gin. The master was letting him learn to read and write, so he could keep the gin records, till the day he lost his temper and knocked out an abusive mulatto overseer. He ran away to save his life and finally found his mother's people in the jungle.

"He lived with them and learned their ways. He was a guide for a Norlan expedition searching the jungle for ruins of the old civilization. They found no gold. The white explorer refused to pay his Hotlan porters. They murdered him. White authorities captured them and auctioned them off in the Periclaw market.

"I don't know how to take him." Ram glanced again at Toron, bent over the paddle, magnificent muscles rippling under the tiger stripes. "I want to admire him for all he's done, but life seems to have left him a cynic, with no loyalty to anybody.

He's a bounty hunter now, running down runaway Hotman slaves."

Ram nodded at the wounded man snoring in the stern.

"That poor fellow has a price on his head for trying to organize a slave revolt. It was crushed, and he was trying to escape through the trilithon. Hoping, Toron says, to bring back that prophesied liberator. A fool's errand, but fools do believe the legend."

Ram slapped at a bug on his arm.

"Toron knows the legend, but he's only half convinced. Willing to treat me like the legendary liberator, just in case I am. Ready to let us hang if I'm not. I don't think I am." He made a wry face. "His main concern is to deliver his prisoner to a government outstation down the river and collect his bounty money."

Next morning the empty loneliness of the river lay heavy on me until Toron made out a tiny puff of black smoke far ahead. We paddled into a thicket of reeds in the shallows and hid there while a small steamer crept by against the current. I made out a long-barreled gun on the flat foredeck and bales of something stacked aft.

"A government packet." Toron spoke and Ram translated. "There's an excise duty on river traffic and a tax on slaves. They'd want to see official permits and search the boat for contraband corath beans."

Toron grew animated when Ram asked about the beans.

"The corath is a sacred tree. He says the first were planted by Anak himself, to show his people the way to paradise. They grow only at a few spots deep in the jungle where the soil is right. He says there's a secret brotherhood that worships the tree. They drink a tea made from the nuts that gives them sacred visions.

"A sort of narcotic, I imagine. He says a lot of whites are now addicted, users evading the taxes. Prices for the nuts are so high that they've become the chief currency here in the forest. The harvest is a risky business, because Sheko breathed death on the sites where they grow."

Three days down the river we reached Hake's Landing.

"A new deal ahead." We were coming around a bend and Toron had pointed at a dull red dot in the green wall of jungle on the bank ahead. Ram gave me a twisted grin. "Another game we've got to play, with our lives likely at stake and rules we'll never know."

He had been an avid poker player. Now, in a better mood, he seemed cheerfully eager to see our new cards as they fell. For Derek and Lupe, the new knowledge they wanted had been worth any risk. For me, the game had become too strange. My own goal was now sheer survival, and I saw little to gain from what I saw as we came to the landing.

A little red brick fort on the point of a granite ridge that thrust into the river bend; a bright sun glint on a brass cannon on top of the fort; a gnarled oak tree on a level drill field; a stake palisade around a few buildings; the dark jungle wall beyond, with all the secrets and hazard it hid: they had begun to prey on my imagination.

Toron had asked to see our papers. We had no papers.

"You'll have to report to the agent," he said. "You'll have to register. But first I'll ask Trader Hake to help you if he can."

Toron beached the dugout below a wooden pier and left us there with a guard while he marched his limping prisoner to the fort. We waited, sweating under the tropic sun and slapping at stinging insects, till he came back and escorted us to a palm-thatched building inside the palisade.

Trader Hake was a tall rangy man with close-set eyes in a long narrow face and a sharp little tuft of iron gray beard. We found him standing behind a cluttered counter, haggling with three black men who wanted to sell him a little black carving they said was a sacred seal of Anak they had found in a hidden tomb. He studied it under a lens and sent them away.

"Made yesterday," he told Toron. "In Periclaw. I know the tool marks."

He listened to our story and scowled in doubt. He wanted more details, tried to question Ram and me, peered through his magnifier at the birthmark, and finally sent us back to the commission agent, who lived in the fort.

A black man in a stiff blue uniform stood guard with a heavy musket outside the agency door. He shouted through an open window and the agent bustled out to gape at us in annoyed surprise. He was naked to the waist, a short bald man with a stubble of beard on a fat red face and pale eyes blinking at us through thick lenses. Strong perfume failed to cover his unwashed odor.

He shook his head at the trader, squinted at the birthmark, frowned over my watch, studied my skin, finally shook his head and called through the window. A sleek black woman came out to join him, a brown-skinned baby in her arms. He had her open our packs and inspect everything we had, and finally took her aside to hear her advice.

Ram motioned Toron aside.

"We're in an iffy fix." He came back to give me a quizzical look. "It's the crown of thorns that worries them. They're afraid of it and afraid of me, afraid I'll set off another slave rebellion. Hake doesn't want anything that might wreck his business. The agent wants no problems with his bosses in Periclaw. They don't quite dare, but they'd love to string the two of us up along with that unlucky jerk they caught."

He nodded grimly at the solitary tree.

"Toron is trying to convince them that we did come through the trilithon, the way the gods did. He's warning them that I might be more dangerous as a martyr than I am alive. They think the birthmark could be a tattoo, a trick they've seen before. You complicate the problem with your white skin and your watch and your clothing. They don't know what to do with us."

The agent and his woman came back to confer with the trader again, and both spoke to Toron and Ram.

"They've reached a sort of verdict," Ram told me. "The agent has put us under house arrest. We're confined to the settlement until he can report the case and get orders from his authorities down the river at the capital."

I asked him what he thought.

"No time for panic." He patted my shoulder. "Our luck has run wonderfully well. We have to hope it holds up."

"That's hard to do."

He shrugged and gave me a thin little smile.

"Think about it, Will. We've made great history if we ever get back to tell it. Derek and Lupe will never be sorry we came, no matter what. We may yet stumble on some way to help them. For their sake we've got to hang on."

He held out his hand and gripped mine hard when I took it.

I resolved to hang on, to trust our luck, to take each day as it came. But next day we found the rebel slave hanging from the oak on the drill field, an iron hook through his ribs. Carrion birds were already perched above him, but he was still alive, whimpering feebly. I found him hard to ignore.

CHAPTER
15

Trader Hake put us up while the agent waited for orders from the high commission.

"Not because we're welcome guests," Ram said. "Toron tried to convince him that we really came here through the trilithon, sent from heaven to change the world. He seems certain we're con men destined to be hanged. Either way, he sees us as a danger to his way of life. Just in case we really are divine envoys, he wants to keep his options open."

The trader's wife, Lela Lu, seemed more cordial. She was a thin blonde with honey-colored hair that hung free below her shoulders. She had pale blue eyes and a wistful smile that seemed shyly appealing, but her fair face showed lines cut by a life that must have been unkind.

She guided us down a long hall to a corner room at the back of the building and called a black maid to bring hot water for the bathtub. We bathed and let a black barber shave us. She brought her son to meet us. A bright-eyed child of seven or eight, he was nearly as dark as Ram.

"My name is Kenleth Roynoc." He extended his open hand

to Ram, palm up, and blinked in a startled way when Ram shook it. "What is yours?"

With no fear of us, he was fascinated. He wanted to examine my watch and touch Ram's magical birthmark, and he asked questions we couldn't answer about the haunted trilithon and how it worked. That night, his mother sent him to call us to the family dining room. Two black waiters served the meal. There was excellent, hard-crusted bread, but most of the dishes were strange, with no names Ram could translate. I was hungry enough to enjoy them hugely.

Kenleth kept asking questions till his mother hushed him. She had little to say. The trader watched us sharply, with shrewd queries of his own, alert, I think, for incriminating slips. When we sometimes failed to understand him, he offered to let his wife teach us the language. Hoping, I suppose, that we would give ourselves away. She gave us lessons for as long as we were there. Never seeming to doubt us, she told a pathetic story of her own exile from civilized society.

"I was born in Periclaw," she said. "My father was a history professor. He was interested in the native culture and the relics of the lost civilization. He took me to hear Gauran Roynoc, a black singer. We met at a dinner after the concert." Old pain pinched her face. "He became Kenleth's father."

She showed us a tiny bust of him, carved in polished jet, that she wore on a gold necklace.

"He was a registered freeman, a native of the Roy-Roynoth tribe, nomads that range the northwest rain forest. An explorer heard him at a tribal ceremony and brought him back to civilization." Emotion softened her voice and misted her eyes. "He had a fine voice, and he sang the sacred songs of his people— oral epics based on myths of the lost empire, maybe composed before the art of writing was lost."

She wiped her eyes.

"I knew him several years. His songs made him a celebrity, but he also took my father's classes, did research in archeology, and finally became curator of the antiquarian gallery at the museum. I was his secretary. We traveled together up the river, collecting historical artifacts the natives sometimes brought out of the jungle. And—"

Her voice broke.

"I became pregnant. That would have been a sentence of death for me and the child. My father wanted to arrange an abortion, but I couldn't kill Gauran's child. I'd met Ty Hake on one of our trading trips, and I came down here to have Kenleth."

Her shrug seemed more resigned than joyous.

"Hake's been good to me, but I do miss the city." She wiped her eyes again. "Gauran was hanged before Kenleth was born."

The agent made a ceremony of giving Toron his bounty money. Ram and I, along with the trader's family, were seated in folding chairs set up on the agency lawn, facing the old oak on the drill field and its evil-odored fruit. The agent's black mistress escorted Toron to join us. The guard detachment, six men in stiff white uniforms, marched out of the fort to the beat of a drum and waited at attention.

The agent came out in a white jacket to stand beside the prize waiting on a little table. He signaled for another roll of the drum. With gestures at the flag flying over the fort and the half-stripped bones in the tree, he read a speech about the dignity of justice and the blessings of life in the World Union.

The drums beat again. He called Toron forward. His black mistress presented the prize. Five burlap bags, each stenciled with symbols Hake's wife read to us:

CORATH

ONE THOUSAND

TOP GRADE BEANS

After we left, she showed us a corath tree growing in a high-fenced yard in the compound, a savage-looking dog chained to it. It had long, leathery leaves and little pink flowers with an evil odor. The flowers and the fruit pods grew directly out of the thick trunk, not from branches. The ripening pods were violet-colored, shaped like footballs and about the same size.

"The agent planted it here, to find if it can be cultivated." She looked vaguely distressed. "That outraged the natives. The corath is sacred. The wild trees grow only in spots called the gardens of Anak, where he is believed to have planted them. Members of a holy brotherhood drink the tea to see their way to paradise. Gauran said corath had been the inspiration for his songs.

"For an unbeliever to touch the tree is a desecration, yet many risk their lives to harvest the beans. They're money here on the river. My husband accepts them for trade goods and grinds them into paste for sale in Periclaw."

She made a bleak grimace.

"A dangerous trade. Forbidden by the natives except in the holy rites and illegal to the high commission unless a high excise tax is paid. But my husband says others would make the profit if he stopped."

She showed us the building where the raw beans were fermented, dried, roasted, and bagged for shipment.

"I think it's our cacao," Ram told me when we were alone. "The source of our chocolate. I've seen the trees back in Africa. Apparently it has mutated or been engineered to carry some stronger narcotic."

We were together there at the landing nearly two weeks. The Periclaw authorities must have been as uncertain what to do about us as the agent himself. The first packet to come up the river brought him no orders for us. Waiting, with nothing better in sight, I grew more and more uneasy.

"Let's learn all we can." Ram was philosophic. "Something we owe to Lupe and Derek."

He asked Hake's wife about the history of the planet.

"Most of it's lost." Wistfully, she shook her head. "Norlan history goes back a thousand years, but the early people were too busy fighting the ice and one another to care about much else. They had no contact with the south continent until white explorers began cruising along the coast and up Blood River.

"My father was a student of what he called prehistory, but nothing to base it on except artifacts from the ancient ruins of the old civilization and the folk tales of the blacks. If you care about those myths and legends, the history of the world began when Anak and Sheko came through that gate on the sacred mountain the way you did."

She waited for Ram to nod.

"They planted trees and put fish in the seas and freed the birds to fly before they brought the first men. Anak ruled the world in peace and shared his powers to let men build the gates to heaven, as well as the cities and temples that the jungles buried after Sheko killed him."

"Myths?" Ram asked her. "What do you believe?"

"My father looked for some truth behind them." She frowned. "I worked with Gauran, collecting for the museum. Enormous ruins still stand. Tombs are found, filled with tantalizing artifacts. Walls are covered with writing nobody can read. There's Anak's pyramid, with Sheko's curse upon it. And the gate to heaven that takes you nowhere."

Trouble seamed her careworn face.

"The blacks believe Sheko breathed death on the world and left her ghost to haunt it. Maybe she did, though that's hard to believe. Perhaps the myth reflects some great natural disaster. My father never knew what to think. He finally called Sheko's curse simply a metaphor for the evil in us all." She sighed. "It's hard to see any good future for my little boy."

It was hard for me to see any good future for us.

For exercise while we were there, I walked with Ram on a gravel path around the clearing, the little fort and Hake's palisade on one side of us and dense jungle on the other. Giant trees with grotesquely buttressed roots towered to a dense green canopy that shadowed the trail. Through gaps in the wall of undergrowth, I caught glimpses of brilliant birds. Enormous orchids blazed with colors and carried scents that tempted me farther than I wanted to go. Now and then I heard an eerie scream from something I never saw.

One morning when we were on the path I heard a cautious call from the jungle. Toron stepped out of the undergrowth to beckon and stepped back again. The fright-mask was gone but he looked savage enough without it, with a bright red turban and a leather vest beaded with brilliant purple and orange. A wicked blade in a blue-beaded scabbard hung at his waist.

We followed him out of sight from anybody. He spoke to Ram, his voice so hushed and rapid that I caught very little of it. Ram kept repeating *Mish*, the word for *no*. Toron's lean black features hardened with anger until at last he drew his blade, slashed a hanging vine out of his path, and strode back into the jungle gloom.

"I don't like it!" Ram muttered. "I think he belongs to the corath cult, though he never said so. He says I was blessed by Anak before I was born, marked with the crown of worlds, and sent through the trilithon to liberate his people."

He shook his head, his face gone as hard and bleak as Toron's.

"Destiny I never asked for and trouble we don't need."

That night I dreamed that Sheko's ghost had slipped into our room. She was skeleton-thin, her head a grinning skull, her deep-sunk eyes as burning red as the hoppers' headlamps. Her bone-thin hand clutched a blade like Toron's, dripping Anak's blood.

A wisp of blue mist, shining in the dark, she came to lean over me. Her breath had the foul stink of the corath bloom. The glare of her eyes felt hot, yet I shivered from her deadly chill. Her bare teeth moved as if with speech, but I heard no sound. She left me in a moment and glided on to Ram.

In the blue of her body I saw him sit up in his bed, blinking at her. Her skeleton arms reached to embrace him. I heard him yelling "Mish! Mish!" He held her off until she offered him a steaming cup of corath tea. He gulped it down. I heard a piercing shriek. She flickered and vanished, but her evil odor lingered in the air, so powerful that it woke me.

I was alone in the room.

The silence hit me first. We had snuffed the candle out when we went to bed—Hake's Landing had no electric lights. I called Ram's name and got no answer. I stopped breathing to listen and heard no sound at all. I groped through the darkness to feel for him and found the empty bed already cold.

With no idea what had happened or what to do, I stumbled back to my own bed and lay there through the hours of another nightmare. Ram had been a strong companion and the best friend I'd ever had. Feeling helpless without him and paralyzed with fear for both of us, I knew I could expect no help from Hake or the agent. All I could do was lie there in the dark, hoping he would come back safe.

Daylight broke at last. The black maid came in with a pitcher of hot water and a tray of ripe fruit. Seeming astonished by Ram's absence, she ran out to report it. Lela Lu came back with two mulatto officers who battered me with questions I seldom understood. They kept an air of distant respect that failed to hide a watchful hostility.

The room had a single outside window with a wooden shutter but no glass. We had left the shutter open for ventilation. They examined the window and found blood smeared on the splinters. Ram, I thought, must have been gagged or knocked out and dragged through the window, but I felt too uncertain of anything to tell them about our encounter with Toron in the jungle.

Lela Lu called me for breakfast after they were gone. I had no appetite.

"Eat," she told me. "You're going to need your strength."

"I'm sorry about your friend." Kenleth eyed me anxiously when I came out to the family table. "I'm afraid for you."

I ate a slice of toast and a few bites of a ripe papaya, and drank a cup of tea sweetened with a little cake of hard brown sugar. Hake came late to the table, with no more appetite than mine.

"An ugly thing." He rapped his cup on the table and waited for Lela Lu to refill it. "I don't care who that Ty Chenji was or where you came from. Ty Toron and his men have inflamed the slaves with their tales about him. They believe you two have come through the gate to set them free."

He gave me a searching scowl.

"Do you know where Chenji went?"

"Mish," was all I could say.

Lela Lu was offering us a plate of fried plantains.

"I'm afraid of insurrection." Impatiently he waved her away. "I had two guards on duty last night, men I trusted. This morning they're gone. You saw that hook in the tree at the agency? Last night somebody cut it off the rope and took it away. A gesture I don't like."

Neither did I.

I was pacing the floor like a prisoner in my room when Lela Lu came to the door to tell me that the agent wanted to see me. His office in the fort was almost a museum of native art.

Bright-woven rugs covered the floor, grotesque wood carvings stood along the walls, his desk was cluttered with strange ceramic figurines that must have come from looted tombs.

The black guards let me in. Seated at the desk, he squinted shrewdly at me through dark-rimmed glasses and spoke to his black mistress. She sat close beside him, nursing the brown baby at an ample breast. The language we had been learning was a lingua franca created by Norlan traders. They must have been using her tribal tongue. I got nothing of what they said.

"Ty!" He stressed the honorific, perhaps in mockery. "We've all heard your unlikely story. Have you anything to tell me about Chenji's disappearance?"

"Nothing," I said. "Ty Chenji wants to make no trouble for anybody. We do come from another world. We left it through an old stone gate we found in a desert there. We've been wandering since, looking for a way back home. That's all we want."

"Perhaps." He squinted at me sharply. "How did Chenji get that mark on his face?"

"He was born with it. He doesn't claim to be the heir to any god. He certainly had no purpose to make trouble here."

"Purpose or not, he's made it." He dropped his voice to confer with the woman, and finally swung back to frown at me. "Ty, whatever he is, his absence leaves you in an awkward situation. If he involves himself in any slave unrest—"

The woman spoke, her voice sharply lifted. The baby was rooting for the other black breast. He smiled at them and turned back to frown at me.

"I don't know who you are, Ty Stone, but if you have any reason to ask me for help, you'd better speak now."

She adjusted the baby and they waited for me to speak.

"I do need help," I said. "So does Ram Chenji. He was taken

out of our room last night. There is evidence of a struggle. That's all I know. I'm afraid for him."

"You ought to be." The agent sat a moment with his troubled eyes on the nursing baby. Very soberly, he turned to me again. "You ought to understand that your association with him could get you charged with treason."

Helpless, I could only gulp at a cold knot in my stomach and try to thank him for the warning.

"You are sure you have no more to tell me."

I shook my head.

"That was your chance." He turned severe. "Perhaps your last. The Hotlan police on duty last night looted the arsenal and deserted en masse. They took side arms, muskets, ammunition, grenades. I don't know what to expect." He made a grim face. "Except more trouble from your friend Chenji, whoever he is."

The woman spoke and he nodded.

"Ty Stone, you will remain here at the landing under house arrest. You will not leave the palisade without my permission."

That was no problem. I had nowhere to go.

I've always been more spectator than actor. I try to blame my nature on an accident that I barely recall. My mother was arranging a surprise party for me at a neighbor's house on my third birthday. My father was driving me there when another car came through a stop sign and struck us.

My father died. I spent several weeks in the hospital and had to learn to walk again. I still have a bad knee, and I envy such men of action as Ram and Derek. I used to enjoy our low-limit poker nights as safe adventures, but sometimes I had to wonder how I'd been able to nerve myself to come with them to Africa.

Now I knew nothing to do except wait for some decision by the high commission down the river in Periclaw and hope for good news of Ram.

Back in the compound, the trader's wife asked me to biscuits and tea in the library room where she kept what she could of her life in civilization: a few books, framed pictures of her family and the home she had lost, a tall harp she had tried to teach Kenleth to play.

She wore a scarf over her untidy hair and her face was tight with tension.

"The agent and his woman!" She shook her head. "How did it go?"

I told her about the house arrest.

"You worry Ty Hake." She frowned. "But I want you to know you're welcome here as long as you can stay."

I tried to thank her, and asked what she expected.

"I don't know." She sat with Kenleth close beside her, her arm around him as if to shield him from the crisis. "It's a bad time. Our living here depends on trade with the blacks. We try to get on. Maybe some of them like us. Most of them don't."

A wide window that had no glass was open to the heavy scents of the jungle. Some wild thing shrieked out in the thick green canopy that hung so near the palisade. I thought she shuddered.

"I long for Periclaw." Absently, she was smoothing Kenleth's hair. "Life seemed good. But here—" Her thin shoulders hunched. "We live on the edge of a Hotman sea that can rise up and drown us."

I asked what she knew about the corath cult.

"Not much." She shrugged. "The Elderhood. A secret society of the blacks. My father thought it might date back to the old empire. They're said to use corath to induce mystic visions. They think they own the jungle, and they don't like us in it."

Far away, something was screaming again, and she listened in silence.

"I used to sit in my father's class on the conquest of Hotlan." Her tone turned ironic. "A misnomer. There was no conquest and nothing to conquer. The blacks live in a thousand isolated tribes, with only trails between them. No vehicles, or roads fit for them. No domestic animals.

"The tribes are independent and often at war, but my father thought the brotherhood was a sort of shadow government, trying to unite them with the secret rites of Anak and fighting the Norlanders with a secret army. Maybe that's true.

"The corath trees are sacred to the blacks, planted by Anak himself, the seed used only in their ceremonial rights. Its abuse by the whites is a sacrilege, but my father thought the brotherhood had made it a weapon, selling it to corrupt and destroy us.

"I don't know." She sighed and drew Kenleth closer. "A bad time, with worse to come. The river is rising, my husband says, and the levee leaking. His business is in danger. Maybe our lives."

I tried to talk to the trader when I saw him at noon. He laughed at his wife's apprehension.

"She's sick with fear for herself and the kid," he said to me, "but I've survived hard times before. I told her not to fret. The agent expects a few more regulars on the next upriver packet. Enough to hold the fort. And we've got nothing here worth a fight. If trouble comes, it will be farther down the river."

Yet her fears were hard to forget. Confined to the palisade, I took uneasy walks along that path between the clearing and the jungle wall, hoping in spite of common sense that Ram would step back out of it as suddenly as Toron had done. He never did.

The storm broke one morning at dawn. A crash like thunder woke me. Some kind of bomb had come over the stakes. I heard men yelling. Smoke stung my eyes when I looked out the window. Yellow flame crackled in the palm-leaf thatch of the corath mill. Warriors waving long jungle knives came swarming into the palisade.

CHAPTER
17

Kenleth darted into the room.

"Ty, quick!" He tugged at my arm. "Mama says we've got to run."

I pulled on my pants and boots, grabbed my backpack, and followed him to the front door. The trader and his wife stood there, his jaw clamped hard on a narcotic wax he chewed, a long-barreled handgun swung at his hip.

"Get to the fort!" he shouted at her. "I'll save what I can."

"Mish!" White and trembling, she clutched his arm. "I can't—I won't leave you to face them alone."

"Think of the kid." He shook her off. "He'll need you."

"Come! Please! They'll kill you."

"Maybe not. I've handled trouble." Tears shone in his hollowed eyes. He brushed at them and reached to draw the gun. "Save yourself. Save the kid."

She hugged him for a moment, kissed his lean cheek, and we ran. Behind us, scores of natives danced around the blazing corath mill. Black half-naked bodies smeared with yellow tiger-stripes, they were screeching out a tuneless song.

I heard a gunshot and looked back again, but nobody followed. We found scores of frightened natives milling around the gate to the fort, clamoring for safety. The agent's black mistress stood there, two mulatto guards behind her, turning most of them away. She met us with a tight-lipped scowl, but our skins were white. She had to let us in.

Inside the high brick wall, we found something close to panic. A mulatto in uniform was trying to drill a few black volunteers the agent had enlisted. A gun crew was loading the brass cannon on the roof. The agent was pale and sweating, shrilling jittery commands. He shouted an order I didn't understand, and the guards hustled me into a concrete cell.

I was there for several days, the worst I had ever known, without much hope of anything better. Alone, I had no contact with anybody who wanted to talk. I longed for news of Lupe and Derek and Ram and felt sick with fear for them. All three lost amid hazards I couldn't imagine, perhaps no longer alive.

With none of Derek's quiet detachment or Ram's ready competence, I found few resources of my own. The cell had only a bare concrete shelf for a bed and a foul hole in the floor for a toilet. The food was tough and tasteless little slabs of something I didn't recognize. I paced the narrow floor for exercise, and spent hours staring at quick little lizards that darted up the walls.

I had one brief break, when my jailers let the trader and his family visit. Hake was limping on a crutch, his head covered with a bandage that hid one eye. His wife looked ill and exhausted. Kenleth hugged me silently, his little body quivering with sobs. The guards stood watching from the door as if ready for some attempt to set me free.

I asked for news of Ram, news of anything.

"Nothing—" Lela Lu's voice quivered and broke. "Nothing

good. The wild blacks were crazy. Stoned on raw corath. They took everything we had. Burned us down. Ruined us."

"We are down." A long red scar ran down the trader's cheek, but he tried to smile at her. "I've been down before. I'll get us up again."

"They were about—" Lela Lu shivered and shrank from the guards. "About to chop his head off, till Toron told them Ty Chenji had been our guest. They think he came to save the world."

"I'm afraid they expect too much."

"They worship him. He's the son of Anak. His touch is pure magic. He can open the eyes of the blind, restore missing limbs, breathe new life into the dead."

Hake made a sardonic face. "They've never seen him do it."

"I'm sorry for you." Kenleth caught my hand. "I begged the agent. He says he can't do anything."

"Not that he gives a spit." Hake shrugged. "He's getting off his hot spot. Transferring to a frontier station far upriver, next to the free tribes. Waiting now for his replacement. And happy to have you out of his hair."

"They're taking you down the river," Kenleth said. "I don't know what they'll do with you there. I wish we could go with you."

He looked at his mother with a silent appeal.

"I told you why we can't." She shook her head, a shadow on her hollowed face. "Periclaw would be worse for us than the jungle."

The jailers rattled the bars, and they had to go. Hake advised me curtly to watch my step. Lela Lu kissed my cheek. Kenleth gripped my hand with both of his and tried not to sob.

"I'm afraid, Ty Will." He swallowed hard and shook his head. "Afraid I'll never see you again."

So was I. I caught him to me and held him close till the jailer shouted for him to go.

The new agent, a burly blunt-spoken veteran of the river patrol, arrived with a little detachment of native troops. He had me brought out of the cell to his office. Stripped of all those native artifacts, it was now severely bare, the desktop empty except for a sheaf of orders. He glanced at me and then at a slate clipboard. A chair stood empty in front of the desk but he left me standing, facing his searching scowl.

"You call yourself Will Stone?"

"Ty Wilston?" He grinned as if the name amused him. "If you were really born a white Norlander, what are you doing with this black witch doctor?"

"Ram Chenji is my friend."

"You've made the wrong friend."

I tried to tell our story, but he was impatient with my halting language.

"That's enough." He cut me off and beckoned the guard to take me out. "You're on your way to Periclaw. You can try your tales on the high commission."

Yet the agent never sent me back to prison. Perhaps Hake's wife persuaded him to hear our story. Perhaps he wanted to look better in his reports to Periclaw. Still with no sign of belief, he had a sudden willingness to listen to our adventures on those other worlds beyond the trilithon on Mt. Anak. I was installed in a decent room and allowed to join his staff at decent meals.

Bound upriver, the former agent was leaving his black mistress behind. I was on the dock when a packet docked to pick him up. Outraged and screaming at him, she thrust the squalling baby at his face. He stalked away. She followed, pleading. He shook her off. She drew a dirk and struggled with the guards until they dragged her and the baby away to the jail.

Though the new agent had only a dozen men, he lined them up for inspection as if they had been a company and assured the refugees camped on the dock that they had nothing to fear from the rebels.

"No organization," he told me. "No discipline. No leadership." He made a derisive shrug. "Your black friend, son of a god or just another con artist, he's leading the fools to the slaughterhouse."

Born in Periclaw, son of a wealthy plantation owner, he had the same contempt for the Norlanders on the ruling high commission.

"White-bellied spiders, fat on the blood they suck out of us! Sky-high excise taxes on river trade. Sky-high duties on every bale of cotton we ship north and every ounce of anything we have to buy. They're bleeding us dead."

The high commission acted at last. A gunboat arrived with supplies for the station and orders to rush me down the river. Half a dozen refugee families were waiting on the dock, hoping to escape with whatever they had been able to salvage from their abandoned homes, but the little boat had no space for them.

The crew was tiny. The mulatto engineer and black firemen had double duty as gunners at the long cannon on the foredeck. The captain was white, a loud angular man with a thick black moustache. Just out of military training, he was inflated with his new authority and proud to be white in a world of blacks.

He had no time for me, no interest in my story. The pilot was a better companion, an affable little man who called himself White Water Kel, so dark I thought he had black blood. He listened to all I had to say about Earth and the trilithons, and liked to talk about the river and himself.

"Water's high," he told me. "Monsoon rains upstream."

The river ran fast where we were, a wide brown flood that lay flat from bank to tree-walled bank. Only a few hours out, we overtook a floating log. A human figure stood balanced on it, waving a broken branch. As we came near, I recognized Kenleth. I begged the pilot to pick him up. He was willing, but the captain balked.

"Let the beggar swim. We've got ten thousand like him waiting on the banks."

I kicked my sandals off as we passed by, dived off the rail, and swam to the log. It was no act of heroism. The water was warm and I'd spent my high school summers as a lifeguard at the municipal pool. Kenleth grinned, dropped his branch, and helped me climb on the log.

The captain yelled lurid curses at me, words I hadn't learned, but he stopped the engine and launched a small boat to pick us up. Kenleth thanked me shyly and said he was starving. I got the cook to bring him a banana and a broiled fish left from breakfast. He devoured them and talked.

"A bad time," he said. "The raiders broke through the fence and got in the house. They took everything. The food off the table. My mother's books and pictures. My father's guns. I was afraid. I hid in the cellar. They burned the house over me.

"The air got hot and smoke got strong. I was caught there a long time, afraid the roof would fall in. It didn't, but I was still caught there in the dark. I tried to get out when things got quiet, but something had fallen on the door. I couldn't get out till I found a tunnel that took me to the well.

"The raiders and my folks were gone when I climbed out. They never took the fort. The flag was still there and I heard the cannon boom, but the new agent called me a mongrel pup when I begged him to help me. All I could do was follow the raiders and try to find my mother again.

"The raiders took a trail back into the forest where we used to go to look for nuts and fruit. I followed all day and the next, with nothing to eat. I was afraid of snakes and crocodiles and jungle fevers, but I went on till I couldn't find the trail any farther. I was lost and hungry.

"All I could do was wander on and sleep at nights on the ground. Finally I came to the river and water I could drink. That log came drifting past. I swam out and climbed on it." He caught my hand. "I thank you, Ty Will. You saved my life."

I gulped and put my arm around him.

"I've lost my mother and Ty Hake." Anxiously, he peered into my face. "Please, can I stay with you?"

It took me a minute to answer. Something about him brought back dreams of my own that had faded long ago. My colleagues and my students had become my family. Lost here, desperate and alone, I was in no position to care for anybody. I had to get my breath.

"Okay," I told him. "If you want to take your chances with me."

He blinked at me through tears in his eyes.

"Thank you, Ty Will!"

CHAPTER 18

Next morning we needed to refuel. White Water followed the
channel markers to a pier built of unpeeled logs. The Norlan
flag flew from a pole over a rough wooden shelter. I saw stacks
of firewood ready, but the place seemed abandoned. The men
tied us up beside the pier and began pitching chunks of wood
aboard. I heard a hail before they were done, and saw a long
dugout coming around the bend above us. The paddlers
brought it near. I recognized Toron in the bow, poling it closer.
Ram stood behind him, waving a palm leaf.

"Will?" he shouted. "We heard you were on the way. We
want to talk."

The captain called his men to the cannon. He found a megaphone and shouted a command for the dugout to stand clear.
Toron stabbed his pole into the mud to stop it where it was. He
was nearly naked, yellow tiger-strips around his torso. Ram
looked just as strange, in a black beret pulled down to his eyes
and a long robe dyed in a pattern of purple, green, and black.
Yet he still carried the battered nylon backpack he had brought
from home. He waved the palm leaf again.

"Toron's speaking for the rebels," he shouted. "They want to offer a truce."

"Black vermin!" the captain snarled. "What sort of truce do they expect?"

Ram beckoned Toron to bring the dugout closer. The captain raised the megaphone. "Keep away, or we'll blow you out of the water."

"I know him," I told the captain. "He's a friend of mine. We came here together from my own world. The rebels captured him. Listen to him, please."

The captain shook his head, with a skeptical scowl at me.

"Tell him I know the rebels," Ram shouted. "Toron's speaking for them. We want to talk to the high commission, if he'll grant us safe passage to Periclaw."

"Hah!" The captain sniffed. "I have no authority to offer safe passage to anybody."

"Maybe so," White Water said. "But let's hear them talk."

"Barter with those black apes? The high commission would laugh."

"Maybe not," White Water insisted. "These men are risking their lives to talk. The intelligence service ought to be interested in what they have to say."

The captain scowled and let them tie up at the dock. White Water had the gangplank lowered. The engineer went down to search Ram and Toron for weapons. Ram laid down his jungle knife. Toron refused to leave his ancient blade. They left him on the dock, but Ram was allowed to climb aboard.

He embraced me.

"A long haul back to Portales! A lot has happened since I saw you."

He offered his hand to the captain.

"Good of you, sir. If you can take us down to Periclaw—"

The captain ignored his hand and had White Water pat him down and search his pack for weapons. He swung to me. "You say you know this man?"

"We came here together," I said. "Through those old stone pillars on Mount Anak. You must have heard our story."

The captain grunted and swung to Ram.

"What's your business with the high commission?"

"Peace," Ram said. "An offer of peace."

The captain bristled. "We'll have peace when these jungle monkeys come to their senses."

Yet he huddled with White Water and let us into his cabin. We sat around a little table, the engineer ready with his gun behind us. Silently waiting, the captain glared at us.

"Believe me, sir," Ram begged him. "I know the rebels. They're fighting to take the river back and throw you whites off the continent. No real good for them. Disaster for Norlan. We want to offer something better."

The captain sniffed.

"Like what?" White Water asked.

"If you care to hear it, sir." The captain kept a stony face, and Ram turned to White Water. "Toron's an envoy from the elders of the corath brotherhood. Not a government, exactly, but it's the organization behind the rebellion." He nodded at the captain. "A force Periclaw ought to respect. They have the gunboats, but the elders have the jungle."

"Bluff enough!" the captain muttered. "What do they want?"

"Respect, sir. Recognition of the brotherhood as a sovereign nation. Liberation for its slave citizens. Fair pay for labor. Free trade on the river. Tax-free exports to Norlan."

"That's all they want?" The captain scowled. "What they get will be the hook through their ribs."

"Listen, sir. The deal they want will be good for them but better for Periclaw. They offer you peace. Security for your colony on the delta and your traffic on the river. Untaxed export of the food and fuel you need in Norlan. Isn't that enough?"

The captain grunted scornfully.

"Look at the alternative," Ram urged him. "I've met the native historians."

"Historians? Black animals that can't read or write?"

"They're learning," Ram said. "They're here on the ground. They study what they find in the ruins of the lost empire. I brought an artifact I think should help us persuade the high commission. Would you like to see it, sir?"

"Jungle junk!" the captain snorted. "They peddle it to tourists."

"Give them a chance," White Water urged. "Intelligence might like to see it."

The captain shrugged and let Ram open his backpack. He dug out a thin little box like the one Derek found in the room where he slept on the planet of the robots. The captain shrank away as if it was a viper.

"It doesn't bite." Ram turned to White Water. "I'm told that it came out of a sealed vault under a ruined temple of Sheko. The natives are terrified by a legend that she breathed death on the place. A white explorer dug it out. His porters stole it. Three of them died of a nasty jungle rot."

The captain blinked uneasily, his hand near his gun.

"I've heard the story." White Water picked up the object, frowned at it, passed it back to Ram. "What is it?"

"Take a look."

Ram lifted the lid. A rainbow of colors lit an array of symbols. Sound pealed out of it, deep notes that throbbed to a rhythmic beat, lifted to a melancholy wail, and slowly died away. The symbols faded into darkness. Stars appeared, and the silver dust of the Milky Way. Bright constellations swam across the screen. One star grew. A planet in orbit around it swelled to show seas and continents.

"Africa!" Ram whispered to me. "They've been there."

I saw the shape of it, then a green plain edged with volcanic cones. It spread wide. I saw animals: wildebeest, antelope, ostriches, elephants. They raised their heads, froze, scattered in panic from a rocket ship descending on a cushion of fire. The rocket dissolved into a tall black trilithon. Strange machines crawled out of it, and then a file of dark-skinned men and women.

"That's us," Ram said. "A couple hundred thousand years ago, arriving from wherever we were born."

They vanished, and I saw a single human figure standing alone on a bare mountaintop. An aged black man, scarred and bent, leaning on a cane. He spoke in a strange high voice, trilling syllables unlike anything I had ever heard. That uncanny music rolled again, and his voice gave way to a page of the symbols we had seen on the monuments of other worlds.

Ram touched a key. The screen went black. He closed the box.

"What's that?" the captain muttered.

"A book," Ram said and spoke to me. "Maybe a computer, if the ancients had computers. It seems to work like an e-book. The elders have recovered several of them. Nothing they can read, but the pictures are enough to reveal something about the Grand Dominion. That's their name for the lost empire."

He turned back to the captain.

"If you will grant us safe passage, we want to show this to

Periclaw. I think it will help persuade the high commission to talk."

"They don't talk to such as you."

"Sir, they should. The Grand Dominion is dead. Something killed it. I don't know what. Neither do the elders, but they have scholars working to recover its lost science."

"Hotmen scholars? They can't read or write."

"But they're learning what they need to know." Ram pushed the book across the table. "Periclaw should give them a hearing. If you'll give us a safe conduct—"

"To that black bastard? I'd hang him first."

"If you feel that way," Ram said, "I'll go alone."

"If you're that kind of fool." The captain shrugged and squinted at the box. "Just get that infernal machine out of my cabin."

Ram went down to huddle with Toron and his men before they climbed back into their dugout and pushed it away. Ram stood watching until it was gone beyond the bend.

"To pay my way." He took off his robe to sweat with the crew, loading the rest of the firewood. When that was done, we steamed on again, down the mud-colored Blood. He shared the cabin with Kenleth and me. I wanted to hear about where he had been, but he was slow to talk.

"Later," he said, and shook his head. "I've learned a lot since I saw you. More of the language, and things you'd never believe." He stood silent for a time, gazing into the jungle behind us. "Too much has happened to me. I need Lupe to help me decide what I am."

He slept most of the afternoon and woke with a haunted face.

"What a dream!" He grimaced and blinked at me. "At first I thought we were back at home at one of our poker nights. Lupe was about to serve her guacamole salad, but then she was Little Mama, reading the script in that artifact. It was a message from Derek and Lupe. They were lost in a stranger world than this, hiding from the hoppers. And then—"

His shoulders hunched uneasily.

"It's all too much. Too much that gets me down." He sat rubbing his eyes as if still half asleep. "I learned my science from Derek and Lupe. It's meant to make life simple. Nice clean answers to everything. But my life was never that simple."

We anchored before sunset in the shallows off a sandbar, where we were out of the current. The engineer dropped a hook over the rail and pulled up a magnificent silver-colored fish that he grilled for dinner. The fireman found ripe papayas in a field on the bank.

I recall that meal as an unexpected moment of pleasure. The fish and fruit were excellent. The captain sat watching Ram with silent suspicion, but White Water opened a bottle of very good wine to play the jovial host. Ram laughed at his tall tales of life on the river as if all his problems had been forgotten.

Night had fallen before we got back to the cabin. While I was fumbling in the dark for a match to light a candle, Ram closed the door and took off his cap. Light filled the room. When he looked at me, I saw that it came from his birthmark, shining like something incandescent.

CHAPTER
19

The anchored ship was soundless that night, except for the muffled thump of the watchman's boots on the deck and the far-off howl of some jungle thing we never saw. The room was dark. When he lifted his wrist to read his watch, it was lit by a glow of light from the birthmark on his forehead.

"The crown of worlds?" I had to sit down on my berth, blinking in startled awe. "Did it ever shine before?"

"Never."

The mark shone brighter when he raised his head to look at me, but he said no more until I asked, "You say things have happened to you?"

"A long story." He paused, and his voice had fallen when he spoke again. "Things I don't understand. I almost hate to tell you. I don't want to make a stranger of you."

"No danger. Just tell me."

"I'll try." He nodded soberly. "If you won't call me crazy."

———

Lying on his berth he began to talk.

"I've been initiated into the corath brotherhood." The birth-mark cast its faint and eerie glow on the ceiling of the hot and silent cabin. He spoke deliberately, as if reliving the story he told. "It was Toron who got me out of Hake's compound. He'd seen the mark, of course, but he took it for a tattoo. Took me for one more ambitious pretender to the legacy of Anak. It wasn't shining then, but he thought he could use me as a figure-head leader for the revolt. I've lived a sort of epic in the jungle since."

A steamy breath of the jungle came through the window, a thin sharp scent of strange blooms and strange decay. I felt grateful for its cool feel on my naked skin. Kenleth lay snoring softly on the floor.

"The whites dread the jungle, but it's a loving mother to the Hotmen. It feeds them, shelters them, hides them from the slavers. Derek and Lupe would give their skins for a chance to learn Hotlan culture and their history. I've tried to pick up what I could.

"Hotlan's huge, bigger than Africa. Hake's wife showed me a map. It sprawls across the tropics. The coasts have been well explored, and the navigable channels of Blood River. The mountain chain on the west coast is higher than the Himalayas. There's a second Sahara across the north and a vast stretch of the south still blank on the map.

"The Blood drains half the continent. Most of it's jungle, still unexplored by the whites but home to the natives. Hundreds, maybe thousands, of tribes. You'd call them savages. No writing, no printing, no metals except scraps they salvage. They've got no government, no cities, and no common language.

"Yet they're children of the civilization that opened the gates and got them here. How they lost it is the sort of riddle that

Lupe loves to solve. She'd find clues everywhere, beginning with the corath elderhood. They worship the little they remember and dream of restoring the great past they've lost.

"That's what Toron's fighting for, his chance to beat the Norlanders and liberate the slaves. The natives are nomads, following the creatures they hunt or the seasons when food plants are ripening, but Toron took me to a permanent center.

"A strange experience—"

Kenleth cried out in his sleep. Ram sat up to look. In the glow of the birthmark, I saw the boy twist and beat at the air for a moment, until he relaxed and lay back with his head in his arm, a slight smile on his lips. I was growing fond of him and worried about his future, half black and half white in this world of bitter race division.

Outside, a long-drawn wail quavered and died. Something answered from farther away. Ram must have seen me shrink.

"Unearthly." The mark lit his grin. "This isn't Earth, but it helps to believe that all of its life originated there. That seems strange, but Derek thought so. The animals and plants we've seen, most of them are more or less familiar. Derek thought the differences must be due to streams of evolution over maybe a hundred thousand years. A lot of it here has become hard to recognize. I've seen things that I hope never lived on Earth. One of them—"

He frowned and shook his head, staring into the dark beyond the open window. Far across the black river something shrieked and shrieked again. His grin was gone. He rubbed at the shining mark as if it hurt or somehow troubled him.

"I'd set out with Toron on a trek to the site for my initiation. A man I wanted to like. I admired him for his courage and his stoicism in the face of pain. He seemed dedicated to the liberation and future of his people, but I knew that he had been a slaver. He was generous and helpful to me, yet I knew he saw me as a tool that might serve his own grand plans.

"We went north from the Blood in a dugout with half a dozen warriors at the paddles. One carried a captured army rifle. The others had two or three handguns or native weapons. For long days we rowed or poled up tributaries that narrowed into gloomy green tunnels and ended finally at the foot of a rocky escarpment, where we had to leave the boat. We climbed that to a trail choked with undergrowth so thick that only Toron could follow it.

"Back at home, I had an excellent sense of direction, a sort of compass in my head, but on this planet—" He frowned again and shook his head, the glow of the birthmark dancing over the walls. "Here it's gone. I felt lost without it, lost and helpless.

"The trail was hard to follow, but Toron knew his way. The going became difficult, a tangle of vines as thick as ropes, undergrowth so dense we had to slash our way with jungle knives. We waded rivers and slogged through swamps. There were trees and creatures I knew, but more I didn't.

"One day I caught a scent—"

He seemed to shudder, the light of the birthmark flickering over the room.

"It turned me sick. A heavy, fetid sweetness that had a carrion taint. Toron held his nose and pointed off the trail.

"'Slubro-Slubroc,' he said. "That translates as gut-worm, though it was a plant. He said Sheko's angel of death had breathed on the seed. She had sowed them to guard her tomb, and Anak's, which stood ahead of us at the end of the trail. I wanted to see it.

"Toron wasn't eager. He said he'd been there, as a guide for a Norlander named Carno Fen, who was a friend of the natives.

He'd made a fortune with a ship line and a chain of trading posts on the river and spent most of it building schools and hospitals for us. He wanted to join the elderhood, and the elders agreed to honor him with an initiation.

"Toron warned him, of ugly spots in the jungle, places still contaminated, I imagine, with lethal agents left from that ancient Armageddon. He was older than you are, Toron said, but still vigorous enough. When he heard about the *Slubro-Slubroc*, he had to have a photo for his journal of the expedition.

"A madman, as Toron tells the story. He had a breathing mask that let him stand the odor. He bribed Toron to go on with him. The jungle thinned. They came through a stand of dwarfed and twisted plants, into a clearing where the rocky ground was littered with the bones of things that had died there.

"Toron kept away from the *Slubro-Slubroc*, but Fen took pictures and Toron got back with his camera. An ugly thing, he said. Its leaves were huge and black, thick as mattresses, scattered with long yellow spines. They lay flat for yards on the rocky ground. A single enormous bloom, purple and trumpet-shaped, crowned a central stalk.

"Fen's mask didn't save him. Toron saw him stagger and tried to call him back, but he went closer for another picture. Toron heard a pop. Something sailed out of the bloom and fell near Fen. A seed, Toron said. He has Fen's picture. It's purple-black, about the size of a plum.

"Toron was sick with the stink of it. Fen was drunk on it, or somehow overcome. Toron says he picked it up, sniffed it, bit into it for a taste, swallowed it whole, and staggered back to Toron. He soon seemed to be himself again. Toron found the trail again and they went on.

"The next day he complained of an ache in his gut. That grew worse. He lost strength until he had to be carried on a stretcher. The pain was so severe he begged Toron to kill him. On the last night he crawled away from the tent to relieve himself and never came back. Toron searched for him when day came, and finally found what was left."

Ram stopped and looked at me with an expression the like of which I had never seen. I thought the birthmark had dimmed. Far off across the river I heard a long-drawn wail that might have been Fen's ghost. A breath of air from the window seemed to have a taint of death.

"I don't know," he muttered at last. "Derek was convinced that all the life here came from Earth. I know evolutionary jumps are facilitated by small gene pools and changed on survival, but Toron showed me the shots he salvaged from Fen's camera. It's hard to believe that thing can exist."

"The *Slubro-Slubroc*—"

He paused again, and shook his head.

"All Toron found was Fen's empty skin. The film shows it lying flat in a puddle of bloody excrement. The flesh is gone, the bones, the skull. Toron says he stood there a long time staring at it, till he thought to keep a record and reached for the camera. The moment he moved, he heard an uncanny sound.

"A shrill cackle, he says, like nothing he ever heard before, but somehow like a human laugh. It came out of the stunted stuff around the clearing. He looked and saw the snake. A monstrous thing, he says, the sleek black coils of it half hidden in the undergrowth, its lifted head as tall as a man.

"The head was shaped like Fen's skull."

Ram shook his head at me, and the glow of the birthmark dimmed.

"Toron showed me the film and tried to describe the head.

He says it stared at him for a minute or two. Its eyes were huge. They never blinked. Fen had worn glasses. Toron swears those eyes were shaped like the lenses. He was trying to steady his hand for another shot when it cackled again, and slithered out of sight."

"The *Slubro-Slubroc*—" Ram sat staring at me, shaking his head, the light of the birthmark flickering across the wall. "If the Old Ones were genetic engineers, they created a nightmare. Maybe to guard forbidden spots. I wish I'd never seen it."

He shrugged and raised his hand to hide the light as the watchman's boots came thumping by. The tiny cabin was hushed except for the murmur of the current against the hull, and sometimes the cry of some far-off jungle thing.

"It's another world," he muttered as the boots receded. "Kin to ours, I know, but still we don't belong. I don't think we ever will, even if we're stuck here till we die. I think we are."

"Maybe not." I tried to cheer him. "If we ever find Derek and Lupe—"

"Don't count on it." His voice was short. "I don't expect them—"

He caught himself.

"But we can't let it get us down." His grim face relaxed, and the crown lit an easy-seeming grin. "Here we are. Maybe in Little Mama's hell. Maybe at the gate to her heaven, if she had a heaven. We've got to make the best of any breaks we get."

"About the corath brotherhood?" I prompted him. "And your initiation?"

His voice grew more sober.

"Toron warned me that Sheko had laid her curse on the land ahead, but I let him lead us on. The lush jungle stuff gave way to a harsher sort of country. The trail spread wider, winding through gnarled and stunted trees. Sometimes it followed a scrap of ancient pavement. We passed a tall black granite stele, the inscriptions eroded away, and crossed a deep ravine on a dry viaduct that once carried water to a field of stony mounds that had been a city once.

"Relics of the Grand Dominion, Toron said. It was a rich and happy land, he said, until the sad day that Sheko found Anak with a human woman. In her rage she tore stars from the sky to hurl at them, and breathed death on him and all the women he had dared to love.

"Yet that vengeance gave her no joy. Mad with grief for the love she had lost, she rebuilt the stones of his palace into a tomb for him and sowed the seed of the *Slubro-Slubroc* to guard it from his bastard half-human sons. When that was done, she built her own tomb and lay in it to die of sorrow."

Ram made a quizzical face.

"Toron's story. Sheer nonsense to me. Lupe says such legends have nearly always grown out of some actual event, but it's hard to imagine any kernel of truth—"

He stopped to listen to a faint and distant banshee wail.

"Sometimes I wonder about Sheko and her breath of death. As we went on, we kept on stumbling on signs of some blight I never understood. The blasted vegetation gave way to stark desolation. The sun seemed hotter. A few high clouds gave no rain. We sweated on across naked rock and dunes of drifted dust.

"Death's dark domain." He gave me a wry little grin. "That was my pet phrase for it. A dead gray waste. No life anywhere. It got to me. Dead stone. Dead sand. Dead silence. No birds sang. Nothing moved, not even a lizard. It left me wondering what killed the Grand Dominion.

"We, ourselves, were close to death, but Toron tramped on till I thought he was mad. My feet were blistered. Our food was gone, the last water canteen half empty. I thought we ought to turn back and asked Toron if we had gone too far for that.

" 'No go back.' He was learning English. 'We get there.' I asked him where.

" 'Place of life,' he said. 'Place of wisdom. Cave of Elders.'

"Next day," Ram continued, "we saw a dark streak across the bleak horizon ahead, and then a faint green line below it. It rose as we neared it, a long escarpment of red sandstone. Next morning we reached another aqueduct. Half ruined, it still carried a thin stream of water from a spring at the foot of a cliff.

"Water! We'd been desperate for it. Toron and his men knelt to kiss the ground and give thanks to Anak. We buried our faces in the stream to drink, splashed each other to wash off all the sweat and grime. Following the aqueduct, we came to a field of growing corn, and then a row of ripe yellow melons as sweet as cantaloupes.

"Heaven!" He shrugged and laughed at himself. "I thought we'd crossed Little Mama's hell and reached her heaven. We stuffed ourselves with those melons and tramped on into that small paradise. I heard what sounded like a mockingbird singing. A man shouted at us from a mango tree. Ram called to him and he climbed down and came to meet us.

"An angel, I thought, in Little Mama's heaven. Or at least a saint. A tall black man in a neat green tunic and turban. His flowing beard was white with age, though he seemed spry as I was, carrying his basket of ripe mangos. They embraced, greeting each other in a language new to me.

" 'Olec Ahn,' Toron said. 'Voice of Elders.'

"He shared his mangos and guided us along the cliffs to an overhang that sheltered the mouth of a limestone cave. He hammered a gong that brought a dozen men out of the fields and the cave.

" 'Elders,' Toron said. 'Leaders of Elderhood.'

"They were an odd little group: all of them black, aged but fit, all of them uniformed in the green tunic and turban. They surrounded us, staring at me, calling questions to Toron in that tongue I'd never heard. We were still famished. At last, when the questions were answered, they set out a feast: dried meat, dried fruit, and hard dry bread.

"As we ate, I had questions of my own for Toron. He was slow to answer.

" 'Place of secrets,' he said. 'Secrets kill you.'

"The Elders do have secrets that I have sworn to guard, but there are things I am free to say. The Elderhood is not a government; the blacks are scattered in hundreds of isolated nomadic bands. They want no government. The Council of the Elders is a little like a college, a little like a monastery, a little like a congress, but without visible power. It has only thirteen members, elected from thirteen secret cells scattered through the jungle.

"The Elders think of themselves as the last surviving vestige of the Grand Dominion. They've been trying to find and preserve relics of it, hoping for some kind of restoration and recovery. Toron sees a new promise in our arrival. There's the legend of a half-god, marked with the crown of worlds, returning through the Gate of Anak to restore the Grand Dominion. Toron saw us appear there. He's seen the mark. He wants to believe.

"Yet he's a realist, a doubter of miracles. There have been known con men tattooed with the crown who proclaimed their own grand schemes. He first took me for another, but that didn't matter. He hoped to use me as a symbol to energize the slave rebellion.

"He took me to see the archives of the Elderhood and relics of the lost empire stored at the back of the cave. The Elders have no real writing system, but he showed me sheaves of little bamboo splints strung on cords and notched along the edges to record names and dates and facts.

"He showed me a shelf of e-books like the one he gave me, and a chest made of something still as bright as stainless steel. It was lined with gold and filled with little crystal rods. Magic sticks, he called them, their magic long forgotten. Transparent as glass, they flashed with colored lights and made musical notes when he rubbed them. Books or records, I imagine, that Lupe and Derek would give their eyeteeth to see.

"My initiation began the day after we arrived. We fasted that night. Drums woke me at daybreak. Seven of the Elders were out on the ledge under the overhang, shuffling around a huge copper kettle of boiling corath, chanting in cracked falsettos. The drummers paused at sunrise, but the chant went on. Olec Ahn came out of the cave to add a cup of brown powder that turned his brew the color of blood.

"He dipped out a cupful, held it toward the rising sun until the chant was ended, and gave it to the dancers. They passed it from lip to lip and back to him. He filled the cup for Toron and again for me. Scalding hot, it had a strange bitter taste. I took a gulp and passed it on."

He made a face.

"Back on Earth I'd tried half a dozen different drugs. They never hit me hard or made me want another shot. That red brew was different. It was slow to act, but the effect of it frightens me even now. The rites are secret, but there's a story I'd tell Lupe if I had a chance. A creation myth she would love. Toron translated it for me.

"All things were born from empty darkness. The first star shone alone until it bore the constellations. Each star burned alone until it bore its planets. They bore no life until the First World hatched worms from its dead sea mud. Those worms climbed into sunlight and evolved the Eternals, who were immortal.

"The Eternals bore Anak and Sheko, who sent robots to open the gates and search the universe for other minds. The robots found life on Earth and carried it to seed the sterile worlds. Anak and Sheko brought the human kind here, and nurtured the civilization that bloomed into the Grand Dominion.

"Unhappily, however, they had left their immortality behind. They fell out. Sheko murdered Anak and herself died of grief. Without them, the Grand Dominion crumbled into a thousand ways of ruin and death. Its few survivors in the Elderhood are striving to restore the world they lost."

Ram paused, his dark face grave in the birthmark's glow, his head tipped as if to listen for those distant jungle sounds. All I heard was a distant splash, as if a fish had jumped in the river. He shrugged. I saw his dark grin, and his voice had fallen when he went on.

"Those words are Toron's, as I recall them. They seem dead when I say them now, but they carried a life and a fire of their own when I heard them chanted to the drumbeat as the dancers swayed around that copper pot. It may have been that blood-red brew, or only my own imagination, but I felt my mind expand in ways I can't describe.

"I shared the awe of the dancers when they saw those first constellations explode out of primal darkness. I felt Olec Ahn's wonder as he watched Anak's robots swarming to open the gates and bearing life to seed the new planets. I felt Toron's shiver of terror when Sheko breathed death upon the world.

"An unsettling experience." He shrugged again, and the birthmark lit a solemn frown. "I've always yearned for truth. I learned first from my Little Mama, who cared for me before I was old enough to care for her. She filled my head with what my father called silly superstition.

"His people had been devout Brahmans until exile and Africa made the American dollar their god. My mother was raised a Moslem. I learned to pray in a Christian missionary school. I came to America with no real faith. It was Lupe and Derek who taught me science, the method of asking nature herself for the truth. But that ritual . . ."

He shivered, the birthmark shimmering.

"The ritual went on till sunset. Olec Ahn gave us cup after cup of his bitter brew till the copper pot was empty. The drums are still beating in my head. The dancers shuffled on till they reeled and fell, chanting things I can't speak about. I found myself with them in the circle, joining in the chant as if I had always known it. I understood it then, or thought I did."

He shrugged, with a bleak grimace.

"We were sweating, limping, dead on our feet. Olec Ahn kept passing the cup to revive us, but one by one the dancers crum-

pled to the ground until only Toron and I were left. The sun was
setting before he fell and left me alone. The drummers stopped.
In my last recollection the world had changed around me.

"I stood alone under a dismal sky, black with smoke, tinged
red with the fire of a great city burning on that empty desert we
had crossed. I heard missiles shrieking overhead, gunfire rat-
tling, great explosions thudding. Lurid flares floated out of the
smoke. They lit great towers toppling, splendid domes crum-
bling into debris. I caught human voices screaming in agony
and terror, faint and far away."

He sighed and shook his head.

"A dreadful thing. I'm afraid it really happened, though I
don't know when or how I saw it. That was the end of—of
whatever that bitter drink did to me. I woke in a cold gray
dawn, lying on the ledge beside the empty kettle, my body stiff
and numb. The drums and the chant had ceased. All I could
hear was some strange bird trilling. The first thing I felt was a
sharp tingle in the birthmark. It became a stabbing pain that
ached through all my body.

"I lay there till the rising sun warmed me and the pain faded
away. The sun was high before I could sit up. I found the
dancers sprawled all around me, seeming as dead as I had been.
A fire was crackling under the kettle, and Olec Ahn came with
a cup of common tea, brewed from dried and roasted corath
leaves. It revived me. One by one, the others groaned and
moved.

"I think we'd all been brain dead. All memory blotted out."
He blinked and shivered, frowning at me. "My mind had gone
blank. Little Mama back in Mombasa, Lupe and her digs, the
years at Eastern, even our Friday poker nights, all my life was
blotted out. I lay there on the ledge the rest of the day, working
to recover the life of my mind and my limbs. By sunset I could

stand. The others were all awake. Olec Ahn gathered them around me. They squatted, open hands spread, and began a chant in that sacred tongue.

"Praying to me!"

He hesitated, eyeing me with a wary expression.

"The words were strange at first, but as dusk fell I began to understand."

He covered the birthmark with his hand and let darkness fill the cabin.

"They were taking me for a god. For the half-human son of Anak, born to liberate the land and lead the people out of slavery."

CHAPTER
21

"What am I?" The light from his forehead left most of Ram's face in shadow, giving him a haunted look. "A demigod, destined to liberate the continent? Or just a mad genetic freak?"

When I had no ready answer, he shrugged and his tone grew graver.

"I've never been sure who I am, or what I was meant to be. In my first recollections, Little Mama is rocking me on her knee, crooning her sagas of Anak and Sheko and the fall of the Grand Dominion, using a language my father called a crazy babble. She told me I was a son of Anak, marked with the crown and born to rule the world in the sky where she was born.

"She believed the emerald pendant was a magic talisman that had guided her out of her own far world and through the Sahara Gate and on across Africa to meet the Portuguese exile who became my great-grandfather. My father laughed at that, but the magic was exciting as long as I believed it. Now I don't know what to think."

He lifted the pendant on its silver chain and sat a moment peering at it.

"Lupe and Derek have taught me a little science. Fireflies and deep-sea creatures have genes for luminescence that can be transposed into other genomes. Could be the work of some master geneticist, back in the age of the Grand Dominion. I'd like to know what it was for."

He shook his head and lay back on his berth.

"Magic?" I asked, as baffled as he was. "Meant to mark you for some special destiny?"

"It's uncanny," he muttered. "A curse I can't understand. I don't believe in magic, and I wish we'd never left the Earth. I don't want any special destiny."

The birthmark lit the ceiling for a time, but it dimmed when he slept. I lay awake a long time, wondering with mingled hope and dread where the crown of worlds would take us. Dozing at last, I had mad dreams of millions of multicellular robots pouring through the Stonehenge gate to conquer Earth. I felt grateful when the sun rose and I heard the steam whistle and the engine puffing.

We steamed on toward Periclaw. Kenleth dreaded the city. Next morning I found him leaning over the rail, staring into the wake. He started when I spoke.

"You frightened me." His eyes were dark and hollow. I saw dark tear streaks down his cheeks. "I was thinking of my mother. After what Ty Chenji said, I'm afraid I'll never see her again. Afraid they'll kill me because my father was black."

White Water saw his mood and tried to cheer him up.

"Don't fret, kid. I've known blacks and whites and in-betweens. Some are good and some are rotten. The shade of color never matters. I can't tell the women apart in the dark. I see no justice in slavery and I hate to see the races at war."

He was young and he did cheer up. The voyage became high adventure for him. He made a friend of the mulatto engineer and learned how the engine worked. White Water let him blow the whistle when we approached a fuel station. The cook taught him to fish off the rail and broiled his catch for all of us.

Around bend after bend, the flooded Blood carried us on between dark jungle walls toward more omens of darkness. We met gunboats cruising upriver and saw a big paddle wheeler aground on a sandbar, refugees waving to us from the deck. We passed a gunboat firing over a burning mansion at some target in the jungle beyond. The forests opened at last, on flat green fields that reached as far as we could see.

"The delta," White Water told us. "All of it worthless salt marshland once, rich plantations now."

When the channel took us near the bank I saw slaves at work. Men, women, little children, stooping in flooded paddies to plant rice. Crawling with baskets to dig potatoes. Swinging bright blades to cut sugar cane. Leaning in harness to pull wagons and carts and plows.

Once, far off, I saw bodies hung like black fruit in a solitary tree.

I found Ram leaning over the rail, staring up the river.

"It has run forever." A bleak look on his face, he turned to shake his head at me. "Beyond control, like history. We can't turn it back." My eyebrows must have risen. "Fighting all the power of Norlan, Toron and the Elderhood are trying to swim against the tide of history."

"We're making history." I groped for a crumb of hope. "They've got a chance."

"Maybe." He shrugged and turned gloomily to peer at the

horizon ahead. After a time he spoke again. "My Little Mama was born here. She called it hell. She used to talk about a blood-colored river and her mother hanged, screaming, in a tree. She found a little mirror to show me the birthmark and quoted her epics about my great destiny."

I had no idea how to break his dismal mood, but I tried not to fret. As we steamed on toward Periclaw, his spirits seemed to lift. That afternoon we were standing with White Water at the wheel, listening to his tales of the river. He gestured at the flat green horizon ahead.

"There's the city."

All I saw was one far dark spear point stabbing the sky.

"That's the Sheko tower," he said. "One ancient monument too solid to fall. It stands on a rock in the middle of the river, at what's now the city center. It was on an island off the coast before the delta built up around it."

"I've heard about it." Ram nodded. "Anak built a fortress there to guard the river. Sheko knocked it down after he was dead. You wonder how I know?" I saw a wistful smile. "My Little Mama told me. Toron says there's still a Sheko cult. Pilgrims from light-skinned tribes up and down the coast that still come to worship there. Tribes with Norlan blood."

Periclaw is really two cities. White Water told us its story as the skyline came into view. Peri is the older, built on the wedge of land where the river channel split on its way to the sea. It began as a stronghold of pirates who preyed on the river trade. Norlan slavers seized it. He called it a mongrel city now, open to black or white or brown. Claw's the new city across the channel, higher up the river and higher on the social scale. Residence is limited to whites and legally registered slaves.

He pointed at a dark bluff that blocked half the channel ahead.

"That's Blood Hill," he said. "It's a fortress, a prison, and the capitol of the colony."

The channel narrowed as we neared it, and brought us close to the fortress wall. Built of enormous blocks of black stone, it towered sheer from the river. Cannon muzzles jutted out of ports high above us. The dark shadow of it chilled me with a sense of cruel and ruthless power.

"The guns command the river mouth," White Water said. "The river commands the continent. And Norlan commands the river."

I felt relieved when we came around the bend, past that frowning wall. White Water pointed at the riverbank just beyond it.

"The fleet yard and constabulary base. The captain says we'll have to leave you there." He shook our hands and gave Kenleth an odd little white metal disk stamped with strange inscriptions. "I found it in a jungle ruin that had been a temple of Anak, the locals told me. It was a Grand Dominion coin, they say. And a symbol of good fortune, if you believe the legends."

I was trying to believe in many things. In the mystic power of the crown of worlds shining on Ram's forehead. In some great destiny for him, and perhaps some final rebirth of the lost splendors of the Grand Dominion. In some happy future for Kenleth in a world with no place for him. In our own final safe return to Earth.

But that was hard when I looked back at that black wall and White Water spoke of all the slaves who had died piling up those huge stones. My faint spark of hope had melted into dark unease. When the cook called us down to our last meal on the gunboat, I found no real appetite.

———

Beyond the fortress we came in view of the Sheko Tower. A windowless cone of some brown stone, it had once marked the center of a long bridge across the river. Most of the bridge had fallen to floods and quakes and endless age, but a few great stone piers still stood, and one magnificent arch.

Kenleth asked who lived there.

"Nobody." White Water frowned. "Nobody would want to. Even the pilgrims stay only to kill their goats, bleed their own privates, and burn their gifts to Sheko's ghost."

Beyond the fortress the river widened into Periclaw Harbor. A seagoing steamer was loading at the commercial docks, across on the other side of the channel. Ant-small in the distance, slaves in endless files were trotting out of warehouses with heavy bags and bales and boxes on their shoulders, toiling up gangways to the deck.

The captain took the helm to dock us at the military wharves below the fortress. He kept us aboard until a subaltern arrived with a squad of riflemen to take charge of us. They were black, and Ram asked White Water if they might desert and join their rebel kin.

"No chance." White Water shrugged. "They're freedmen. Disciplined well and paid to forget who they are."

The subaltern was a lean young redhead from the north continent, his fair face spattered with gold freckles from the tropic sun. The name on his badge was Enec Hawn.

"Ty William Stone?" He read our names from a slate, stumbling over the "W" phoneme, which is strange to the Norlan dialect. Well briefed to receive us, he stepped close to give me a piercing look, and made Ram take off the black beret to let him study the birthmark. I heard no warmth in his crisp official voice.

"Ty Ram Chenji?"

"Yes, sir," Ram said.

"Where were you born?"

"On another world," Ram said. "We call it Earth."

He blinked and scribbled on the slate.

"What purpose brought you here?"

"No purpose," Ram said. "We've been lost, wandering through this system of connected worlds, looking for a way back home."

He looked at me. "Where is this Earth?"

My mouth was dry. I had to swallow before I said, "In the sky, far from here."

He squinted again at the birthmark and studied us both. Ram, with his multicolored robe and long jungle knife, might have been another native, but he examined my skin, my glasses, my wristwatch, my worn hiking boots. Keeping a sternly doubtful face, he shrugged and scribbled on the slate.

"Ty Hawn." Ram's voice lifted, "We have found a new purpose since we came through that stone gate on Mount Anak. I've met the Elders, the elected leaders from the rebel tribes. They've seen this birthmark." He touched the crown. "They take it as a sign that I was born to lead a rebellion to free the slaves. They've sent me to negotiate for a truce."

"So?" Hawn's face went hard. "What sort of truce?"

"Justice, Ty." Ram flinched from Hawn's sneer. "Right. The Hotmen have been exploited too long."

Hawn's sunburned face flushed redder with anger.

"Go slow." I caught Ram's arm to draw him aside. "We've got no gunboats. You can't run a bluff with nothing in the hole."

"Right?" Hawn was exploding. "Justice? Norlan doesn't treat with beasts out of the jungle."

Ram straightened boldly, turning back to face him. Perhaps

he thought the birthmark could serve him as an ace. Perhaps the Elderhood's corath tea had merely made him reckless. I felt sick with dread but he seemed strangely cool.

"Hear me, please." He found a tone of calm conciliation. "I'm speaking for the Elders. They're asking Norlan to recognize the Elderhood as an independent republic. They ask for an end to slavery, for guarantees of equal rights for their citizens, for free trade on the river, for untaxed exports to Norlan."

"An end to slavery!" Hawn clenched a fist. "What sort of fool do you take me for?"

"Listen, Ty Hawn," Ram begged him. "You don't know the Elderhood, but I think they'll be able to take the river back, unless—"

"Hah!" Hawn cut him off. "We don't dicker with ape men. We've seen a dozen slave rebellions in the last hundred years. We've put them down and hanged the leaders."

Kenleth caught my hand and shrank closer to my side.

"You Norlanders have been on top too long." Ram shrugged and grinned at Hawn. "Ty, I've come to bring a warning and offer you a chance. The Elders have resources you don't imagine."

"Resources?" Hawn sniffed and gripped the handgun at his hip. "What resources?"

"Better for you if you never have to know."

"Get this, Chenji." Hawn looked at his slate. "The officer who picked you up had no authority to offer you any sort of amnesty. You offer no certificate of legal registration. Your ridiculous demands are high treason."

"I understand the risks." Ram nodded gravely. "I knew we were risking our lives to come here, but we were hoping to avert devastating tragedy. For Norlan as well as Hotlan."

"You'll get the hook through your ribs!" Horn snorted. "Hooks for all your outlaw slaves. If you didn't know, the

North Sea Fleet has already steamed from Glacier Gulf, bringing enough constabulary forces to recover control of the river and put this madness down."

I saw a flash of pity when he glanced at Kenleth, clinging to my hand in wide-eyed anxiety, but his blistered lip had curled when his narrow eyes came to me.

"If you say you came from a star, Ty Stone, you'll wish you'd never left it."

CHAPTER 22

"Ty Hawn—"

Ram had begun one more appeal, but Hawn frowned at his slate and turned to me.

"Ty Stone, if that really is your name—" He scowled and raised his voice. "Come along. I'll see you in my office."

The rifle squad in step behind, he escorted the three of us off the dock and through a guarded gate in the fortress wall. Inside, we climbed a steep pavement to a second gate in an inner wall that enclosed the whole hilltop. Ugly red brick buildings surrounded a drill field perhaps a mile long. The cannon muzzles we had seen jutted from a third wall around a knob on the crown of the hill.

All three walls were built of the same enormous black stone blocks.

"New to you?" Hawn gave me a sharp look when I paused to study them. "You'll get to know them."

"They're huge," I said. "I've never seen building stones so large."

"If you've never seen them—" He looked at me again as if

suspecting that I had. "I had to ask about them. They're relics of what the blacks call the Old Dominion. They were found scattered across the delta, half buried in the silt that had been laid down around them. Quite a riddle to historians."

He halted the rifle squad while he spoke.

"Where were they quarried? No source has ever been discovered. How were they worked? They're harder than granite. How were they moved? Every block weighs a dozen tons. Special equipment had to be built and shipped down from Glacier Point to dig them out and lay them in the wall. I've tried to question the natives. They tell me a fairy tale as fantastic as your Earth."

He gave me another searching look.

"Their black god fell out with his white wife. She invented weapons, raised a great army, and fought a war against him. These stones were in the walls of a fortress he built for his last stand. She won the final battle, killed him, and scattered the stones where we found them.

"Not that I believe it." Hawn shrugged and ordered his men on. "But those stones are still a mystery."

We climbed a flight of steps to a high terrace that looked over the outside walls and across the harbor to the Sheko Tower. Hawn dismissed most of his squad, but brought riflemen with us through a narrow door at the base of the central fortress.

Inside, we came into a dim twilight. Electricity was unknown here and the giant black blocks had been laid with no space for ground-floor windows. A few gas lamps, high and far apart, left dismal gloom in a cramped hallway. Guards saluted Hawn, patted me down for weapons, and kept my backpack.

Leaving Ram and Kenleth sitting on a stone bench, Hawn

took me down a narrow hall. Sharply, he ordered Kenleth back when he tried to follow me. I love the vast open spaces of New Mexico. His office was a tiny, windowless box that felt like a tomb. A small black boy squatted in the corner, hauling languidly at a rope that swung a big fan back and forth above a bare stone desk.

He nodded at a chair in front of the desk. "Sit down."

I sat, but he stood behind the desk, watching with a wary hostility, as if I had been some uncaged and dangerous animal. Feeling terribly alone, I longed for Ram's cheerful competence, Derek's grasp of science, Lupe's easy way with people, even Kenleth's childish trust. In spite of the fan, I felt sweat trickling down my ribs.

"Ty Stone." His sudden voice startled me. "I've seen the intelligence reports on you and your black companion with the headlamp on his forehead. The commission takes no stock in the tale that he's a god come down from the sky to liberate the blacks. They certainly won't discuss the truce he demands.

"As for you—" He searched my face again and his voice grew stern. "You appear to be white. Your association with him and the insurgents makes you a traitor to your race and your nation. Governor Volmer, however, has authorized me to offer you a chance to save your life."

He sat down, frowning at me.

"Are you willing to answer questions?"

"I am."

He clapped his hands. A slender pale brown woman came to perch on a stool at the end of his desk, a pen poised over her notebook.

"You say you come from a place you call Earth. Where is that?"

"It's another planet, sir. Many light-years across the universe."

Hawn and the woman seemed baffled by the English words and I knew no translations. When I tried to explain what a planet was, he cut me curtly off, as if he doubted that other worlds existed.

"What's your age, Ty Stone?"

"Fifty-seven Earth years, sir. I don't know how many of yours."

He asked what an Earth year was. I tried to explain that it was the time the planet Earth required to complete its orbit around the sun, but I was lost for words he could understand. He stopped me curtly.

"Enough of your clever jargon. I want the simple truth."

"I'm trying, sir, but I'm too new here to know your language."

With a helpless shrug, the brown woman laid her pen down. Hawn sat for a time glaring at me, but finally shrugged and nodded for her to continue.

"The inquiry will proceed." His tone was sardonic. "My orders are to hear your story and advise further action. Describe this planet Earth."

"It's another world, sir. About the size of this one, far off among the stars. Our plants and creatures are pretty much like yours."

He scowled, shook his head, and finally spoke again.

"It has people? Whites like you? Blacks like Chenji?"

"It does."

He sat in stony disbelief till the woman murmured something.

"The blacks—are they slaves?"

"Some were, long ago. We have abolished slavery."

The woman lifted her pen, waiting for his response. His own gaze sharpened.

"You did?" He shook his head. "What did you do with the slaves?"

"They are citizens, sir. Legally, all of us are equal."

"Equals?" His eyebrows lifted in irony. "You call yourselves fellow animals?"

"Blacks are human, sir."

"I must warn you." His voice rose and he began to lecture me. "Any such claim is the crime of sedition, punishable with prison. Blacks may have human forms, but they are a failed creation, stupid, lazy, and lawless, animals by law and in fact."

The woman murmured and he slowed his hot voice to give her time to write.

"Whatever fiction you may invent, the world was a special creation, designed to cradle humanity. The sun moves to light our way through it. Plants on land and fish in the sea are there to nourish us. Animals, even your pet blacks, were made to serve us."

His voice rang strong again.

"If the seas are sometimes stormy, if the jungles are sometimes deadly, if the black animals sometimes rise against us, those are trials to test our strength and make us stronger. The blacks are said to hold secret ceremonies for the worship of their black god and a white whore that murdered him. We worship the nature that made us. Heresy is a felony. Preaching heresy is punishable with death."

With nothing to say that might change such opinions, I sat sweating in uneasy silence until he shrugged and spoke abruptly.

"This mongrel child? What's he to you?"

"A friend. He was lost and alone in the jungle. His parents may be dead. I'm caring for him."

"Do you have a license to keep him?"

"If I need a license, how do I get it?"

"I doubt that you can. Such licenses are limited, their possession restricted and rarely granted." He frowned severely. "If you claim not to know the law, any close association would make you suspect. Any coupling with animals is strictly forbidden. Guilty females are destroyed, along with the offspring. So are black males, when identified."

The pale brown woman held her pen ready. He waited for a moment, as if expecting me to speak, but the narrow gas-lit office was suddenly a prison cell, he my vigilant jailor. With no key to freedom, I could only long for the sunlit campus back home.

"That's your situation." He gave me a piercing glance. "If you want to save your life, I want a full confession."

"Sir," I tried to protest, "I have nothing to confess."

He raised his freckled hand to sweep my words aside.

"I'll be honest with you, Ty Stone. Frankly, we're asking for your aid." His tone had suddenly warmed. "We, ourselves, are facing our own ugly situation. Black hostility is nothing new, but remote free tribes are hearing of Chenji and sending men to join the war. Planters and traders have already suffered heavy damage.

"The rebels and their allies are hard to fight. They're using terror tactics. They hit us where we don't expect them and then melt back into the jungle. Our problem is intelligence. We get lies and rumors enough, but no hard facts. That's what we want from you. A full and honest report on your black companion and the outlaws around him.

"In return for your help, the high commission is offering you total amnesty from the charge of treason." He was fleetingly sardonic. "Nothing is likely to win you any popular welcome as the savior of Periclaw, but we can give you bodyguards if you need them, or arrange a disguised identity. We can even save that mongrel pup, if you like."

Sitting there under the flicker of a gaslight set on the ceiling of that dusky little room, I felt frozen, numb, trapped, helpless. All I could do was listen to his hard, tyrannic voice.

"Forget your tales of other worlds in the sky and the myth of Chenji's holy destiny. We want to know who you are, where you came from, how you got involved with Chenji."

"We came from Earth, a world that moves around a star too far to see from here. He and I were teachers at a school there."

"That won't save your skin." He barked what I thought must be an expletive and paused to let the woman struggle with my words. "We are not stupid. We are not naïve. We have native agents in the field and competent intelligence men here at headquarters. We aren't children. We're not that easy to deceive."

"You say you want the truth." I spoke from baffled desperation. "The truth is all I have to say."

He shrugged and waited for the woman to nod.

"This is your chance, Ty Stone." He stressed the honorific. "We want what you know about these so-called Elders. Their organization. Their leadership. Their weapons, if they have better weapons than their jungle blades. The whole truth."

He waited. The woman looked at me, her pen poised. Thinking of Ram's story of the Elders and his secret initiation, I shook my head.

"If that is all you want to say—"

His face set hard, he clapped his hands. The woman folded her notebook and the soldiers came to take me back to the anteroom. Kenleth was there alone, huddled down on the long stone bench.

"Oh, Ty Will!" He ran to put his arms around me. "They took Ty Chenji away, they wouldn't tell him where. I was afraid I'd never see you again."

He peered at the guard and uneasily back at me.

"What will happen to us now?"

"I don't know," was all I could say, but I put my arms around him for what comfort that might give him.

CHAPTER
23

The prison stood behind the long row of red brick buildings we had passed, its tall brick wall capped with blades of broken glass. The warden was a fat mulatto in a brown uniform, his skin a milky chocolate, a license number branded on his forehead. I asked about Ram.

"Special guest." He smiled and spread his hands to greet us, but I wondered what he meant. "No contact with anybody. Orders same for you and unlicensed child."

More amiable than Hawn, if not so literate, he kept us an hour in his office, listening to my story with such close attention that I thought he meant to check it against Ram's. He thanked me as if half inclined to believe it, and put us in a cell on the ground floor, a level reserved for whites.

We were there nineteen days. The cell was clean, the food edible, but those were endless days of uncertainty and dread. The guards were blacks who never spoke. I paced the floor for exercise, but we were never allowed out of the cell. Kenleth wanted to learn English. On the nineteenth morning, to relieve the deadly tedium, I was teaching him to recite lines I knew from Shakespeare's *Tempest*.

The locks clanked. The guards called us out, took us to a conference room, and left us there without a hint of explanation. We sat at a long table there, waiting uneasily, until I heard the guards again. The door opened. An attractive young woman stood there, looking us over with intent blue eyes.

We stood up, staring back. Her skin was fine and very fair, the cheekbones high, her eyes wide-spaced. Straight platinum hair fell free behind her back. Her short white dress looked like silk. On a thin gold chain, she wore a large teardrop shape that glinted with a smoky opalescence.

A faint fragrance came with her into the stale prison air, a fresh sweetness like the lilac blooms in the spring in the bushes my grandfather planted along the gravel walk in front of the house. It was a ray of sunlight in the gloomy prison room.

She spoke to the guards. They went out and closed the door.

"Hello." Well-briefed, she knew the English word. "Ty Will Stone?" Waiting for me to nod, she scanned me again. Her eyes were blue and keen, her oval face quick and pleasant. I thought of Shakespeare's Miranda.

She turned to Kenleth. "Ty Kenleth Roynoc?"

He spread his open hands and bowed to greet her, beaming with instant adoration.

"I'm Celya Crail, from the Museum of Ancient History." She gestured for us to sit. "I've read Officer Hawn's report and spoken to Ty Chenji. He tells a remarkable story. I wish to confirm some of the details, if we may speak."

Her interest gave me a spark of hope, though her eyes had a glint of wary caution.

"Certainly," I said. "I know the story may be hard to accept."

"He says you came together from a world he calls Earth? Did you come alone?"

"Two others were with us." I had to assume that Ram had been honest with her.

"What were their names?"

"Dr. Derek Ironcraft and Dr. Lupe Vargas."

"Where are they now?"

"I don't know. We lost them on other worlds before we got here."

"Lost them? How?"

"They were captured and carried away by strange creatures."

"Can you describe those creatures?"

"They were enormous. Their bodies looked to be partly metal. They hopped on great legs and flew or glided on narrow wings."

Watching my face, she asked for more about Derek and Lupe. How old were they? How tall? How long had I known them? Did they have living parents or children? If they had been teachers, what had they taught?

She asked to see my glasses and inspected them closely. She asked about my watch. I told her it measured Earth time, and gave it to her. She peered at the jumping second hand, held it to her ear, and listened gravely while I tried to explain why the days of Earth were different.

"A clock." She nodded and gave it back. "I never saw one so small."

She paused to search my face again, and nodded as if with decision.

"Thank you both." She smiled at Kenleth to his delight, and turned back to me. "You seem to confirm Ty Chenji's story."

The smile disappeared when I asked if I could see him.

"I'm afraid that's impossible." She paused to frown at Kenleth. "I was allowed to interview him, but he is held in strict isolation, under extreme security."

"Ty Ram?" Kenleth's voice was an anxious wail. "Will they hang him?"

"I hope not," she told him, and turned very gravely to me. "Your corroboration of his narrative may save his life."

She was with us there in the prison for over an hour, asking more questions. She wanted to know about Earth and our lives there. She asked how Ram had been able to open our way from world to world. What kind of magic had kept the moving roads in motion so long after their builders were dead?

I had no explanations.

My attempt to describe the virtual world and the hidden battlefield bewildered her. She opened a notebook and had me try to draw a diagram of the twin planets and the skywire between them. She wanted a drawing of a multicellular robot. She asked what had killed the extinct civilization.

She seemed disappointed when I could only shrug and shake my head.

"That's a mystery that haunts us all." She frowned and shook her head. "I'm a historian. My field is prehistory, especially the evidences of the culture that left those monumental ruins buried under the jungle. I had no idea their power extended to other worlds. You and Ty Chenji have revealed exciting hints to the answer. I thank you."

A quick smile dimpled her cheeks. She looked far younger than most historians I had known, and her air of scholarship astonished me. When I asked for more about those hints, she sighed and shook her head.

"We have riddles enough, but no real answers. Explorers

have described the ruins and collected native folktales and myths about them. At the museum we are gathering artifacts for a hall of the Grand Dominion. Scholars have tried to decode the writing, but they have as yet found no key."

She sat for a moment frowning at Kenleth and turned back to me.

"On all those worlds, you found no clue to what destroyed them?"

"War, perhaps. We found an enormous cannon or missile launcher beside a road that was itself an amazing riddle. The road was still moving through a dead world, even though sections of it had been destroyed, apparently by great explosions. We found weapons and human skeletons in the crater-pitted battlefield hidden under that virtual world."

"That must be the answer." She nodded. "The natives worship a black god who came down from the sky with a white consort to create mankind and rule the Grand Dominion of mankind. A golden age endured until he fell in love with his own creation and took human women.

"In a jealous rage, the consort turned his white offspring into demons and raised an army of them to revolt against him, finally killing him and destroying all his works. The myth may reflect actual events, though the logic of it seems a little twisted. There's a lot of evidence of violent conflict: broken walls, fallen towers, enigmatic ruins buried ages ago.

"I think there was a war between the races."

Trouble on her face, she glanced at Kenleth and shook her head. He squirmed uncomfortably and gave me an anxious look. She turned soberly back to me.

"Thanks to Ty Chenji, I'm afraid it's happening again."

"Don't blame him," I begged her. "He was born with that birthmark, but we didn't come here to make any kind of trou-

ble. The gates were a trap that caught us. We've been lost, wandering, looking for any way back home."

"That's what he keeps saying." She shrugged. "It doesn't
matter. He has that shining crown on his forehead. The natives
believe he's the predicted son of Anak, sent from heaven to free
the slaves and lead them in a conquest of the world."

"The slave rebellion?" I waited for her to nod. "I suppose it
is a real threat to Periclaw, but Ram Chenji came out of the jungle at the risk of his life to bring an offer to end it. Isn't there a
chance for any sort of truce?"

"He's a fool!" Her voice turned violent. "A fool to leave his
jungle hideout. The slaves will never be freed. He's asking to
hang by his ribs with the rest of the rebels."

She clapped her hands and rose. The guards opened the door.

"Thank you, Ty Stone." She spread her hands and bowed.
"You and Ty Chenji have answered questions for me. The
Grand Dominion must have been greater than I ever imagined.
You've brought tantalizing hints about what brought it down."

"A war? What could have been the cause?"

"A black rebellion." Her face went bleak. "It killed the
Grand Dominion. The civilization that left its ruins in the jungle here. It nearly wiped out all humanity. In spite of the myths,
the Dominion was never black. It was a white empire, based on
slavery. Nothing else could account for all the engineering
wonders it created. Minds dulled by manual toil could never
have reached the other worlds you describe."

The idea startled me.

"That's hard to believe." She paused to let me continue. "We
saw no hint of human slavery on those other worlds. No evidence of any human labor. Those strange roads moved them-

selves. The skywire had no human crew. People like us must have lived on the last planet we saw, but they needed no slaves. We found those robots instead, mechanical slaves, waiting to work for whoever knew how to command them."

"That's the point." She stabbed a slim finger at me. "As I told Ty Chenji. The robots must have left the blacks with nothing to do. Unemployed, with no place where they belonged. Like idle kids, they turned to mischief. I think they tried to seize the power of the whites, without brains enough to use it. It was their animal stupidity that destroyed the Grand Dominion."

She shrugged and moved to go.

"Tyba Crail?" Kenleth rose anxiously. "Are we in bad danger?"

"Perhaps." She nodded somberly but gave him a wistful smile. "I'll help you if I can."

His gaze followed her fondly as she left the room, and a trace of her lilac scent lingered in the air.

CHAPTER
24

My breakfast next morning was ham and eggs, with a sort of toast, and orange juice, a feast I might have enjoyed back at home. Kenleth's dish held a thick yellow slab of something with an uncertain odor. I shared my tray with him.

"A special order," the fat black warden said when the guards brought us to his office. "Compliments of Tyba Crail." He grinned. "You have a friend." I wasn't sure of that, even when he added, "She wants to see you again."

Two rickshaws stood waiting outside his office, each with two Hotmen yoked to the pole. He released us to a pale brown officer sitting in one. Kenleth squeezed with me into the narrow seat of the other. The men ran with us to the prison gate and out through the avenues of Periclaw, which I had never seen.

"It's exciting!" Eyes shining, Kenleth looked to the right and left. "My mother lived here."

It was a white stone city, roofed with clay red tile, the balconied buildings no more than three or four stories tall. The streets were wide, lined with trees and blooming shrubs. They swarmed with slaves yoked to rickshaws, slaves harnessed to two-wheeled carts and heavy wagons, slaves carrying jars and boxes on their heads.

Yet, save for the muffled hum of human voices, the city seemed strangely silent. Muscle power is noiseless, and Periclaw had no mechanized transport. Silent, and strangely peaceful. If the black rebellion was a threat, I saw no shadow of it. From a street that took us to a higher level, I caught a glimpse of the harbor and the twin city on the other side. Freighters lined the docks, but I saw no battle craft, no hint of coming war.

An artist might have made it a scene of peace: The silver-bright canals branching from the river bank. The white Sheko spire standing on its river islet beyond the ruined bridge and causeway. The flat green delta plantations stretching on as far as I could see. Nearer, slaves at the commercial docks were as busy as ants, loading cargos for Norlan. Our black runners seemed docile, even cheerful, calling soft greetings to friends they met.

Periclaw looked secure, Ram's peace mission tragically forlorn.

The museum stood beyond a long pool of water lilies and well-cut lawns. We left the rickshaws at the white-columned entrance. The officer escorted us up the wide stone steps. Inside, we waited at the doorway until a yellow-clad mulatto girl brought Tyba Crail to accept our custody.

In a neat white cap and jacket, she was still brightly attractive, still an enigma to me. She had a quick smile for Kenleth, and opened her hands to me in a brisk, official manner. I caught a hint of her lilac scent. She took us into her office, itself almost a museum. Native artifacts hung along the walls: reed baskets, enormous hats, colorful rugs, knives and spears, and prayer mats.

She nodded me into a seat before her desk, which faced a

great window that looked out across the harbor. The desk held a sheaf of papers, a stack of slates, and an odd, two-handled drinking cup. Standing by my chair, Kenleth saw it and caught his breath.

"My mother!" he whispered. "She had that."

"Lovely, isn't it?" She picked it up very carefully and held it for me to see.

It looked like fine white porcelain, the lip rimmed with gold. The handles were green, shaped like palm leaves. One side held the image of a black head that looked almost like Ram's, even to a golden fleck for the crown of worlds on the forehead. The woman's ivory head, on the other side, could have been modeled from hers, a flake of black for the crown.

"Sheko and Anak." She turned to Kenleth. "You've seen it before?"

"My mother traded her diamond ring for it," he said. "It came from a tomb. Ty Hake sold it to a man from Periclaw."

"A unique item," she said. "We bought it for the Grand Dominion collection."

Kenleth's eyes were still fixed on it.

"My mother." He made a sad face. "I think she's dead."

She set it back on the desk and turned gravely to face me.

"I'm removing you from the prison," she said. "For your own safety."

"Who would hurt us?" Kenleth asked her. "We aren't hurting anybody."

"People who fear Ty Chenji. They want to believe his story is a lie. If they got rid of him and silenced you—" She paused to frown at me. "They think that could end the slave rebellion."

"I'm afraid for us." His anxious eyes fixed on her face. "I'm afraid for Ty Ram."

"You are in danger." She nodded soberly. "But you should be safer with me."

"Thank you." A wistful smile lit his eyes. "I love you, Tyba Crail."

"Don't say that." Her face hardened as if he had offended her. His smile went out. His color was wrong for such emotion. She turned the cup on her desk and sat for a moment with her eyes on the black god's image before she looked back at me.

"You understand your danger?"

"With the little I know, I'm trying to."

"I've talked to Ty Chenji." Her smile held a flash of warmth. She paused thoughtfully and I saw her glance at my watch. "You've confirmed what he tells me. I suppose our planet is as much of a puzzle to the two of you as your Earth might be to me."

"Puzzle enough." I'd begun to like her.

"I've been briefing Ty Chenji," she said. "Perhaps we should review a little more of our history."

She pushed the cup back to its place and sat a moment organizing what she meant to say.

"The Hotlan continent was discovered ten generations ago. The jungles and people here on the east coast seemed so hostile that the first explorers passed it by. The west coast seemed more inviting. Gold was discovered in the sands of the dry riverbeds in the narrow desert strip between the mountains and the sea. Adventurers came to wash out the gold and abandoned their shantytowns when it was gone.

"Settlement of the east coast didn't begin until generations later. One of my own forefathers was on the first ship to sail into the Blood. He led a group ashore on the delta and stayed behind to live with a native tribe. He learned languages and guided later expeditions up the river.

"He left two sons who became captains in the Norlan fleet. The elder turned pirate, preying on the river commerce. He built the first fort on the delta. The younger stayed loyal, captured the fort, hanged his brother, and became one of the first delta planters.

"His son organized the first colonial assembly, to speak for the planters' rights. The high commission, appointed by Norlan, stands against the Blood River Authority, which is elected by the planters. My father heads the authority now. He tries to keep some kind of peace with the commission. Never easy!"

She shrugged and made a face.

"Norlan claims the whole continent, but it has never actually controlled anything beyond Periclaw, the delta, and a few spots along the river. The commission tries to prohibit, tax, and control everything it can reach. The authority fights for free speech, free trade, free traffic on the river. We dream of total independence, which Norlan will never grant.

"The slave rebellion is the big issue now. Norlan sneers at Chenji and his talk of a truce. They want to believe he's a fraud, that his shining mark is some kind of weird tattoo. They want to hang him and crush the revolt with military force. They expect an army and a fleet from Glacier Bay."

She was speaking freely now, as if quoting arguments she had made to some Norlan authority.

"We colonials feel a little differently. The Norlanders might go hungry if their food imports were cut off, but their lives are not in danger. Here on the river we live side by side with the slaves, at their mercy if they want to kill us. Planter families have already been slaughtered. And Chenji—"

Absently turning the cup to study the black god's head, she frowned and sighed.

"I want to trust him, but he's a problem I don't know how to solve. He denies that he's any supernatural being, but he can't explain the way that sacred mark glows at night. The natives are convinced that he was sent down from the sky to lead the rebellion and restore the Grand Dominion.

"And you, Ty Stone—"

She looked up from the cup to frown at me.

"You and Chenji will live or die together. Without you to prove his story of the sacred gates and all those other worlds beyond them, he'd hang today. Without your tie to him, you could die for sedition. The two of you have persuaded me. Others are harder to sway, but most of those who want to hang him now are willing to listen when I tell them that a dead martyr could do more for the rebels than a live captive."

Turning the cup again, she shook her head at Sheko's image as if it had spoken.

"So what will happen now?" I couldn't help asking that anxious question. "What do you expect?"

"Who knows?" She shrugged, her lips drawn tight. "Chenji sees no peace without a truce, with some plan to end slavery. We can't afford that. Our lives depend on slavery. Our whole culture is built on it. Yet the revolt is already killing us. Responsible planters in the assembly are hoping for some sort of compromise that will bring peace with the free tribes and let their lives go on.

"Feelings are high. Norlan could lose the continent that feeds it. We colonials could lose our lives. No matter whether Chenji is a divine son of Anak or just a clever liar, both sides blame him for the crisis. Those who fear him fear you just as much.

"That's the way things stand." She pushed the cup aside. "No good for anybody, but I thought you ought to know."

She had smiled again at Kenleth.

"Anak aid you, Tyba Crail." Voice quavering, he opened his hands and bowed to her. "If you can save us."

"I have your custody," she said. "I'm taking you to my home."

Rickshaws waited at the museum door. She got into one and led the way. Kenleth and I followed in another, with two branded mulatto guards running behind us. We came into a section of wider streets and impressive mansions with garden parks or high stone walls around them. We stopped outside a thick-barred wrought iron gate.

"You'll meet my people." She spoke while we waited for a black keeper to open the gate. "My father is chairman of the assembly. He owns a delta plantation, with two thousand slaves. My mother's an Icecape heiress. She didn't want you in the house, but my father insisted and people are curious. She has invited guests for dinner."

Eyes narrowed critically, she surveyed me, my ragged beard and uncut hair, my soiled and tattered clothing.

"Dress for the affair is formal."

The gate swung open. Inside, a wide pavement curved to a marble-columned portico. A black butler in spotless white met us at the door and fixed Kenleth with a scornful stare.

"You will leave the boy," she said. "He is not permitted in

the house. He will sleep in the slave quarters."

"He's not a slave," I told her. "He stays with me."

She frowned severely.

"Residence in Periclaw is limited to whites. Others are not allowed."

"His mother was white."

"He is not." Her voice grew sharper. "Resident nonwhites must be registered, licensed, and numbered. They are commonly branded."

I saw Kenleth flinch as if he could see the hot iron coming.

"His mother was born here in Periclaw. Her father was an Authority official. She had to leave the city before he was born, to save her life and his. He didn't choose the color of his skin."

"His misfortune." She shrugged. "The law is the law. Custom is custom. Our ways are our own."

"Kenleth stays with me," I said. "Or I stay with him."

"Out of the question." Her face set. "I have your custody. I am responsible for your security."

"I'll take my chances." I put my arm around him. "He's with me. Call him my son."

She shook her head, sternly impatient. "That could cost you rights you're going to need."

I drew him closer. She faced me for half a minute, anger smoldering in her eyes.

"Your choice." At last she shrugged. "His registration can be delayed."

"Thank you, Tyba Crail." He tried to smile at her, but she had turned away.

At a sharp word from her, the black butler shrugged and escorted us up a marble stair to a corner room on the third floor.

He shut the door and left us there alone. Kenleth put his arms around me. I felt his heart thumping.

"Thank you, Ty Will," he whispered. "I don't like it here."

He stared around him in uneasy wonder. The walls were high; the room seemed enormous. Mosquito nets hung around a huge four-poster at the center of the floor. White lace curtained tall glass doors that looked across a railed balcony to a sea of red-tiled roofs that ran down to the broad brown river and a far line of green plantations.

"My mother had pictures," he said. "She lived in places like this. She grieved for her twin brother and the friends she had to leave. I think she was sorry she ever had me, but I do miss her. Terribly."

I myself was longing just as keenly. For news of Ram. For news of Derek and Lupe, wherever they were. Longing even for my students and my university friends and the tiny crises we used to debate in the faculty senate. Earth had become an impossible dream.

The lock had clicked when the butler left. I tried the door; it didn't yield. I felt a sudden sense of suffocation. We'd been confined too long. Wanting to get out and walk, wanting sun and space and air to breathe, I rapped on the door. After an endless wait, a huge mulatto guard appeared.

"To go outside?" His eyes rolled in astonishment. "Ty, you have no permission."

He closed the door and the lock clicked again.

To endure the empty time, we gave each other language lessons. I recited my scraps of Shakespeare and we tried to translate. Kenleth listened avidly when I tried to answer his questions about Elizabethan England. Earth must have been as strange and wonderful to him as the universe of the trilithons had been to me.

The door opened, late that afternoon, and quiet black servants came in to ready me for dinner. A silent barber shaved me and cut my hair. A black valet measured me as carefully as a tailor back at home and came back with the Norlan equivalent of a tux. A tight white jacket, tight white hose that came above my knees, a green silk sash embroidered with the Crail monogram.

The butler escorted me down the spiral stair to a spacious hall and steered me to my place at a long dining table, elaborately set with hand-painted china and gleaming silver that had come from Icecape. Scented candles already burned in the gold chandelier above it.

The guests had not arrived. I stood behind my chair until Celya Crail appeared. In a white silk gown, she looked as fresh and chic as a film starlet back home. She inspected me critically, adjusted the sash, and showed me around the hall.

The high walls were hung with solemn portraits of the Crail dynasty. In a moment of family pride, she pointed out paintings of a Crail freight steamer, the Crail sugar mill, and a steam locomotive on the Crail railway, which ran out of the delta to the coal fields and silver mines a hundred miles north.

Her family came in. Her father was a tall, austere white-beard, who eyed me sharply through a gold-rimmed monocle he wore on a chain. He gave me a stiff formal bow and turned to mutter sharply at her. She murmured something that made him smile.

Her mother was a lean, hawk-featured woman who wore chalk-white makeup and a crown of bright orange hair. With only an absent nod for me, she turned angrily to scold the butler for a fault I couldn't fathom.

Celya introduced the guests when they came in. A uniformed commander from the constabulary. An intelligence officer and his wife. The secretary of the River Authority. Two commissioners from the High Council. A wizened river magnate who owned a stable of racing slaves. Crail's banker, a licensed quadroon whose fat fingers glittered with diamonds and gold. They gave me casual nods or searching squints or formal bows or stares of cold disbelief, but never an open hand of friendship.

Ram's testimony before the Council was still in progress. Some of the guests had questions of their own. Was it true, the intelligence officer asked, that we had come together from that magic planet in the sky? Had I seen any actual evidence that Chenji's great-grandmother had been an escaped delta slave? Had he brought magic weapons with him?

With his shrewd eyes on my face, he asked about our missing companions, the magician Ironsmith and his female assistant. Did they really know the secrets of thunder and lightning? Had they really been able to speak to each other around the world? Where were they now? Hiding in the jungle perhaps, casting evil spells for the rebels? He shrugged at last and walked away.

A scornful engineer probed me for more about the magic gates. How had we been able to jump between those worlds in the sky with no wings to lift us or bridges to walk across? The commander had searching questions about the Elders. Were they themselves warriors? Or priests of Anak and Sheko? Did they command the rebels?

It was a grim little comedy. None of them believed anything I said. They were trying to trick me into contradicting Ram's testimony. If the situation hadn't been so terrible, I could have laughed at the technological backwardness that made fairy tales of all I tried to tell them about the Earth and all the marvels we had seen since we left it.

A red-haired quadroon artist made me pose for a quick char-

coal sketch. She worked for the Crail newspaper. Seeming a little more open than most of the others, she wanted to interview
me about Earth and my life there when she could get permission. She never did.

Waiters were offering glasses of some fiery stuff from the
Crail distillery. With no response at all when Celya tried to in-
troduce me, the River Authority executive reached for a glass
and turned to ask the commander about harbor security.

"No concern." The commander shrugged. "The fleet will
soon be here with troops to reclaim the river and put the trouble down."

Standing near, Crail had overheard.

"We do need support from Norlan, but mark my word." He
raised the monocle to glare at me and turned to shake his head
at the commander. "I've heard too much of that odd blackbird
and his puppets. We'll have no peace on the river so long as they
are allowed to sing."

"True, sir." The commander raised his glass and shouted for
a toast. "Death to that black demon and all the witches with
him! Death to all their jungle thugs and every traitor who seeks
to aid or arm them!"

People turned to stare. I felt relieved when a troop of black
musicians filed in. They were natives, Celya announced, that
the museum had brought to display the culture of an isolated
tribe in the northwest mountains. Their tunes were a harsh ca-
cophony to me, but they must have expressed their loyalty to
Periclaw. They got polite applause.

The butler held a gong for Crail to strike. His voice high and
thin with age, he asked us to stand and began the meal with
thanks to the Unknown Creator for all his bountiful blessings
and a prayer for him to cleanse the errant soul of every traitor
with the pain of holy fire.

"Please remain standing," he said, "for a moment of silence in memory of Benkair Var, a daring explorer and a great friend of mine. You may have seen his collections of prehistoric antiquities in the hall of ancient art. He never returned from his last expedition into the unmapped area north of the Blood. I've just learned that he is dead."

"Killed by the *Slubro-Slubroc*," Celya told me. "A jungle parasite. Also called the gut worm."

A young waitress, uniformed in something stiff and white, stood rigidly silent behind every chair. I was placed at the foot of the table, between the intelligence officer and the engineer. The engineer shuddered and asked if Var's party could have brought infection back.

"No danger," Celya said. "None of them got back. A rescue expedition has just returned with the tragic news. They found Var's records and cameras in his last camp. Fortunately, they escaped infection."

"A nasty bug!" the officer muttered. "Chenji himself makes no threats, but he suggests that the rebels might attempt to use disease as a weapon. The medical corps is considering that possibility."

He turned to me as if he expected some response. Afraid anything I said might somehow damage Ram, I kept silent. With nothing to say that he might believe, I felt relieved when the actual meal began. The waitress at my place was young and lovely, probably an octoroon, her license number tattooed on her pale cream forehead. She bowed and smiled and said her name was Sherleth.

"I serve you, sir," she breathed at my ear. "Ask for what you wish."

What I wished for at the moment was Norlan table manners. My place was set with a vast gold plate surrounded with a be-

wildering array of silk napkins, bowls and cups and glasses, silver knives and forks and spoons. With no skills for them, I
watched the engineer for clues.

He seemed amused when he saw me aping him, and I relaxed
a little when it struck me that really I need not worry. Good eti-
quette could have condemned me as a native Norlander, a traitor to my race.

The meal came in many courses, elaborate dishes accompanied with a series of alcoholic drinks. Sherleth served me with
an eager zeal, refilling every glass or dish I touched, asking
what was wrong when I could only taste the liquors and toy
with the food.

A hopeless depression had killed my appetite. No matter
whether the Council hanged Ram or set him free, I saw that he
could never bring an end to slavery. This whole world was built
on it. Call these people good or evil or in-between, they would
fight to the death to defend it.

CHAPTER
26

The screams of a woman under torture woke me next morning. They continued for nearly two hours, broken with sounds of strangling and gasping cries for mercy. I felt sick and jittery before at last they ceased. Kenleth had slept on the floor, but he woke, crawled into the bed, and lay trembling against me.

It was Sherleth who entered with our breakfast tray when the guard unlocked the door. She looked drawn and nervous, her eyes puffy and red. Silently, she set our meal on a little table. I couldn't help asking if she had heard the screaming.

"Nobody screamed," she whispered. "Perhaps a happy child was singing."

"She was hurting." Kenleth shook his head. "Bad. Maybe dying. I was frightened. I have no license. Could I be next?"

"You won't be." She tried to smile. "Not now."

"What happened?" I asked. "Can't you say?"

Her swollen eyes fixed on me.

"You are a friend of Chenji?" I heard a desperate plea in her voice. "He is the true son of Anak and will set us free?"

"If he can."

"I pray to Anak." Her slender fingers made a fleeting sign. She paused to peer into my eyes. "You will not speak?"

"I promise."

She glanced at the door to be certain it was shut.

"My sister." Her voice fell, and her words came fast. "Ty Crail chose her to bathe him. Favored her too greatly. Tyba hated her for that. Tyba told butler she found her coupling with him in the tub. Not true, but butler fears Tyba. Ty Crail—" She tried to stifle a sob. "He wants no quarrel with Tyba."

She stifled a sob and dropped to her knees.

"Ty," she whispered, "may I serve you now?"

Kenleth tried to put his arms around her. She shook her head and pushed him away. I let her serve our breakfast. Her hands shaking, she spilled a few drops of tea and cried out as if in pain. She wiped her eyes when we had eaten, gathered up the dishes, slipped silently away.

Next morning another woman brought our breakfast. We never saw Sherleth again. Kenleth was not allowed out of the room, but the valet appeared every afternoon to dress me for dinner. The intelligence officer, Ayver Krel, was always there to update Crail on the slave rebellion. A wiry little fox-faced man who spoke a dozen native tongues, he had been a corath trader and a collector for the museum.

Day by day, I saw Crail's nerve melt away as he heard the news from Krel. The revolt was spreading down the river toward his delta holdings. The River Authority reported more violence than they could contain. More planters and traders had been murdered. More towns and factories burned. More refugees were waiting on the riverbanks for rescue.

Krel always tried to lift his spirits.

"We're secure, Ty. They can't storm Blood Hill with jungle knives. The constabulary can certainly contain any trouble on the delta. The advance flotilla of the North Sea fleet is already steaming up the channel."

Crail asked about Chenji.

"His fate is still uncertain, sir. The council would vote to hang him at once, if not for—"

He stopped with a frosty stare toward the foot of the table.

"Frankly, Ty, we face a nasty stalemate. The blacks take Chenji for a son of Anak, sent to throw us off the continent. That white—" He shrugged and scowled at me. "He doubles the dilemma."

I drew a long breath and tried to keep a blank expression. The whole group sat gazing at me until at last Krel proposed a toast to Crail's wife, the "uncrowned queen of Periclaw."

Glasses clinked, and her cold smile wrenched me with thoughts of Sherleth's sister slave and her shrieks of torture.

Krel was back a few nights later with news that the whole fleet was now at anchor in the harbor, with ten thousand men aboard the troop transports under command of General Arka Zorn.

"Periclaw's now secure," he told Crail. "And we're stabbing at the heart of the rebellion. Tribes we never conquered, up north in the Black River basin, are joining the rebels. Their heads are filled with the poison notion that Chenji's here from heaven to create a new Black Dominion."

The Black River was a major tributary of the Blood, navigable for a thousand miles into territory that only a few explorers had seen. General Zorn would be pushing up it, with a dozen gunboats and four thousand troops.

"With victory on the Black, we can hang the traitors and snuff the trouble out like a dying candle."

With no news of Ram, I dreamed that night that we were back at the trading post upriver. I saw him hanging from that twisted oak, blood dripping from the hook through his ribs. He was gasping for water, but blood filled the cup when I got it to his lips.

At dinner the next evening, the guests included the Admiral Kuch, General Zorn, and their staff officers all in full uniform and gleaming with jeweled swords and medals. Zorn was a bronze-haired giant in starch-creased whites and a crimson sash, his voice a raucous bark.

A mulatto guard and my nearly white waitress alert behind me, I sat alone at the foot of the table, empty chairs on either side of me. Laughing with the officers, Krel gave me a mocking introduction as "the honorable ambassador from the magic planet Earth." When the meal was half over, a sudden silence fell. People turned to stare at the door. Celya Crail and Ram stood there, two guards with them.

"Ty Ram Chenji." She caught his arm and turned to face her parents. "Governor Volmer has released him in my custody."

In the startled silence, the butler escorted them to the empty places beside me. Limping, leaning on a cane, Ram wore yellow-striped prison coveralls. His face bruised and swollen, he had a white bandage taped across his forehead where the crown of worlds had been. He stopped behind his chair and gave me a dismal shrug.

Krel murmured to Zorn and the admiral.

"That black devil!" Zorn was on his feet, stabbing a furious finger at Ram. "What's he doing here?"

Crail gaped at him and then at Celya.

"General, Ty Chenji is my guest." She caught Ram's arm. "The council inquiry is still in progress. We have evidence that he and Ty Stone are what they claim to be, travelers from another world who meant no harm to us."

"A monstrous fraud!" Zorn blinked at her, then at Ram and me. "They'll hang for it."

"Perhaps." She shrugged. "Charges have been filed against both him and Ty Stone. They are not yet convicted of anything, but their lives have been in danger. I have accepted custody to protect them."

"Wasn't Chenji safe in prison?"

"Not safe, Ty. Intelligence exposed a plot to kill him."

"Is that true?" Zorn swung his fury to Krel. "In prison?"

The little intelligence man cringed and braced himself.

"Ty, a guard was bribed to knife him. He disarmed and disabled the guard. His food was poisoned. He lay near death in the prison hospital until Tyba Celya brought her doctors to save his life."

"Who would kill him?"

"The culprit has not been identified." Krel glanced down the table at us. "These men have enemies everywhere."

"General Zorn." Beside me, Celya raised her voice. "Ty Chenji is more than my guest. He is a weapon against the rebels. He has traveled in the jungle. He has met the Elders, leaders of the wild tribes that support the enemy. He has given us valuable information about their positions and resources."

"Or misinformation?" Zorn huffed.

"The story of his arrival on Mount Anak has been well substantiated."

"By that white traitor?" He glared at me.

"And others, Ty. His best witness is the double agent known as Toron."

"A double agent?" Zorn scowled at her. "Whose agent? Yours or theirs?"

She looked at Krel, who flushed and caught his breath before he spoke.

"Ty, we trust the man. He has been a useful asset for many years. He led the group that saw Ty Chenji and Ty Stone appear on Mount Anak. He has penetrated the rebel leadership. His reports have been reliable."

"If you think they are actual magicians from this magic Earth—" Zorn glowered at him. "I think they've enchanted you. I know they've inspired the rebellion. They're a blade in our gut."

A troop of waiters had appeared with platters of broiled quail. The scent sharpened my appetite in spite of the tension, and Crail rapped a glass.

"Gentlemen, can't we let the meal continue?"

"One moment, Ty." Zorn glared at Ram. "If this splendid son of Anak has appeared to arrange the surrender of Periclaw to a horde of black savages—" He clenched his jaws in indignation, and stopped to squint at Ram. "Can't he speak for himself?"

Celya nodded at Ram. He gave me a wry shrug and turned to face Zorn.

"Ty." His voice rasped and he cleared his throat. "Ty Stone and I never asked to be here. I'm not the son of any god. I never claimed to be."

"Yet you wore a mark of magic power."

"The birthmark?" He touched the bandage across his forehead. "I've always had it. A small pale freckle. Nothing uncommon, though it had the shape of a crown. Only an accident, I think, but it has been taken for the fulfillment of a prophecy."

"Nothing uncommon?" Zorn's harsh voice sharpened. "Wasn't it shining in the dark?"

"That's why they cut it out."

"How did you get it?"

"I was born with it."

He said nothing of his black great-grandmother and her story of escape from another world. Zorn scowled at him and bent to hear something from Krel.

"I am told you command the rebels."

"Not true, Ty. Some of them may claim me for a leader, but I have no authority. I have met native people and heard their legends of a great civilization destroyed by war. I came out of the jungle hoping for a peace that would stop it from happening again."

"I think you're a liar or a fool. Likely both."

With a nod to Crail, Zorn sat down. Crail clinked his glass. Frozen waiters came to life, refilling glasses and serving the quail. The silent guests relaxed and talked again. Ram grinned at me. I reached to take his hand. He stiffened and drew back. Celya frowned at me, her lips set tight.

"No contact between you is allowed."

CHAPTER 27

Ram was back every evening at dinner, the guards and Celya with him, seated near me at the foot of the table. A white bandage still crossed his forehead, but the bruises had healed. The prison stripes were gone, but he looked no happier in his starched and creased formal attire.

Sometimes he winked or gave me a grim little nod, but we were not allowed to speak. Her parents coldly ignored him, but she sat beside him, smiled at him, introduced him to other guests as if he were a welcome friend. The guards were always close.

We saw no more of Zorn. Determined to stab the rebels to the heart, he had gone up the Black River with his gunboats, an infantry battalion, a long-range rocket battery, support troops, and a shipload of "crawler cannon." His gunboats, meeting no resistance, were already near Sheko Falls, at the head of navigation.

Krel, the intelligence officer, was always there to share war news with Crail. A second flotilla was steaming up the Blood River to pick up refugees and relieve besieged outposts.

Admiral Kuch was often back. A heavy, deliberate man with a hearty appetite and shrewd green eyes in a smooth bland face, he was full of good humor and basking happily in his popularity as the champion defender of the nation. Careful with his ships and his men, he would have been a winning poker player. He held half his fleet in reserve, still at anchor in the harbor.

He had spoken in the council to oppose Zorn's adventure.

"I've known Arkkie Zorn since we were cadets," he told Crail. "He always liked a fight, and fought to win. He half killed himself, working to stay at the top of his class. But I'm uneasy for him now. He's never known the jungle. Fighting jungle blacks is like boxing with smoke. They're nomads. They've got no towns. No forts. He can fire his cannon. Maybe hit some savage in his hut. More likely nothing. The jungle doesn't care."

Celya was back with Ram every evening. At first he was stolidly silent, she warily alert. I saw them change. In my freshman classes back at home I had watched a hundred new romances bloom. I knew the signs. The tender glances, the gentle touches, the secret smiles. Like a Romeo reborn and an alien Juliet, they were falling in love.

Her parents were no happier than the Capulets. I saw their hostile stares at Ram, their cold frowns for her. Tears filled her eyes when she looked back at them. Sometimes I caught a grimace of pain. They must have tried to reason with her. She would have said she was an agent of intelligence, assigned to pry for anything that aided the cause. What had they to fear from a prisoner under constant guard?

She must have felt torn between conflicting loyalties, but I saw more tender smiles for Ram as the romance ripened. I'd first seen her in a plain white dress, her long hair straight and free. It was soon cut shorter, curled, sometimes with flowers in it. Her lacy gowns were styled to reveal sleek white flesh that must have tempted him.

He was silent and restrained, nodding impassively when curious guests wanted to meet him and she had to explain that the terms of his release didn't let him speak in public. They spoke enough to each other, murmuring softly, heads bent together. Their shoulders touched. She often caught his arm. Once I saw his hand on her thigh. I felt apprehension for him, and sharpening unease for Kenleth and me.

Days went by with no fresh news about the war. Periclaw and the delta were still untouched, the commercial docks still busy. Freighters still slid down the channel to the sea, laden with grain, sugar, and rum for Norlan. General Zorn had reached the Sheko Falls at the head of navigation on the Black River. At the last report, he had led his ground forces up the cliffs beyond to attack a reported native stronghold.

Crail was an optimist.

"Like us or not," he told the admiral, "the rebels will come to see the fools they are. They can torch a few buildings and leave good crops to rot, any time they want to hang for it. They forget that they'd be back in the stone age without us. They've got to have our metals for every tool and pot they use, our drugs to save them from their jungle fevers, our faith to keep them out of hell."

He raised his voice, staring down the table at Ram and his daughter.

"If you want to see our actual danger, look at those deluded few who want an end to slavery. They call it cruel. Call it wrong. They're blind to the facts. The workers on my plantations live better lives than their jungle kin. They get food and shelter, medical care, safety from their jungle brothers who'd hunt them down for trophy skulls."

Celya flushed and bit her lip. Ram stared coolly back. The shrieks of Sherleth's dying sister echoed in my mind.

Confined to our room, Kenleth was as restless as a caged monkey. He tried to talk to the maid who brought our trays and cleaned the room. She would only touch her lips and shake her head. We played catch with green apples. He learned to juggle them. We carried on our language lessons. He asked a thousand questions about the trilithons and the worlds we had seen and Earth itself.

If I ever went back there, could he come with me?

I told him he could, if we could ever escape from the Crails. If Ram came with us. If we could find Derek and Lupe. If they had discovered some way home. If Ram still had his emerald key. If we could find an intact trilithon programmed to take us in the right direction.

That seemed a wild dream, but it brightened his troubled face. Sometimes, in the long and anxious nights, I almost believed it. After all, miracles sometimes happened. Nothing was ever quite what you expected. The Sahara gate itself was proof of that.

The war picture suffered a sudden change. One evening Krel and the admiral arrived late for dinner. They burst in together, pushed past the butler, and rushed to whisper at Crail's ear. He rose to huddle with them. We sat waiting until he rapped his glass and looked down the table.

"Sad news." His old voice was nearly too faint for me to hear. "Sad news."

He sat again as if his knees were weak and let the admiral talk.

"Until today, nothing had been heard from General Zorn since he left his boats below the Sheko Falls."

He spoke slowly and carefully, perhaps repeating testimony he had given the council. Pausing from time to time, he turned to Krel for a word or a nod of support.

"We sent three courier craft upriver to ask for information. The first two never returned. The third has just come back, bringing a man they met on the river in a small boat. He tells a story I didn't want to believe until intelligence could confirm its accuracy."

"Convincing detail came from native sources," Krel said. "The wild tribes keep in touch with drum talk. You hear the drums at night."

"This man had been Zorn's orderly," the admiral continued. "He'd gone on with Zorn above the falls. They'd heard tales of a ruined temple of Anak and a center of native power around it in an area that had never been explored. The orderly says their native guides took them out of the jungle and on across a barren plateau where the vegetation was scant and strange. He describes a plant the blacks call the gut worm."

"Also called Sheko's flower," Krel said. "Or the flower of death. Sheko is their goddess of death."

"A peculiar plant," the admiral said. "It lies flat on the ground. The leaves are black and enormous. A short center stalk carries one huge purple bloom that has a powerful odor. Nauseating, the orderly says, but intoxicating. The natives warned Zorn to stay clear of it, but he felt safe in his armored crawler. He made his driver bring him close.

"The orderly says the stink of the thing made them all so woozy that he's not sure of all that happened, but the flower spat something that hit Zorn and stuck to his face. Maybe some sort of seed or fruit. It looked like a ripe plum, but he says it intoxicated Zorn. He sniffed it, tasted it, swallowed it whole.

"He seemed to sober up, the man says. He was able to go on to the ruins, which the orderly describes as a mountain of broken stone. Great black blocks, he says, like those the constabulary center is made of. He believes the place had been a fortress rather than any kind of temple.

"Zorn got sick there. Out of his head and finally so weak they carried him in a litter. On the last night he was screaming in agony. The orderly called an army surgeon, but Zorn ordered them both out of the tent. Next morning he was gone.

"The orderly left the details out of his written report, but under oath he swears that he found an enormous black-scaled snake coiled on Zorn's cot. He claims he wasn't drugged or drunk, but he swears that the snake cursed him in Zorn's voice before it crawled out of the tent and disappeared into the ruins. Nothing was left of Zorn except his empty skin."

The admiral hesitated and turned to Krel.

"The surgeon failed to save the skin," Krel said, "but the orderly did get back with his journal. The illness is diagnosed as an internal parasite. He never saw any snake. A paragraph of speculation is broken off, unfinished. The final entries in the journal are devoted to another jungle illness that nearly killed the orderly himself."

The admiral shook his head at Crail. His voice stuck when he tried to speak. He picked up a glass and gulped something that wasn't water. Strangling on it, he coughed and wheezed and gasped for breath.

"A frightful thing." His voice was a husky squeak. "I hope it never gets here. The native name for it translates as blood rot. It hit them at the ruin. The first symptoms were a high fever and a burning rash. The victims went fast, the surgeon writes. They bled profusely in the final hours, from all body orifices. The entire bodies—"

The admiral lost his voice again and clutched the table to keep his balance through another fit of coughing.

"The entire bodies dissolved into blood. The orderly swears that it was fatal to every white who caught it. He says the blacks were immune. The hybrids were commonly sick. Quadroons and octoroons had high fevers and sweated blood, but they nearly all recovered. The surgeon hoped to use black blood to develop a vaccine, but he was dead before he had a chance to try."

"Dead?" Trembling, Crail caught the admiral's arm. "Dead of what?"

The admiral had to cough again.

"That jungle fever. They retreated and took the infection with them. The orderly is an octoroon. He was sick with it when he got back to the falls, but he survived. He says it swept the crews and troops waiting there. He says he was out of his head, but he remembers panic, with mutiny and fighting, before he was carried on a hospital ship.

"Recovering, he found himself the only man left aboard. The ship was aground in the channel. He says all the ships were empty, most of them beached or burned. Any other survivors must have disappeared into the jungle. When he was strong enough, he found a boat and came on down the river."

Crail gulped something that took his voice and left him doubled over the table.

"Survivors?" he gasped at the admiral. "Where are the survivors?"

The admiral turned to Krel and waited for his helpless shrug.
"Ty, there were no white survivors."

CHAPTER 28

The table was silent, stunned, until somebody dropped a glass. It shattered on the floor, but nobody moved to clear up the fragments. Crail's wife opened her mouth to scream and clapped a hand over it. I saw Celya's searching glance at Ram. Grimly, he shook his head.

We watched the admiral huddle with Crail and Krel. He nodded at last, cleared his throat, and spoke to the table.

"A terrible loss." He managed a feeble smile. "But it happened a thousand miles away. Officer Krel believes we are safe here in Periclaw. He says the very deadliness of the fever limits our danger. Victims are dead before they can carry it far."

"The sick orderly?" Crail's wife shrilled. "Where is he?"

The admiral turned to Krel.

"Here in the Blood Hill hospital," Krel said. "Still confined to an isolation ward, but he appears to have made a full recovery. If he had been a carrier, we wouldn't be talking."

"After all, Tyba," the admiral told her, "it's nothing new. It was described long ago, but it has never spread beyond a few remote locations. Historians have suggested that it originated as a weapon of war in the final years of the lost empire. If that's true, its range may have been deliberately limited. It appears to have been endemic so long that blacks have developed a natural immunity." He shook his head. "Zorn was simply too stubborn to accept the warnings from his medical staff."

Whispers rustled around the table and he paused to rap his glass.

"May we have a moment of silence for him?" A shrug of solemn regret. "I've known him since we met back at the academy. A tough old bird, rough on his men. He always pushed too hard, but he deserved a better end."

He bowed for a long moment. Crail clapped his hands, and the grilled quail was served at last.

Late that night a muffled rapping woke me. I heard the click of a lock. The balcony doors swung open. Light shone into the room. Ram and Celya stepped inside. Kenleth slid out of bed, darted to meet them, and stopped with a gasp. The bandage across Ram's forehead was gone. The light came from the mark on his forehead, larger than ever, burning like molten gold.

I sat up on the side of the bed, blinking at them.

"Quiet." His finger on his lips, Ram nodded at the hallway door. "The guard's just outside."

Celya stood close beside him. The revealing gowns were gone. She wore a plain jacket and slacks of something like gray denim. She looked pale and tense, but her face was set with determination.

"A miracle?" His voice hushed, Kenleth stared at the shining mark. "You really are a god!"

"I don't know what I am." Ram touched the mark, grinning

bleakly. "They cut it off to defang me. It grew back again." He shrugged at me. "I guess Derek would explain it. He'd say the builders of the trilithons were also genetic engineers. Here the Hotmen take it for a sign of destiny. The whites as a death warrant if they catch us."

He slid his arm around Celya.

"She's had a hard choice, exile or death."

She smiled into the light from his face and turned gravely back to me.

"The council met tonight. Emergency session. They voted to revoke my custody and hang him. We're running for our lives."

"Can we?" Kenleth breathed the words. "Can we come with you?"

Ram shook his head and frowned at me.

"You're safer here. We have no time. No plans. Nowhere to go. We're climbing down the fire escape. Celya knows the city. We may find friends if we let the right people see the mark." He shrugged. "Hard luck if we don't.

"We stopped to give you this."

He slipped off the emerald pendant on its thin silver chain.

"The intelligence men ripped it off me. Celya had it in the museum."

He handed it to Kenleth, who goggled at it and brought it to me.

"You can't," I protested. "It was a gift from your Little Mama. It's somehow magic, and it means too much to you."

"Magic?" With a wry little shrug, he touched the mark. "It's a key to the trilithons. I'll never need it again. There's a chance it might save your life. Or maybe get you back to Earth. The cards are falling wild, as Derek might say."

He strode across the room to grip my hand. Kenleth was

staring at Celya, tears running down his face. She hugged him, set a kiss on his cheek, and followed Ram back through the balcony door. He closed it silently, and they were gone.

Early next morning we saw uniformed officers on the balcony outside, squatting to inspect the floor, leaning to peer over the railing, squinting at the lock with a magnifying lens. They unlocked the doors and came inside. Ignoring us at first, they searched the room, looked into the closets and under the bed.

Finding nothing, the man in charge glared at us and gripped Kenleth by the shoulders. Had he seen anything unusual? Anybody on the balcony? Had he heard any unusual sound? Had he seen Ram Chenji or Celya Crail? Had they been in the room? Did he know where they had gone?

Bravely, he played the wide-eyed innocent. He had slept through the night. He knew nothing at all. The officer shrugged and turned grimly to me. My pulse throbbing, I tried to seem as innocent as Kenleth. What were they looking for? Had something happened to Ty Chenji or Tyba Crail? The door had been locked and guarded. Who could have got in?

He was not convinced.

"We'll be back. If you're hiding anything, we can make you sorry."

They never came back. We spent the rest of the day anxious and alone. The valet never came to dress me for dinner. Instead, a pretty quadroon housemaid brought us a tray. Looking as stressed and desperate as Celya had been, she shook her head when Kenleth begged for news.

"I'm afraid," I heard her tell the guard. "Afraid of Sheko's breath."

The valet did come to dress me next day, as silent and nervous as if grooming some dangerous predator. Ram's place and Celya's were empty; I sat alone at the foot of the dinner table. The admiral and Krel were there, offering sympathy to the Crails for the loss of their daughter. In funeral black, Crail's wife looked sick and wasted, suddenly old.

Crail pressed Krel for word of Celya.

"Not a clue, sir," Krel told him. "Except that a rowboat is missing from your landing down on the beach. We have to assume they went downriver with the current. The constabulary has five hundred men combing the delta. We're posting rewards. A hundred slaves for your daughter. A thousand for that black devil, dead or alive."

I was left in limbo. Perhaps intelligence had left me as bait for Ram, on the chance that he might come back to rescue me. Or perhaps I was just forgotten. I had no way to know. A strange way of life. The valet dressed me every day. The guard brought me down to dinner and stood behind my chair. Not allowed to speak to me, the guests could only stare. Sitting in silence, I tried to overhear whatever I could.

One day Krel was elated. The hunters had caught Ram and Celya, hiding in a delta cane field. Next day he was gloomy. Taken to a constabulary station, they escaped when it fell to rebel commandos. A captured slave claimed to have seen the Lord of Worlds in a rebel camp, the crown shining on his face, drilling a rebel army.

"Propaganda," the admiral scoffed. "He'll hang high when we catch him."

Yet Ram was never caught.

"The natives take him for their prophesied messiah." Krel scowled in frustration. "They think he's come to wipe us out and build a black empire. They'll give their lives just to touch him."

Slaves broke their chains and flocked to follow him. The rebellion spread across the delta. Rebels burned Crail's cotton gin, his sugar mill, and a warehouse where he had stored baled cotton worth five hundred slaves. He commonly accepted his losses with stolid shrugs, but the strain told on him.

He burst into fury one evening when a waitress dropped a dish, cursing her and ordering her whipped till she bled. The girl fell to her knees, whimpering for mercy. Relenting when his wife protested, he muttered an apology and let her stand behind him, sobbing silently, until the meal had ended.

Kenleth listened hungrily to every scrap of news I brought him.

"Ty Chenji must be proud and happy."

For the moment Kenleth was happy. Dark eyes shining, he turned from me to the windows, gazing across the river to the delta's vast green sweep. He seemed not to see the plumes rising from the fields or the black hulk of a grain freighter aground on the rocks of the old causeway.

"People worship him like a god. Warriors follow him. Celya's the prettiest girl I ever saw. She loves him. Really. She gave up everything to run away with him. He's a very lucky man."

I felt far from sure how happy Ram could be, but the tides of war seemed to have turned for him. The admiral reported his gunboats busy on the river channels and canals, hunting the rebels, but Crail got him to admit that men hiding in the cane fields were nearly impossible to hit.

General Gurnash had taken command. He landed an armored constabulary brigade to hunt the rebels down, field by field. Fresh from Icecape, he hadn't known that half the delta was reclaimed land below sea level. The rebels cut the dykes, flooded roads, bogged the armor down. Trapped, helpless, surrounded, Gurnash refused to surrender.

"A hero!" Krel said. "The slaves want his guns. He'll never give them up."

In a midnight assault, the rebels wiped out the brigade and took the general's head. In a fever of revenge, the council ordered the commander of the river island camp to hang half his prisoners, and cut the hands off the other half, and turn them loose to show the price of freedom.

Out of desperation, the council began liberating slaves to fill black battalions. Any able-bodied man willing to join was offered a certificate of registration and the promise of all the land he could till for himself.

In the admiral's sour words, such measures were spit on the wall. The new recruits deserted as fast as they were trained and armed. Black commandos brought captured gunpowder to knock down the stone pillars of a viaduct that supplied the city water. One night they set fire to an oil barge moored at the commercial docks. The blaze swallowed ships and warehouses, and spread into the city. From the balcony window we saw a sky dark with smoke by day and flame yellow at night.

One evening Krel brought a special dinner guest, a constabulary lieutenant the rebels had captured and released. He had seen Ram, and he brought another request for a truce.

"They still offer peace and open trade," he said, "if we'll set them free."

"Never!" Crail's sick face was grimly set. "Our whole world stands on the system. Without it we are dead."

CHAPTER 29

On the night of Crail's final dinner, Krel came late, brushed past the butler, and handed him a scrap of yellow paper. Crail rose to scan it, lost color, and sank back into his chair. An uneasy hush filled the room until he stood again.

"Intelligence report." He read broken phrases as he squinted at them, the paper quivering in his fingers. "Delayed for confirmation . . . now verified . . . blood rot . . . deadly contagion . . . cause unknown."

The room was dazed. I heard gasps, whispers, curses. Anxious voices lifted and jangled. Crail's wife rushed out of the room, her napkin over her face. Another woman shrieked and fell to the floor. A constabulary captain tossed a glass of liquor into his throat and gagged on it. Most of the meal was left uneaten. Guests pushed their plates away, made quick farewells, scattered to their fates. The guards hustled me back to our room.

Shut up there with Kenleth, I listened and watched from the windows as Periclaw died. The maids still brought our meals and now they told us what they knew. The infection began on a

delta island. Krel believed the rebels had brought it out of the
jungle as a weapon of war. More likely, the admiral thought,
death had drifted down the Black River on the vulture-picked
skeletons in a native dugout the tides left on a delta beach.

The house grew strangely silent. The Crails had left the city
for refuge in their summer home in the hills, taking most of
their servants and a small army of licensed guards. My own
guards were still on duty, never speaking to us but watching me
as warily as if I had the infection.

The contagion struck hard and fast. Retreating from the delta,
constabulary forces brought it back to Blood Hill. It spread
from there into the city, panic with it. People fled when they
could. We saw craft of every sort carrying refugees upstream.
The infection went with them.

We heard an ocean liner whistle and watched tugs pull it
away from the commercial docks. It steamed down the channel
almost to the Sheko tower, started to list, finally capsized and
sank. Refugees had bid fortunes for places aboard, the maids
told us. The council ordered it scuttled, hoping to save Norlan
from the plague.

With city water cut off, the fire set at the military docks had
never been controlled. The smoke of it gave the air a biting taint
even in the room, and became so thick outside that it hid the
river. One night a high wind carried glowing embers past our
windows. Kenleth crouched against me, quivering.

"Will it burn the house?" he whispered. "And us inside?"

"We can hope for luck," I told him. "Back on Earth we used
to play a game called poker. We always trusted luck."

He knelt by the bed to murmur a prayer to Anak.

"My mother believed," he told me. "She said he has no

color. He can be black or white. He loves us all, when we love each other." He made a grimace. "Ty Hake laughed at her. If he had a god, he said, he wouldn't be black."

Our luck came with the monsoon rains. They began that night with blinding lightning and crashing hail. The sudden downpour quenched the flames and washed the city clean. Half of it had escaped destruction. The smoke was gone, roof tiles clean and bright, the streets and the river empty, no traffic anywhere.

That day the maids never came. The stillness chilled me. I'd sensed the pulse of the city in the murmur of mingled far-off voices, the muffled rumble of toil, all the echoes of unseen life. Now the breathless silence became its dying scream.

Late that night the lock clicked on the inside door. Nobody entered. The room was pitch-black. We had a snuffed-out candle, but no way to light it. I lay there in the dark, listening to Kenleth's quiet breathing, till daylight came at last and I got up to try the door.

It opened. The guards were gone. We dressed and went down the stair and through the silent house. An aged, crippled cook was still at his duty in the kitchen, perhaps out of loyalty to the Crails, perhaps merely unable to leave. Limping about the stove, he was making breakfast for Ram and Celya Crail.

We found them sitting at the table, eating a ripe papaya. Ram was in mud-stained constabulary fatigues, blood dried black around a bruise on the side of his chin. Even by day, the crown of worlds still shone with a golden glow. Celya wore the same yellow fatigues, now tattered and stained with blood, a red band around her close-cut hair. Her face looked thin and pale but lovelier, I thought, than ever.

Ram shouted when he saw us, and came grinning to meet us. "Will?" He scanned my face. "Are you okay?"

"So far," I told him. "We've been shut up alone. I'm not sure I've been exposed."

"You will be," he said. "It's everywhere. Lethal to whites, but I think you have a chance. If Lupe was right, a geologic age has passed since our own forefathers got back to Earth. We're all the same race, but our immunities may be different."

"I hope."

I gripped his hand and looked at Celya. She was still at the table, staring as if we were strangers. I moved to greet her. She drew back, shaking her head.

"Keep away." Her voice was a raspy whisper. "If you're afraid."

I turned to Ram. He nodded silently. She was white, and the pathogen was striking everywhere. I turned to offer her my hand. She rose to put her arms around me. I felt her slender body trembling, felt a silent sob. Yet she managed a wan little smile and kissed my cheek. Ram nodded at the table and she called the cook to take our orders.

The papayas were fresh and delicious. The bacon and eggs might almost have come from the Wagon Wheel, back in Portales. The meal was half over before we felt ready for talk of anything else.

"While it lasted, we had a golden time." Ram spoke slowly, with a bitter little smile for Celya. "We were in love. The crown of worlds was magic, and triumph was in sight. The constabulary blacks were burning off their tattoo numbers, ready to follow us out of hell. We dreamed of freedom, peace, even the chance to start rebuilding something like the Grand Dominion must have been. But then—"

He gulped and slid his arm around her.

––––––

The cook had brought us huge mugs of bitter black corath tea. They smiled into each other's eyes and clicked the mugs together before Ram turned back to me.

"An old friend brought us back. White Water, the river pilot. Remember his complexion? All his life he managed to pass without a license, but the genes from his black grandma saved him. He has a neat little steam launch. The owners hired him to take them upriver. The boat fell to him when they died."

When we had finished eating, Celya showed us the house. Her own room was almost a museum, the high walls hung with collected artifacts. Mats and hats and baskets, knives and pots and fishing spears, prayer sticks and divining rods, counting cords and funeral masks, tiny images of Anak and Sheko carved from jet and alabaster.

"The black culture." She gestured at the walls. "It's richer than you'd think. Ritualistic and well diversified. There are scores of cults to the divinities and mythic human heroes. I was trying to understand them, preserve what I could."

For a moment she seemed forlorn, but she smiled at Ram when he put his arm around her.

He nodded at a library table. "We've something to show you."

I saw the ancient laptop he had brought back from the place of the Elders.

"From Derek and Lupe?"

He shook his head. "Something else."

Celya lifted the screen and turned it to let us see.

"Krel seized it," he said. "He gave it to the museum when it baffled his experts. Celya had it here at home when I got to know her."

She tapped keys to open pages of hieroglyphs.

"The text is still a riddle, but she's found an interesting map."

She touched the keys again, to show the prelude we had seen before: black space and new constellations, the rocket pioneers and a strangely tipped Milky Way, the fine green lines I thought must have been spaceways, our own solar system and its planets. He stopped her on Africa.

"Notice the coastlines. That's the way they were when Homo sapiens got back from the Grand Dominion, two hundred thousand years ago. The oceans are lower. It must have been an ice age. A lot of water frozen on land, and the Sahara region wet enough for the trilithon builders." He grinned at me. "That's your chance to beat the odds."

He turned to Celya.

"Let's see this world."

She was gazing at him, her face fixed and grave. She seemed not to hear until he asked again. She started, and found us an image of the planet, slowly rotating in dark space.

"The two continents." He pointed. "Norlan, spread over the pole. Here's Icecape, Southpoint, Glacier Gulf. And Hotlan, the equator across it. Iron River. The Blood. Periclaw, here on the delta."

He asked Celya for a flat projection.

"Here's what I wanted to show you."

Hotlan spread wide. The legends across it were riddles, but I found the rivers, the delta, a brown mountain ridge down the west coast. "Mount Anak, where we got here." He pointed at a tiny black trilithon symbol north of the Blood. "And look at this."

He jabbed his finger at another like it, in the mountain chain that curved down the west coast.

"A way out?" It took my breath. "Home to Earth?"

"Maybe." Ram shrugged as if it didn't matter. "If you could

get there. Celya says the site's unknown. It's in high mountains, far beyond the head of navigation on the Blood." He frowned. "It could be a chance, if you want to gamble on it."

He looked at Celya and I saw his lips twist.

"We have other plans."

"I want to see my parents." Her face drawn with pain, she took a long breath. "If they're alive."

"The railway isn't working," Ram said. "The rebels burned a bridge. White Water can take us up the river."

She clutched at his arm as if she needed support.

"They couldn't—wouldn't understand how I love Ram. They were bitter. It hurt me to hurt them. And now—" Her shrug was almost apologetic. "I have to see them if I can."

Kenleth had been staring at a display of native weapons, but now he turned eagerly to them.

"Can we come up the river with you?"

"I wish you could." Ram shook his head and turned to me. "They wouldn't want you."

CHAPTER
30

That day was almost happy for Kenleth and me. The sun was warm and bright, the fresh air sweet, songbirds aloft. Rejoicing in freedom, we walked in the orchard at the back of Crail's walled compound. Cherry trees were loaded with blood red fruit. We filled ourselves and went on down to the riverside dock where White Water was overhauling the launch, replacing a broken paddle and melting metal to pour a new bearing.

I saw no change in his worn leather garb or his weather-beaten face. He was chewing cinnamon sticks. They left an amber stain on his tuft of chin whiskers, but he said they cleared his head. Kenleth embraced him happily, glad to find him still alive.

"The fall of the bones." He shrugged. "Bad times come and bad times go. I've been up and I've been down. I live as I can, but we aren't here forever."

He stopped to gnaw at his stick.

"The bones fell wrong for most of the world." He made a dismal grimace. "Wrong for Celya Crail and your friend Ram. With a better break, they might have been rulers of a great new kingdom. Might have been, if General Zorn hadn't been so hungry for glory. Might have been."

He shrugged and grinned at Kenleth.

"You and I are the lucky ones. We're alive, here on the river with a great little boat."

He showed us over the launch and explained the engine to Kenleth. It had two cylinders, with drive shafts that turned two paddle wheels at the stern, the rudder hinged to the keel between them. Delighted, Kenleth sat at the wheel and hissed through his teeth with the sound of steam.

I asked White Water what sort of future he saw for Hotlan.

"Don't ask." He shrugged. "I've known black seers with their divining rods and white scientists with their statistics. They had one thing in common. Their forecasts very seldom hit the mark."

Reflecting, he chewed his cinnamon.

"It's hard for me to see anything good to come. Periclaw spat in Ram's eye when he brought them a chance to save themselves. They've paid a bitter price. Sheko breathed her deadly breath on the whites, and her worshipers are burning their bloody wafers in thanks. Admiral Koch scuttled every seagoing ship, hoping to save the Norlan whites. They may survive, but they'll go hungry.

"As for you, Ty Will—" He squinted at me, shrewdly. "If you got here by magic, you might do well to try your spells again."

Ram and Celya were going on next day to look for her parents.

"An idiot mission," White Water called it. "The Crails were king and queen. I've had my fill of the type. Owning men gives the mind an ugly set. They might forgive their daughter, but you—" He looked at Ram. "You're pure poison. It's you and your shining sign that killed their world. They'd kill you if they could."

Ram shrugged. "Celya has to go."

They spent the day preparing for the trip. With so few left to use it, city water was running again. They showered and found clean clothes. White Water finished his work on the launch. The cook packed them a basket of food and served a farewell dinner at the kitchen table.

It was simpler than those at Crail's formal dinners, but for Kenleth and me it was a banquet. A platter piled with something like fried chicken, cousins, I guess, to the chickens of Earth. Another platter of crisp brown pones, rather like the corn bread my grandmother used to bake. Crail had an ice-house, stocked with ice shipped from Norlan glaciers, and there were bowls of ice cream.

We toasted Ram and Celya with a bottle of wine from Crail's cellar. She sat close to him, smiling fondly at him but ignoring the rest of us. Toying with her food, she barely tasted it. Her face was pale and she seemed unsteady when she walked. I wondered if she would live to see her parents.

I'd almost enjoyed the day, but that night I had a dreadful dream. After a long search, we'd reached that trilithon in the high mountains west. The great square pillars of black granite rose out of a frozen lake rimmed with towering, snow-capped peaks. Ram and Kenleth were somewhere behind me. I started through the gateway, holding Ram's green pendant before me, and stopped when I saw a naked body.

It lay sprawled on the ice between the columns. Blue with cold, the limbs jerked suddenly, twitched, stiffened, turned slowly red. Thick dark blood oozed out of them. All at once the whole body melted into a wide red puddle, spreading slowly toward my feet. In terror of it, I tried to back away.

I couldn't move, because I knew the body had been my own.

"Ty Will?" A hollow voice boomed out of the dark beyond the trilithon. "Ty Will, are you okay?"

Kenleth caught my arm and dragged me out of the nightmare.

The cook had an early breakfast ready. Kenleth and I went down to watch Ram and Celya board the launch. White Water had it ready, with fire under the boiler and a head of steam. He cast off the mooring lines. The paddle wheels spun. Ram waved good-bye as they swung into the current. Celya sat staring blindly at us, without expression.

Kenleth turned to me and whispered, "Will Ty Ram come back?"

"I hope so," I said. "I hope his Little Mama made him immune."

Waiting to know, we stayed inside the walls. From the upper windows, the river looked empty. The streets were deserted, except for now and then a furtive survivor risking Sheko's wrath in search of plunder. Kenleth found a hook and line in the boathouse and fished off the dock. Cheerfully, the cook fried or grilled his catch.

At last the launch came back. Ram and White Water were aboard, Celya wasn't. Ram looked bleak and sleepless. He didn't want to talk. White Water did, after Ram walked out to see what was left of Periclaw. Kenleth and I were alone with him.

"Upriver, we had to fight the current. It took us all day to reach the canal. Celya was already too sick to travel, really, but she had to see her folks before they died. Ram was her slave. We had food enough, and a case of wine, but she couldn't eat or drink. I thought we'd never get her there."

We were in the boathouse, with the launch tied up at the dock below it. White Water had been grinding a leaky steam valve, but he sat down on the workbench and bit the end off a cinnamon stick.

"The infection made her crazy. Ram got half drunk with old Crail's wine. He sure had reason for that. All she wanted was him. They made love on the boat. Why not? He tilted the awning to screen them and told me not to look. With the whole world gone, who was left to care?"

He shook his head and stared out across the empty river.

"I care," Kenleth said.

"Matter of fact, so do I." He shrugged and resumed his story. "Forty miles upriver, we reached the first lock. It looked abandoned, but we found the lockkeepers still at the gates. Still proud of their licenses, proud of their posts, proud of the locks. Seeming not to mind that the old world had come to an end, they let us through. We tied up for the night.

"Next morning Celya was so fast asleep I thought she was already done for. Wet with sweat. Stiff and hardly breathing. Ram finally roused her. A few swallows of wine revived her enough to sit up. She raved wildly about the war ruining their honeymoon cruise to Icecape. At noon she drank another glass of wine and tried to sing him a song. Her voice turned to a wheeze. He took her in his arms. She cried herself back to sleep.

"That day the canal took us on through what had been great plantations. Grain. Cotton. Sugarcane. All left to waste with the harvest workers gone and blown flat by monsoon storms.

Two more locks got us up to the edge of the foothills and the Crail landing. Their country place was another great mansion. Not quite so fancy as this city house, but grand enough.

"Crail came out to meet us. Looking older, limping on a cane, but fighting death like a wildcat. Celya begged him to let her see her mother. He waved the cane and called her a filthy black-loving slut. Said she'd shamed herself and fouled the family name. If she had the fever, she'd got it from the devil with her. He yelled for his guards.

"They came out of the house. A squad of mulattos and quadroons, all branded with their license numbers, looking fit as ever. Crail's wife followed them, carried in a chair, white as chalk and shriveled to a wisp. She wiped her eyes and waved the handkerchief and beckoned Celya to her. Crail yelled at her to get back in the house.

"Celya fell to her knees, trying to climb out of the boat. Ram helped her to the dock. Crail struck at her with his cane. As weak as he was, he staggered. One of the guards caught him to keep him on his feet. Ram picked Celya up and carried her to meet her mother. Crail yelled again. The guards snatched her out of his hands and got her to her mother. They hugged, but she looked back at Ram.

" 'Wait for me, darling. Just a minute, till I can say good-bye.'

"Of course we couldn't wait. He knew Celya was dying. Crail ordered his guard to give us ten seconds to get the hell off his dock. They hustled her into the house, her mother with her. Crail ordered the guards to fire. Ram jumped back in the boat and grabbed an oar to push us off. The guards fired a volley. The bullets whistled over our heads. All we could do was get away."

White Water got off the bench, turning back to grinding the leaky valve.

"I think Ram's immune to the rot." He paused to spit a brown jet at a fly on the floor. "But still it nearly killed him."

That afternoon Ram went for a swim in the river. It was muddy and high from the monsoon rains, the current fast. White Water warned him of crocodiles swarming up from the delta lagoons, drawn by all the corpses. He shrugged as if he didn't care.

We stayed on the dock, watching for him till the sun went down. Kenleth kept asking about the crocodiles, and I had to wonder if he meant to come back. Dusk had fallen before Kenleth shouted and we saw him wading ashore, the crown of worlds glowing to light his way. He was breathing hard, but I thought that bitter set was washed off his face.

"She loved me," he muttered to me. "I can't be sorry we came."

He spent all the next morning in Celya's room, poring over that electronic book, and finally slammed it shut.

"The text is chicken tracks. The video sections make it look like a history of the planet. There's just enough to tease us in the maps and that trilithon symbol in those high mountains west. A crazy bet, but it's the only chance I see."

"Chance?" That startled me. "You mean you want to go there?"

He nodded, his face still bleak and strained.

"There's nothing for us here. No reason not to try." He shook his head, his face drawn grim again. "Don't bet on it. The map was drawn when the planet was younger. No delta yet. The mouth of the Blood is far down the coast. That trilithon has likely been knocked down by a quake by now, or buried under a lava flow."

That afternoon Kenleth and I went with him back to the

academy complex, which held the museum, the Crail library, and the concert and lecture halls around them. He wanted modern maps of the upper river and the records of any expeditions into the mountains on the map.

Vandals had been there before us. We found doors battered in, display cases smashed. There were no lights, but Ram found a candle lantern a little brighter than his birthmark. The storm had damaged the museum roof, and the floors were carpeted with rain-sodden waste.

"The Grand Dominion." He stopped us at the entrance to a gloomy hall. "This was Celya's treasure house. Her prize collection from what she thought had been imperial tombs. Personal ornaments, weapons, tools. Tantalizing objects she had no names for." His shoulders hunched and the birthmark dimmed. "Relics of Celya." His lip quivered like a hurt child's. "Relics of death."

A long moment passed before he drew his body straight and turned to leave the building.

"All precious to her but no good for us." He shrugged and gave me a bitter little grin. "If the Hotmen ever reached the spot, they never made maps, not any kind we can read. White Water never heard of any expeditions far beyond the head of steam navigation. We've got a long way to go."

That night a stabbing headache woke me. I lay sweating and shivering till day came at last, and I wanted no breakfast. Blood rot had hit me.

CHAPTER
31

I tottered down to breakfast. The cook was serving ripe mangos, boiled eggs, and fried slices of something like plantains. They looked good enough, but one taste of the egg wrenched me with nausea. I staggered when I tried to stand, and Ram helped me back up the stair.

I thought I was dying.

"Not quite yet." He grinned at me bleakly. "You're white enough, but Earth has its own evolutionary tree. You could still draw an ace."

I don't know how long I was sick. My watch still ran, but the days of Earth meant nothing here. Sometimes I was conscious. I remember Kenleth holding my hand, his warm touch a lifeline out of the darkness. I remember Ram lifting my head to give me water I couldn't swallow.

Sometimes I was back on Earth. Once we were flying into Lubbock and they wouldn't let us land because I had blood fever. We flew on into a thunderstorm, with no destination. Once we were back at home. Lupe had called the media to a press conference to announce our return. Derek tried to give a slide show, with shots of the Sahara gate and all the strange worlds we had seen. The reporters laughed and walked out, and the campus cops were called to arrest me for bringing the fever home to Portales.

Sometimes I was lying in the bottom of the launch, listening to the steady puff of the little engine, staring up at the awning. It was woven of coarse strips of some straw-colored reedy stuff, with herringbone stripes of orange and rust. Sometimes they made patterns like the glyphs in the e-book, but never anything sane.

But at last a morning dawned when a breath of wind felt gratefully cool and I heard birds singing somewhere. A bright sun rose in the blue sky above the awning. Kenleth was at the wheel, White Water warning him to steer clear of a snag. My head was clear again. I could breathe without coughing. I knew where I was and I wanted to live. Before noon I could sit up and look around us at the wide brown river and the green forest walls. Periclaw was already far behind. White Water was taking us up the Blood River.

"To look for that trilithon, if you remember," Ram said. "If it's anywhere near where that old map shows it."

I grew stronger. I was able to swallow a few sips of the hot black corath tea when Kenleth offered it, and finally felt eager for another full mug. Kenleth fished from the boat and Ram broiled his catch on the boiler door. They discovered ripe papayas in the abandoned fields, and yams Ram could bake. Once Kenleth found bees in a hollow tree. Ram built a fire to stun them with smoke and brought back a basket filled with delicious honeycombs.

I grew ravenous for any food they offered. I was able to stand, able to climb out of the boat and walk on the sandbars when we stopped to gather driftwood for the boiler. My recollections of sweat and pain and dread began to fade away. I felt alive once more, alert to things around me. The river was lower now, as the monsoon wind had changed. It was empty of traffic. The banks looked empty of people.

"Sheko breathed death on the river," Ram said. "They've gone back to the jungle."

Thoughts of his parents filled Kenleth's eyes with tears and he showed me a ring his mother gave him the last time he saw her, after they had followed Toron into the jungle. Her last relic of his father, he thought it had come from some jungle tomb. A wide gold band, it was set with three polished black stones to make a tiny trilithon. It was too large for Kenleth's finger, and he wore it on a cord around his neck.

The old brick fort was abandoned, but he wanted to see his old home. We tied up at the empty dock. I was able to limp ashore with him. Kenleth ran ahead of me to the scraps of the stake palisade that still stood where the compound had burned, and found only a new jungle of ferns and vines inside. Nothing was left that he remembered. He came back clutching the ring in his fingers.

Pushing on upriver, we passed tributaries, one so wide that White Water seemed uncertain which branch to follow. Ram frowned over the maps in his e-book, and found no useful clues.

"We'll trust our luck," he said. "Or White Water's hunch."

We stopped when we had to, for driftwood or fallen logs we could cut, and steamed on when we had steam. The channel narrowed, cut through rocky hills. The vegetation changed, rain forest replaced with evergreens. We found mountains ahead, blue in the distance.

Day by day, they rose higher. We came out of barren hills into a high-walled canyon cut through black granite. It narrowed till the sky was a thin bright strip we had to crane to see. The current grew too fast for the toiling engine. Thunder boomed against the cliffs. We came around a turn and found a waterfall ahead.

I'd seen Niagara. This was wider, higher, the thunder louder. Kenleth stood up in the boat, gaping at the crashing water and the canyon walls that boxed us in.

"Is this the end?"

I thought it was. I still felt weak. I saw no way out. The water fell over an enormous dam, roaring down into a cloud of white spray lit with a rainbow arc where a shaft of sunlight struck it. White Water steered the launch to a tiny strip of gravel beach and eased us to it. He and Ram jumped out and pulled the launch half out of the water.

We stood there on the beach, craning up at the dam. Built of something smooth and black, it curved from wall to canyon wall. I felt shut in, caught in closing granite jaws.

"They were giants!" White Water shook his head at it. "The magicians of the Grand Dominion."

Ram was scanning the dam's long curve.

"The map shows it," he said. "There's a long lake above it. It must have been built for power. There should have been tunnels to carry water to turbines and generators somewhere. Or maybe not?" He shrugged and turned to scan the walls around us. "So much has been forgotten."

"Far enough?" White Water gave him an inquiring frown. "Is it back to Periclaw?"

"We can't stop here. Not with the trilithon just beyond the lake."

"I can't leave the boat," White Water said. "It's all I have."

Ram stood a moment frowning at me. Kenleth shrank against me, groping for my hand. Feeling helpless, I could only shrug.

"We've nothing here." Ram winced as if from a stab of pain. "We've got to go on."

"I don't see how." White Water gestured at the black cliffs and the narrow far scrap of sky. "You've got rough country ahead. We've been living on the land, but we've left the easy pickings behind us."

"Will?" Ram turned to me. "Are you fit to climb?"

"I'm stronger," I told him. "I'll do my best."

"If you're that crazy," White Water said, "I'll wait for you here."

"Thanks, my friend." Ram gripped his hand. "But don't wait too long. If we find the gate, if it lets us through, we'll never be back."

"You will be." White Water frowned at Ram's face and the golden birthmark. "Your destiny is here."

"I've had my destiny." Ram flinched as if from an actual stab. "It's over."

We shook White Water's hand and left him with the launch. Ram loaded himself with fruit we had dried, fish we had smoked, yam-like roots we could bake. Kenleth carried blankets. I had a water jug and a strip of the awning, with ropes to stretch it like a tent.

The dam builders had left us a way around the fall, a sloping ramp that led us behind that roaring water to a narrow crevice in the canyon wall. In single file we followed it for hours, uphill and down, until at last we came out into twilight on a windy ledge, the lake a thousand feet below us, so vast that most of it was lost in the dusk.

The wind had an icy bite. We retreated into the crevice and spread the blankets. I slept and dreamed that Ram had left us there alone. He had gone back with White Water to rule a new Grand Dominion. I felt relieved to find him still with us, kindling a tiny fire to make hot tea.

By daylight, we saw a range of snow-clad peaks beyond the lake, blue with distance. We were already high above timberline. I wondered if the trilithon might be beyond our reach, but we made a frugal breakfast and took the trail again, over barren ridges and through rocky gorges.

By noon, we were down to the lakeshore, the water so crystal clear that Kenleth wanted to swim till he dipped a foot and felt how cold it was. The trail went on, cut into the cliffs just a few yards above the water level. We followed it all day, to a narrow in the lake and a bridge across it, five long arches of some dark stone, hardly scarred by time.

We camped in a shallow cave where an overhang jutted above the path, and crossed the bridge next morning. The lake widened again beyond it, reaching far toward those snow-topped peaks. We left it there, climbing the path to a stony, treeless tableland.

Next day we saw the trilithon, toy-small in the distance, so far that another noon had come before we reached it. It stood alone, the only feature on a scrap of barren plain. It had grown enormous as we finally neared it, the twin black pillars towering out of a broad black pavement.

Ram opened his e-book and craned to study the symbols cut deep into the huge crossbar a hundred feet above us. He sighed at last and snapped the book shut. Kenleth stood gaping at the pillars and the bleak landscape beyond them. The path had ended and it looked like the road to nowhere. In a mix of awe and disbelief, he turned to Ram.

"It's a door? Where does it go?"

"*Quien sabe?*" He shrugged. "That's what a friend of ours would say. With luck enough, we can hope to find her somewhere on the other side. We've got no way to know except to try it." He turned to Kenleth. "Are you ready?"

Eyes shining, Kenleth caught my hand.

"One more shuffle, one more deal." Ram shrugged and grinned at me. "If you have the magic key."

I'd worn the emerald pendant since the night he gave it to me. I slipped the silver chain over my head, and gave it back. He held it in his right hand and caught mine with his left. I got my balance and held my breath. Grinning at Kenleth, he chanted his Swahili numbers. His hand gripped harder. We stepped through together.

The sunlight dimmed and reddened. My ears clicked to the air pressure change. The ground jolted as a different gravity caught me. My right ankle failed. I staggered and went down, my breath knocked out. I lay gasping for air that was suddenly oven-hot and bitter with dust.

"Will?" Ram and Kenleth had my arms, trying to help me up. "Are you hurt?"

I tried to say I was okay, and found no voice. I tried to stand and fell back against the black stone column. Sitting propped against the column, I gasped for breath and gripped the ankle to ease the pain.

"Where?" Kenleth sneezed and coughed from the dust. "Where are we?"

"My Little Mama always said she'd run away from hell." Ram stood gazing around us. "I think we're there."

The trilithon stood on a flat stone bench. The land around it was pocked with craters but almost level to far dark mountains. Wind-blown dust lay piled around scattered boulders of rust red stone. The sun was huge and high, the color of red-hot iron, so dim that it didn't hurt my eyes.

"Mars?" Ram shook his head. "We couldn't breathe on Mars."

"What's that?"

Kenleth was pointing back through the trilithon. The paved trail we had followed was gone. All around us, that lifeless waste of rocks and dust and crater pits reached away to dark and distant mountain peaks bare of snow. A gust of the burning wind stung my eyes with dust.

"That thing?" Ram turned to me. "What could it be?"

I blinked and rubbed my eyes and found the object. Far away among the craters, it was a great thick octagon of some dark stuff, something no natural force could have shaped.

"A building?"

"Odd, if it is." Ram shook his head. "No doors or windows I can see." He shaded his eyes to study it again. "Something the trilithon-builders left? Maybe the ship that brought them?"

He sat down in the shadow of the high lintel stone and opened his pack to find his e-book. The script pages flickered across the screen. He stopped on the image of a planet that might have been a second Mars, waterless, cratered, the color of dust.

"I wish we had Derek here." He frowned a long time at the image and finally looked back at me. "But I think the book's a history of the Grand Dominion and its founders. I can't read the text, but the planets we've seen are all there, even the twin system. I think they had to reach the planets with rocket craft before they built the trilithons.

"This planet is the first one in the book. Could be it's the first one they reached. Not fit for life." He scowled at the red desolation around us. "They would have gone on from here.

Found better worlds, but barren of life. Finally Earth and life they could transplant from there."

He touched a key. Lines of golden hieroglyphs flashed across the image. He pointed at a tiny black trilithon symbol in a wide crater at the center of it.

"That could be where we are." He shook his head. "Or I could be wrong. No way to know."

"An ugly place." Kenleth shivered in spite of the heat and shaded his eyes to stare back through the trilithon at the dead waste beyond it. He turned anxiously to Ram. "Can we go back?"

"I wish we could." Ram touched the pendant. "We've tried. The key never lets us."

"So what can we do?"

"Not much." He shook his head, with a wry glance at me. "Not till Will can walk."

He touched a button to close the book. It stayed open. A bell-tone pealed. The dead screen flashed red and green, red and green again. It froze, amber-hued. English letters scrawled themselves across it unsteadily, as if written in haste.

RAM AND WILL, IF YOU EVER READ THIS, YOU HAVE REACHED BETA CENTRAL TRILITHON. WE ARE GOING ON TO PLANET ALPHA. WE NEED YOU WITH US. IF YOU CAN FOLLOW, TAKE THE SOUTHWEST ROUTE TO THE MOUNTAIN GATE.

LUPE AND DEREK

I read it to Kenleth.

"Can we follow?"

"If we could." Ram made an ironic grimace. "If we had a taxi and knew where to go."

Kenleth blinked forlornly at the red desert around us.

"Is there any southwest here?"

"Derek explained directions," Ram told him. "When you face a rising sun you're looking east. The north pole is on your left, south on your right. But I don't see any road or any signs to get us to the southwest route."

Ram shut the e-book and turned to frown again at that great black octagon.

"I could walk out for a closer look. I don't know what we'll find. Likely nothing, but I wonder if it could be the workshop used and left here by the trilithon builders. Interesting, maybe, if we could get inside." He shrugged. "I see nothing else for us to do."

I tried again to stand. Again a stab of pain brought me down. My ankle was swelling, turning purple, painful when I touched it. I looked around for anything that might make a cane or crutch, but all I saw was useless stone and dust. The effort to move left me breathing hard.

"Oxygen." Ram grimaced. "It's short here. No green life to set it free." He gave me a wry grin. "Just wait right here."

"Can I go with you?" Kenleth turned to me. "Or do you need me here with you?"

"Go," I told him. "Ram could need you more than I do."

Kenleth put his arms around me. Ram grinned and told me to call an ambulance if I needed help. I tried to laugh and felt tears on my cheeks. Helpless to do anything else, I sat back against the pillar, sweating in the heat and coughing from the acrid dust.

"Back by sundown," Ram called. "Or light a lamp if we are late."

I watched them walk away, picking a careful path through

the rocks and crater pits, raising puffs of orange dust the wind whipped around their feet. They went slowly. Once Kenleth tripped and fell. Ram picked him up and gestured as if trying to send him back, but they went on together.

The black octagon was larger and farther than it looked. They were a long time on the way. The huge pale sun crept across the dusty sky. The shadow of the lintel shifted. I crawled on hands and knees to move our gear back into the moving shade.

They diminished in the distance. Gusts of yellow dust hid them and hid them again. They became tiny insect figures dancing in the shimmer of heat on the horizon between dark red desert and red-lit sky. I lost them altogether. The great dull sun sank into what I thought should be the west.

My ankle throbbed. The dust turned bitter in my throat and I took a careful sip of water. I dozed, and the sun was suddenly lower. I thought they had gone too far to be back before it set. I was wondering dismally if they would ever be back at all when I saw a bright flash above the octagon and then a tiny black grasshopper soaring in silhouette against the sun's great face.

The hopper spread and beat its stubby wings, climbing higher, gliding down across that vast red disk. Small and far as the creature was, I knew the shape: the long narrow body and blunt silver head, the short wings, the black lever legs. It was another like the one that snatched Lupe out of the trilithon circle on that first planet, like the one that seized Derek on the planet of the robots.

I watched till it rose back across the sun's dull face and glided down toward me. I counted five flights before it dived at the point where I had last seen Kenleth and Ram. It soon soared again, away from me now, soared and soared again, till I lost it in the sky above that strange black structure.

I waited but saw nothing else before the sun went down. Purple dusk faded into moonless, starless darkness. I lay there on the hard stone floor, my ankle throbbing. The hot night wind took my breath and stung my throat with dust. I longed for Kenleth's bright laugh, for Ram's calm courage, for Lupe and Derek, for any spark of hope.

Yet somehow I slept. I dreamed that I'd somehow got back home to the university and called a press conference at the Campus Union. Reporters jeered at me. NASA scientists called my story a hoax. Our instant skipping from planet to planet was forbidden by Einstein's laws of space and time. A chartered radar plane had flown over the Sahara and found no trace of any trilithon buried under the sand.

Skeptics demanded evidence, but I had no written records, no photos of the skywire or the robots or the hoppers, no artifacts from the fallen Grand Dominion. The university president wanted to know what had become of his missing faculty members.

Refusing to believe anything I said, he called the campus cops and then the state police. I was arrested and tried in district court. The judge was a tall black-robed man who had Crail's sick and angry face. In a funereal voice, he stated the case against me.

"William Martin Stone, you are charged by the state of New Mexico with the murders of Dr. Derek Ironcraft, Dr. Lupe Vargas, and Dr. Ram Chenji. You are charged with destruction of evidence, obstruction of justice, and perjury in the fourth degree. What is your plea?"

My attorney rose to plead not guilty by reason of insanity. My only witness was Kenleth, still in the muddy rags he had worn when we picked him up out of the jungle. The prosecut-

ing attorney ridiculed him. What court would accept the lies of
a scrawny little black kid, a minor and an alien from nowhere?
His testimony was stricken from the record.

The prosecuting attorney called a clever dark officer from
Interpol, who clinched the case against me. Ram had been the
kingpin of a plot to overthrow the government of his native
Kenya. Derek and Lupe were his allies. They had infiltrated a
terrorist group to obtain high explosives, and they were flying
to Nairobi to assassinate the president.

Kenyan intelligence officials had bribed me to nip the plot. I
planted a stolen bomb in Ram's briefcase. Their plane crashed
in the dunes of the Grand Erg Oriental, where searchers could
never reach it. All three were certainly dead. The prosecutor
called me a criminal idiot, if I expected a fairy tale of magic
trilithons to shield me from the justice I deserved.

My attorney rested his case. The jury glided in, six glittering
snakes shaped of glittering diamonds. Climbing into the jury
box, they flashed their scarlet eyes at the lawyers and took half-
human forms. The foreman's head became White Water's, and
he read the decision from Ram's e-book.

Death by lethal injection.

I woke drenched with sweat and parched with thirst. The giant sun was rising, veiled in wind-whipped dust that dimmed it
to a great copper plate and burned my eyes. The courtroom and
the cellular robots were gone, but that sentence of death was
still with me.

It would execute itself when my food and water were gone.

CHAPTER

33

I was there an endless week as my watch measured Earth time, fifteen of the planet's days. It spun fast, its day hardly a dozen hours, but each of those dragged on forever. I watched the path Ram and Kenleth had followed and searched the dull red sky in the direction the hopper had flown. I ate when hunger drove me. I hoarded water till the last drop was gone. I slept when I could, and endured evil dreams.

"Ty Will?" I heard Kenleth's anxious voice and felt his finger on my arm. "Are you okay?"

For a moment I thought he was another dream, but I opened my sticky eyes and found him leaning over me, clad in new white garments. Ram stood beside him, garbed in the same tight jacket and ballooning pants. Behind them I saw the machine that had brought them.

The size of a van, it had no wheels, resting instead on a thick mattress of something that shaped itself like a black rubber balloon to fit the ground. It was topped with a dark oval shell that gleamed like glass. A door in the end had swung down to make a ramp.

"Will?" Ram helped me up. My ankle felt stiff, but I could stand. "How are you?"

My dry throat made a hoarse rasp when I tried to answer. I swayed on my feet and the trilithon spun around me. I tried to swallow when Kenleth held a cup of cold water to my lips, coughed and strangled on it, finally washed my mouth, took an uneasy sip, then reckless gulps.

"Better," I managed to whisper. "Since you got here."

"We tried to come sooner," Kenleth said. "The hoppers kept us in the octagon."

Ram helped me into a small space at the end of the machine. The ramp lifted to seal the door behind. Air hissed, suddenly dust-free and cool. A second door opened into a larger space that had seats rather like those in a small RV.

"An air lock," Ram said. "And our own ventilation system."

I sank into a seat. Kenleth folded a little table down before me, brought a basin of water and a sponge to let me wash the dust out of my eyes, the sweat-caked grime off my hands and face. He brought a cup of hot soup and a tray of crisp little biscuits. It was the banquet I'd longed for. I breathed the good air, sipped and nibbled, collapsed suddenly into a fit of sobbing.

"What's wrong, Ty Will?"

Kenleth hovered over me, but I could only lie back in the seat, shaking, struck with a wave of terror that this was only one more dream, that I would wake still alone. He brought the sponge to let me wipe my eyes again. I'd nerved myself to die, and relief had overwhelmed me. I sat up at last, caught my breath, and found life enough to ask questions.

Had they found humans?

"Not yet." Ram frowned. "This machine seems designed to fit the human form, and we've found traces—"

"Of Derek and Lupe?"

He nodded, with a wry little shrug.

"We found their backpacks in a sort of museum. Hung up for display, along with their clothing and possessions. Marked with labels we couldn't read. Nothing else."

"You saw a hopper?"

"A monster!" Kenleth went shrill. "As big as a ship! It came down at us out of the sky. I was terribly afraid, but that was exciting. It had arms like slick snakes and hands with a dozen fingers. It grabbed us up and carried us back to the hive." He looked at Ram. "If that's what you'd call it."

"The place does seem to be a sort of hive." Ram nodded, frowning. "Or maybe a factory. We saw what I think is a baby hopper. A big, pale gray slug, floating in a tank of liquid. Part of it was wrinkled like a brain. Something was pulsing like a heart. It had no eyes, no limbs.

"Next to it was a big workshop, where a gang of those multicellular robots were turning out parts for it. Making them out of metal and some sort of plastic. The hard body shell, those long legs, the wings, the silver-colored skull. I think the hoppers are half machine, half alive."

"Are they intelligent?"

"Their creators certainly were."

Eyes narrowed, he sat staring out across the craters toward the far black bulk of what he called the octagon. A gust of wind lifted a veil of yellow dust that hid it. Those creators haunted me. Their vast age, their works, their absence. I shivered to a chill of dread.

"Engineers," he muttered. "Master engineers. They must have designed the hoppers and the robots to explore the galaxy. To build and operate the trilithon system. Maybe to bring life from Earth and populate the planets where we've been. But then they went away, as if they were never here."

His shoulders hunched as if he shared my dread.

"I don't know. I tried to talk to the hopper. The best response I ever got was a bellow that made me shake. The robots might be better if we knew the language."

"What about us? Why did they pick you up?"

"They wanted to study us," Kenleth said. "Like bugs under a lens."

"They examined us." Ram nodded. "Stripped us. Weighed and measured us. Tested our vision and our hearing. Ran us through a sort of maze, I guess to test our own intelligence."

"That's how they found my ring."

Kenleth showed it to us, still hung on the cord around his neck, the gold band set with the tiny black trilithon.

"The one his mother gave him," Ram said. "I don't know where she got it, but it must be a relic of the Grand Dominion. The robots found it and took it to the hopper. It examined it under those big eyes that shine like searchlights and let the robots give it back to Kenleth."

"And they worshiped me!" His eyes had lit. "Bowed to me and gave me a gift. A wonderful toy."

He showed it to me. A crystal tetrahedron, clear as glass, two or three inches on a side.

"A lucky break." Ram shrugged, with a puzzled frown. "I don't understand the toy, if it is a toy, but the ring's magic. It must come down from the time of the Grand Dominion. It carries authority. They gave us the machine and let us go."

"Derek and Lupe?" I asked. "You say you saw their packs?"

"They must have been here. They had no magic ring, but they should have scored well on the I. Q. tests. I'd like to think the hoppers came to respect them. Fitted them out and let them go on."

"Where could they go?"

"Not back to Earth. Not if I know them. I think they'd want to go on to look for the creators."

That shook me.

"Where?" I whispered. "Where could they be?"

"Not here, for sure. This planet never cradled the evolution of anything. A riddle Derek and Lupe would love if they got a chance to tackle it. A chance for us if we can follow them." He stopped to frown at me. "If you're game for it, Will."

I caught my breath and asked what he meant.

"The hoppers run the trilithon system. They take orders from Kenleth since they saw the ring. I think we could get them to take you back to Earth. Kenleth, too, if he wants to go with you."

That hit me like an unexpected fist. Emotion choked me. I broke into another fit of sobbing.

"Don't you want me with you, Ty Will?" Kenleth put his arms around me. "You don't have to take me."

He brought me a cup of water. I took a gulp and found my voice.

"I want you with me when we go," I told him, and turned to Ram. "I wish we were home, but I won't—I can't run out on you."

Soberly, Ram shook his head.

"Better take time to think about it, Will. If there's a chance to find Derek and Lupe, I have to go on, but it won't be a picnic. The message said they needed us, but we might never find them." He studied me again. "You've been through rough times. I don't think you're really over the fever. Frankly, you don't look fit to go."

"We're the Four Horsemen, remember?" I tried to grin. "I can't go home alone."

———

We stayed in that odd vehicle, there in the shadow of the trilithon, through two more of the planet's windy days. Ram spent most of them at the controls in the nose and at a navigation screen, with what he thought was an operator's handbook. It seemed to show routes across the area and views of destinations.

"Imagine a chimp in a car, with no instructor and a book he can't read." He mocked himself. "The robots don't give driving lessons."

Kenleth spent hours absorbed in his new toy, the crystal tetrahedron. I began to see what made it wonderful. Changing colors flashed through it when he pressed the points. I glimpsed fleeting images of human-seeming faces, strange creatures, symbols from that script we had never been able to read, all gone before I could really see them.

"It's a game," he said. "I have to learn the rules."

I asked how the vehicle moved with no wheels.

"It crawls." Ram shook his head. "Don't ask me how. Never very fast, but it's fit for rough country. No tires to puncture. You couldn't make it collide with anything or turn it over. I think it's also a boat, if we had water to float it. There's a sort of autopilot. And something that looks like our satellite navigation systems back at home.

"I can't read the legends, but the screen shows a map of the crater, with a red dot for the big disk and a trilithon sign for the point where we are. Routes across the area are marked in yellow. One runs southwest to the mountains. Maybe a couple hundred miles."

He stopped to frown at me.

"Southwest. That could be the route Derek and Lupe took. One more gamble, if you really get fit for it."

I ate, drank, dozed, ventured outside for short walks in the dusty heat, and finally convinced Ram that I was fit for travel. He drove us by the octagon. It was even more enormous than I'd thought—maybe a mile across, the long black wall towering several hundred feet above us.

As we came near, a tiny-seeming door opened down on the ground level. A robot marched out, an orange-colored light flashing on the crown of its plastic head. Ram answered with a light on the nose of the machine. It made an about-face and flashed a green signal. Its plastic arm pointed and froze. Ram drove us on.

"Slow," he said. "But it sure beats walking."

There was a sort of joystick, but he let the machine steer itself. Turning away from the octagon, it found a path that ran the way the robot had pointed. Wind-drifted dust covered any pavement it might have ever had, but it was level and smooth enough, curbed here and there with ragged rows of boulders that had been moved to level it. It led straight across the red-lit desert as far as I could see.

"Where are we going?" Kenleth was flushed with excitement. "Where do you think?"

Ram was tapping the keys of his e-book, squinting at the flicker of script and image.

"We'll see." He frowned at the long road ahead. "The book's still Greek to me, but the pictures begin to make a sort of sense. I think we're in a vast depression, left early in the planet's history by the impact of something big. It's deep. Maybe a couple hundred miles across. We're on a route toward the mountains around it."

He and Kenleth took turns in the driver's seat, but the machine left nothing for them to do. I sat watching the rocks and craters slide past. The machine moved without jolts or vibration, but it had a gentle sway that finally lulled me to sleep.

It had stopped when Kenleth woke me. We had reached a towering precipice. The road came to a dead end against a tall trilithon carved into the cliff, and solid rock ahead. Crater pits had been smoothed to level a space below it. I saw no other path leading away.

"We're here!" he was shouting. "Breakfast, and then we're going into the mountain!"

He and Ram were busy with a little device that dispensed hot tea and crisp little cakes. We ate. Ram studied his e-book and sat again at the controls, his birthmark glowing. He fumbled under his white jacket for the emerald pendant and raised it.

"Ready?" He looked around at Kenleth and me.

"Ready!" Kenleth shouted. "Go!"

He touched something. The machine lurched ahead.

CHAPTER 34

Black midnight fell. The rock-carved trilithon was gone, the dull red sun, the lurid sky, the wall ahead. Ram stopped the machine. The pale green glow of the instrument lights went out. The crown of worlds shone golden on his forehead, but I saw nothing else. We sat lost in suffocating darkness.

"What happened?" Kenleth whispered. "Are we dead?"

"Not yet," Ram said.

We sat there while our eyes adjusted to the dark. Stars came out one by one as we sat there, waiting, wondering. Kenleth sat close beside me, silent. A faint blue spark burned low in the east, a white spark to its right, a dim red point below it. More and more came behind them as we sat there, rising so slowly I thought they were never really moving, all low in the east, none overhead or north or south or west.

"Strange!" Ram shook his head. "We've seen half a dozen skies from planets light-years apart, but all somewhere in the galaxy. They all had our own Milky Way. But none like this."

Hours passed. My legs cramped from sitting too long. Ram turned on the inside lights. Kenleth worked the dispenser to bring us cups of a tart amber drink and a tray of crisp almond-flavored biscuits. With lights out and our eyes adjusted again, we found a star cloud in the east, thousands of stars, bright and faint, a luminous haze behind them.

"Look!" Kenleth caught Ram's arm. "Your birthmark!"

I saw an odd constellation. A compact cluster made a level bar. Brighter stars made an arc above it. They formed the crown of worlds. I turned to stare at the glowing pattern on his forehead.

"The same!" I couldn't stop myself. "What does it mean?"

"Nothing." Ram shrugged. "Nothing I like. Derek said it had to be a genetic artifact created by the trilithon builders. Maybe it is. I don't know."

We sat in silence till I heard Kenleth's awed whisper.

"My mother thought you were born to be a god."

"No!" The word exploded in the dark. "I'm no god!"

He moved abruptly to turn the headlamps on. Blazing ahead, they flooded a flat wasteland, white as new snow. Nothing broke it, as far as I could see. Not a rock, not a building, not a tree, not anything at all.

"Where?" Kenleth's voice was hoarse and hushed. "Where is this?"

"I'd like to know."

Ram started the crawler again, turning to let the headlights sweep all around us. There was no trilithon, nothing but that flat white waste. I shivered, as if its dead desolation had crept into the machine.

"Let's take a look," he said. "A look outside."

He went back to the air lock. The door thumped and sealed

behind him. Air hissed. We waited a long time until at last it hissed again. He stumbled dazedly back, shaking his head.

"We're stuck," he muttered. "The outside hatch won't open. A safety lock, I guess. I can't be sure how to read the instruments, but I think they show air pressure zero and outside temperature close to absolute zero. That would mean the planet has no sun."

His face turned harder in the birthmark's glow.

"If Derek and Lupe got here ahead of us, I'm afraid they're dead."

Kenleth looked at me, his eyes huge. "Will we die?"

All I could do was put my arm around him.

Ram was peering into the pool of light ahead of the crawler.

"See that!" Suddenly he was pointing. I saw a faint gray trace across it. "Derek and Lupe did get here. They left a track in that white stuff, which I guess is frozen air. A trail I think we can follow."

We set out along it, the machine crawling a little faster than a man could walk. Ram let me take my turn in the driver's seat, but that faint gray trail ran straight forever, with never a turn or a break, and the machine drove itself.

"A frozen world." Ram hunched his shoulders as if he felt its bitter chill. "Frozen nearly forever, but it must have been alive. With air until it froze. Water and weather, to wear the surface smooth. How long ago—" He shook his head. "I can't imagine."

Kenleth served our meals from the food and drink dispenser, which fascinated him. The strange textures and flavors turned me off at first, but hunger was a great appetizer.

"Synthetics." With a grin of relish, Ram finished a chocolate-colored bar. "But I've had worse. Those old engineers had human tastes."

Very slowly, the crown of worlds rose higher in what we came to call the east. Crowded constellations followed it. Hot red stars. Cold blue giants. Stars yellow-white as our own sun. Crowded closer and closer together till half the sky blazed with diamond fire.

"Imagine Derek!" Ram shook his head at the sky and the faint trail ahead. "If he's okay. He used to teach an astronomy course back at Eastern, with a little telescope of his own. This sky should drive him wild."

By my watch, twenty hours of Earth time had passed by then.

"A lazy planet," Ram said. "The day is maybe eighty hours. The ages must have slowed it down."

The machine crawled on and on. We slept, stretched out on seats that folded flat. We ate when we were hungry. We scanned that great swarm of stars rising out of the east, climbing till it covered all the sky and flooded that empty white infinity with starlight brighter than our own moon had been.

Nothing changed it until Kenleth, sitting at the joystick, cried out.

"There! See!"

It was hard for me to see, but at last I found a saw-toothed break in the straight horizon. Hour by hour it stretched longer. The tiny teeth became towers, climbing higher and higher against the bright mosaic of varicolored stars.

"A city?" Kenleth was enchanted. "Have we found a city?"

It had been a city. A wall had stood around it, half of it leveled now with gaps that let us see the buildings. Climbing taller as we neared them, they became magnificent and strange. Slender pyramids stabbed spearlike toward the star-packed zenith. Hexagonal columns clustered among domes and spires and soaring shapes I knew no names for. Their splendor awed us into silence.

Ram stopped the machine.

"A ruin!" he whispered. "I wish we could have seen it whole."

Half of it was gone, reduced to stumps and rock piles and bare foundations. Deep canyons yawned between rubble mountains. All of it was shrouded under hills of frost-white dust.

"Dead!" Ram shivered. "It was dead before our world was born."

"Were they people?" Kenleth whispered.

"The doors look human-sized," Ram said. "That's one good sign."

"What killed them?"

"A falling meteor?" Ram shook his head. "A missile attack? Or maybe they just got tired of living. We may never know."

We sat there a long time before he moved the machine again.

"A field day for Lupe!" Ram swung the headlights to scan the way ahead. "She was wild for anything prehistoric. Just imagine her here!"

The trail was hard to follow. They had gone through a gap in the wall and into a magnificent avenue. A ridge of toppled masonry had turned them back. Our own tracks were laid over theirs until we lost them altogether. We ourselves were lost.

A dozen hours were gone before we found a gap that took us back out of the wall. With the constellations for a compass and starlight over the ruins, we picked up the trail. Again the faint gray track ran straight into a world dead forever. Frost crystals flashed and vanished in our headlights, but we saw no other change.

The star clouds covered all the sky with diamonds and crept slowly on until they slowly sank into what we called the west. Outside again, we crawled on and on and on through a darker midnight than I'd ever imagined, with only the headlights to keep us on the trail. We took turns at the joystick, turns at staring into darkness, turns asleep. We ate again and still again. I asked Ram how long he thought our water and food might last. He didn't know.

Another day of starlight dawned at last, the crown of worlds climbing again out of the east.

"There!" Kenleth pointed ahead. "What is that?"

His eyes were sharper than mine. I saw nothing until an hour later, when the stars were bright enough to show me a tiny pyramid on the horizon. Ram woke to watch it with us. It grew until I saw that it was no pyramid at all, but a vast cone-shape instead, towering alone out of infinite flatness.

"A mountain?" Kenleth asked. "Is it a mountain?"

"Not here." Ram shook his head. "Not likely, though it's high enough."

It was a thousand feet tall, he guessed, half a mile across, the surface sloping smoothly up. Kenleth made out a spiral path that wound around from the ground to a railed platform at the top.

"Something built," Ram said. "Likely when the city was."

Like the city, it was rounded under heavy frost and dust.

"Can we climb it?" Kenleth was eager. "To the top?"

"If Derek and Lupe did," Ram said. "We'll follow till we find them."

———

They hadn't climbed, we found, but had gone down instead. The track took us past a long ridge of frozen air that had been bulldozed to clear a wide open ring around the cone. I saw a dark archway in the foot of it. Light flickered there, and a long crystal robot crawled out to meet us.

It reared in front of us. The little cubes and disks and pyramids and cones and shapeless masses morphed into a glittering travesty of Lupe in her jeans and field jacket and even something like her wide-brimmed field hat. The eyes flashed red, and it beckoned us to stop.

"Lupe Vargas!" Ram stopped the crawler and sat gaping at it. "We've found them!"

"Found what?" Kenleth goggled at it.

Its eyes flashed again. Ram moved abruptly to answer with our headlights. Its eyes shone green, and it stepped aside to beckon us through the arch. Ram drove us past it into a wide tunnel that sloped gently down. The walls were high and our headlamps glinted red and gold on tiles that made intricate patterns of interlocking rosettes.

"A paradise for Lupe!" Ram whistled. "What a culture to explore!"

The tunnel curved, always sloping down. We followed for several miles, finally out into a cavernous space with a circular floor. A blue dome arched above it, softly luminous. We saw no exit. Ram stopped the machine. We sat there waiting, hoping to see Derek or Lupe.

Kenleth fidgeted, staring uneasily around at the featureless dome.

"What's this—"

It flickered before he could finish, and became a bright blue sky with a warm sun rising in the east. The crawler sat on a grassy plain with clumps of trees around us. Smoke climbed from a brown lava cone on the north horizon. A small stream ran past us toward a distant water hole. Far off to the south, veiled in the mist of distance, a taller cone was capped with white.

"Kenya!" Ram gasped. "We're on the rim of the Rift." He shook his head and pointed south. "That's Kilimanjaro."

"Where's this?" Kenleth gaped at me. "What happened to us?"

"It's a picture," Ram told him. "A living picture of the world where I grew up." He caught his breath and turned to stare at me. "But how did it get this far from Earth?"

I had no idea. We sat there drinking it in. A little herd of zebras was grazing near us, a few impalas among them. A pair of giraffes browsed treetops beyond. A great, white-tusked elephant ambled around a clump of the trees, half a dozen more behind it. Ignoring us, they stopped to drink from the stream. A dark-maned lion lay on a rocky hill, its great head lifted, watching sleepily.

"People!"

Kenleth pointed. They came toward us, wading the stream in single file. Naked and hairy, but walking erect, they were certainly human. In the lead were three or four black-bearded men, carrying long spears and stone axes in rawhide pouches slung from their shoulders. One carried an impala hindquarter on his back, still in its hide. Another had a little boy with a missing foot astride his neck.

Two of the women carried babies, one a full water skin. A tall girl had golden fruit in a fiber bag. A younger girl led her little sister by the hand. A wisp of smoke drifted from a little pile of ashes in a bird-nest of mud and woven grass on an older woman's head. She was the keeper of fire. Two boys had slings and bags of pebbles. One ran to the front, whirled a rock around his head, and let it fly. The other darted to look for what it might have hit.

Kenleth blinked at Ram. "Who are they?"

"Us," Ram said. "The way Lupe thought we were two hundred thousand years ago, when somebody brought us back to Earth from wherever we were evolved or engineered."

They vanished. The dome around us was smooth and blue again. A door slid open ahead of the crawler to reveal another wide tunnel mouth ahead. A vehicle glided out, a crawler like ours, perhaps a little larger. I glimpsed the man at the joystick.

Derek Ironcraft.

The machine crawled closer. Derek waved a greeting. Lupe sat in the seat beside him. In an odd white outfit like Ram's and Kenleth's, she was almost a stranger. Her field hat was gone. Her hair hung behind her shoulders in a long black braid. Derek had grown a thick beard and long bronze hair secured with a red headband.

"Derek?" Ram bent over the instruments and pulled out a knob that looked like a microphone. "Lupe? Do you hear me?"

Derek waved again, but I heard no answer. Lupe shaded her eyes to see us. Ram shook his head and edged us closer. Derek gestured for us to stop. He backed away and turned his machine to bring the rear doors together. The air locks thumped and hissed. Suddenly Derek and Lupe were coming through, a gleaming metal and crystal robot gliding behind them.

"We were hoping." Derek gripped my hand. "It's great to see you here."

Lupe hugged us. I introduced Kenleth. Lupe gave him a smile. He burst into tears.

"I—I'm sorry," he sobbed. "You look like my mother."

She put her arms around him. Ram beckoned them into the seats. He huddled against her, gazing up at her face in instant adoration. Derek studied me sharply and asked how I was.

"Okay," I said. "Since we've found you."

"We're all better now," Ram said. "I thought we'd lost you forever."

We asked a thousand questions. Where had they been since the hoppers picked them up? What was this place? How had they found their own way here? How did they control the robots? What had they learned about the builders of the trilithons, the frozen city, the towering cone above us?

"Big questions." Derek shrugged them off. "We keep looking for answers and always find more to ask. Most of what we have is guesswork. You've seen the cybroids. That's what we call the hoppers and the robots. You've seen the empty sky. You must have come through Omega. That's Lupe's name for the city. You know as much as we do."

"You got here," Ram said. "All we've done is follow."

"Tell us how you managed that."

"A long story." Ram's face went bleak. "It wasn't easy."

Lupe worked the dispenser and brought us a plate of little lemon-flavored cakes and yellow globes that had almost the taste of ripe peaches. Derek opened a cabinet and came back with a tray loaded with pitchers, glasses, and a bowl of ice.

"It's not quite the Kentucky bourbon we used to drink on poker nights." He held a bottle of amber liquid up to the light. "But the cybroids make a fair mint julep when you can teach them what you want." He filled our glasses. "Here's to Planet Alpha and the Omegans."

"To the Four Horsemen!" Lupe waved her glass. "Together again!"

I sipped cautiously. It wasn't bourbon, but it had a hint of mint and a fiery bite. Kenleth wanted a taste. Derek gave him a little of it, mixed with water. He sipped and made a face.

"You came through Delta?" Lupe asked.

"Delta?" Ram shook his head. "We never knew a name for it."

"We tag them in Greek," Derek said. "In the order in which we think the Omegans reached them. They must have evolved here, which makes this Alpha. The octagon's on Beta."

Ram summed up our story. His voice grew hoarse and slow when he came to the slave rebellion, our captivity, the blood rot pandemic, our escape with White Water up the Blood River. He broke it off with not a word about the Crails.

"Celya?" Kenleth said. "Don't forget her."

Ram's face went hard. He gulped and said nothing.

"She was beautiful," Kenleth told Lupe. "We lived in her home."

"She was white." Ram spoke at last, his voice quick and sharp. "We fell in love. She's dead. I can't talk about her now."

Kenleth sat playing with his crystal tetrahedron while we talked. Lights flashed in it, sometimes a shining hieroglyph, sometimes a shape that baffled me. Now and then an identical tetrahedron sprang from of one of its faces and vanished again, a second pyramid of golden light with some momentary image inside it. Once a chord of strange music pealed out, so loud it startled me, and I saw the tiny image of a woman's head, fair-haired and entirely human. She was singing to the music, the rhythm strange, her voice loud and clear. He pressed a point that muffled it to a whisper.

"Sorry," he said. "It surprised me."

Ram caught his breath, staring at the little image. Derek and Lupe leaned to see. The woman was young and very blonde. She looked much like Sheko in the colossi we had seen on Delta, almost like Celya Crail herself.

"Amazing!" Lupe turned to Derek. "Is she an Omegan?"

"Maybe." He shook his unkempt head. "More likely an Omegan creation, engineered to populate the new worlds. Maybe a distant cousin of our own. I'd like to know."

Kenleth pressed another point, and the image was gone.

"A holographic projector?" Derek took it, squinted at it, tried the points. Nothing happened. "We saw a rack of things like it in the octagon." He grinned at Kenleth. "I hope you learn to work it."

"We've seen a thousand artifacts we didn't understand." Lupe nodded. "Enough to fill a museum if we could get them back to Earth. Enough to keep a hundred scholars busy for the next hundred years."

I wondered if we could ever get back to Earth with anything at all.

Derek offered his juleps again. Ram took one and sat sipping it slowly, staring at Kenleth and his toy; thinking of Celya, I imagined. I declined the julep and asked them to say more about the Omegans and Planet Alpha.

"It gets me. That black sky with no sun. The frozen air. The dead city. Earth so far away. I feel—feel like I was lost in Dante's hell."

"So did we. Lost in Little Mama's hell."

Derek nodded at the robot still at the air-lock door. It stood rigidly motionless, but its eye disks seemed to follow when he moved. A slow pulse of dim green and orange light beat from its head down through the crystal bits that made its body.

"The cybroids gave us rough times. They guard the gates. We had to pass tests to convince them we're human. Lupe was there first, of course. She helped me through."

"Stiff tests," Lupe said. "But the cybroids were never vicious. And I had a bit of good luck. The bad luck of an Arab who died a thousand years ago, back when he must have been carrying Islam across North Africa. He blundered on the Sahara gate, and a hopper picked him up. He flunked the tests and never got beyond Beta, but he left useful clues for me."

"Poor guy." Derek grinned. "He must have thought they had him in his Moslem hell."

"I found a few useful items in the octagon," she went on. "It's hard to be sure how they got there. I imagine his disciples could have made the Sahara gate a sort of shrine to him and left offerings the hoppers picked up. There were weapons, a few gold coins, an ancient manuscript of the Koran that a true believer would die for. The cybroids learned a little Arabic in the course of his interrogation, and they don't forget. I have a smattering of Arabic, enough to help me get past the hurdles."

"Enough to get us here to Alpha, just a few weeks ago." Derek shook his head in awe. "The sky's a wonderland! I wish we had a telescope. The seeing would be splendid."

He saw me shiver.

"It's no tropic paradise." He grinned as if amused at me. "That's because we're outside the galaxy. Outside a globular cluster. I think our Milky Way is hidden behind it. It's probably older, formed before the galaxy was. Not the best place for life to begin, because the cluster stars are poor in the heavy elements it needs, yet Omegan life was born here."

"Here?" Ram turned to stare at him. "On this dead planet?"

"It's been a graveyard for the last few hundred million years." Derek nodded. "The tomb of the Omegans. But it was somewhere in the cluster once, with suns enough to warm it."

"How did it get out here?"

"It must have been ejected." Derek paused to gaze at Kenleth, who had laid his magic toy aside and moved to snuggle up to Lupe. "Stars are crowded in a cluster. Their chaotic gravitational forces can toss a planet out."

"And cold killed its people?"

"Not the Omegans." He shook his head. "Rather, I think it must have forced their evolution. We don't know what they knew or remembered, but their history could have made an epic. They had to change with the changes in their world. They invented the science and the high technology that kept them alive—and finally let them send the cybroids out to explore the galaxy and build the trilithons."

He sighed and shook his head. "I'm sorry they died."

"What killed them?" Ram stared at him. "After they'd hung on so long?"

"We hope to find the answer here. Or maybe out in the old city, if we can ever get back to Earth and return with a team and equipment to begin the excavation."

"I hope to!" Lupe's lean face lit. "I've spent my life digging for our own prehistory. In Asia, Chile, Kenya, New Mexico. But Omega City! It's an incredible treasure! Whole buildings there under the frozen air that look still intact. Who knows what we can uncover?"

"A wild dream." Derek grinned and shook his head at her. "Imagine the problems of working there. Maybe a billion light-years from Earth, in high vacuum at absolute zero."

"Problems enough." She nodded. "But I believe the Omegans left us solutions, if we can just learn a little of what they knew."

"A great game." He shrugged, laughing at her. "If we can learn the rules. We'd be gods. We might make ourselves immortal. We might restore the Grand Dominion. We might make ourselves the lords of Earth and turn it into a real utopia."

"We dream." She smiled at him fondly, with a wry little quirk of her lips. "We do collide with awkward realities, but the hopes and visions keep us going. And what we're learning is wonderful enough."

"I've still got questions." Ram frowned. "If the Omegans were really immortal, how come they're dead?"

"That is a paradox." Derek nodded soberly. "But look at the logic of it. Immortals can't afford to replicate themselves. Their progeny would supplant them. They have to stop reproduction. I think the Omegans conquered death. I think that did them in."

"Tell me how."

"If you want a guess, perhaps they'd lived as long as they wanted to. The cold hadn't hurt them. Their cybroids had found warmer worlds where they might have gone. Even out to Earth if they found it fit for them. They chose to stay, chose to die. That's just my guess. If they left any records of the reasons why, we haven't read them."

He shrugged and grinned at Lupe.

"If they'd learned everything and done everything, perhaps

they were simply bored with everything and found no reason to go on. Or maybe—" He stopped to study Kenleth, who was absorbed again with the images and symbols flickering in his crystal pyramid. "Or maybe they are still alive in us,"

Ram blinked and his eyebrows lifted.

"We are their children," he said. "We know they were skilled genetic engineers. We know the cybroids picked up prehuman hominids and brought Homo sapiens back to Earth. You've had a glimpse of the new arrivals, there in the shadow of Kilimanjaro. I think the Omegans left their own genes in us."

Ram stared, shaking his head.

"The answer to an old question in human evolution." Lupe nodded. "Early hominids had small skulls. The sudden enlargement of the brain has been a puzzle. Maybe the Omegan genetic engineers enlarged the human skull to make room for gifts of theirs that our first forebears had never needed. Language, art, abstract thought. We may be the new Omegans."

CHAPTER
36

"So much we'll never know!" Derek's shoulders sagged to a weary shrug. "Not if we could work here another hundred years."

"But we're learning fast." Lupe was more cheerful. "The Omegans may be dead, but the cybroids are still with us and we're on the road to wonderland. I think the cone above our heads is an interstellar signal tower in instant touch with all the trilithons. It must have been the nerve net of the Grand Dominion."

"Guesswork!" Looking out at the mosaic riddles on the tunnel wall, Derek shook his head. "Chicken tracks! We've tried, but we'd get more out of the omens on the entrails of a goat."

"It's frustrating." Lupe nodded. "Sometimes we fail, but we've got to look at what we have. The Omegans knew the Grand Dominion might not be eternal, but they saw farther. They stored the records of their culture here, a gift to whatever future they hoped for. Here outside the galaxy, the planet's a deep freeze that ought to be perpetual. A fabulous bonanza."

"If we can get at it." Derek stared out at the riddles on the wall and turned at last with a thoughtful nod for Ram. "There are tunnels filled with what must be libraries and museums. Enormous halls filled with artifacts that stump us. Miles of mosaic print we can't read. The whole place is what old Egypt was before Young and Champollion deciphered the hieroglyphics on the Rosetta Stone." Behind the unkempt beard, his face set tight. "We've found no Rosetta Stone."

"But we've just begun," Lupe said. "The job took them a good many years. Let's look at the site for a hint of all we hope to find."

Derek raised his hand to signal the robot, which was waiting at the air lock like a human helper. It made no sound, but its eye disks flickered and the pulse of light quickened through its limbs. Moving with a swift economy of action, it uncoupled the crawlers.

Leaving ours there in the dome, Derek drove us farther down the corkscrew curves. Huge yellow glyphs blazed out of a spot on the wall ahead, changed slowly to others in blue, changed and changed again, faster and faster until they became a shimmering sun. They winked out, and the same sequence began again. Beyond it, a ragged patch rippled with waves of rainbow light in a way that hurt my eyes and left me giddy.

"Look at that." He stopped the crawler to grin at me. "It's driving me crazy."

"It's a tough nut to crack." Lupe nodded in grave agreement. "I'm not even sure we have the right senses to get the full signals. Or the minds to read them if we did. Our brains were shaped to make specific responses to specific challenges in our own environment. To find food, defend territory, defeat rivals, win mates, interact with others."

"We can do a lot more," Derek said. "Do higher math or write symphonic music or build the Hubble telescope. But we aren't Omegans. Evolving in their own very different environment, they had to cope with another set of challenges. They must have had different brains. If that's a message for us, we haven't got a clue to what it is."

He gestured at the mosaics we were passing.

"More chicken tracks. Lupe says they have to be symbolic of what the Omegans knew and felt and believed, but we simply weren't evolved to grasp them. We'll never think like the Omegans did."

He sighed again and drove us on. Those perplexing images gave way to panel after panel that shone with lines of symbols like those in Ram's e-book. Some of them had graceful flourishes that reminded me of Arabic, but they flickered in a way that made my head ache.

"That's their writing." Derek frowned. "A code without a key."

"But we can look for repeated patterns." Lupe made him stop the crawler and pointed to a green-lettered panel with a line below it set in tiny ruby-colored stones. "See those symbols in red? The text is in sections, separated by breaks like that. Each one has that sort of centered heading. Just maybe, those repeated symbols could be chapter numbers."

"They are." Kenleth looked up from his toy. "That's number two hundred and seven in Omegan. I think it would be more the way we count. The Omegans count to eleven before they come to ten."

"So they used base twelve?" Derek stared at him. "Instead of base ten."

"Kenleth!" Lupe blinked. "How do you know?"

"I'm taking lessons." He held up the crystal tetrahedron.

"I've learned the numbers. I've begun to get words. Water sounds like *scheeth,* though I can't say it quite right. A river is *en-scheeth.* A sea is *ru-scheeth.*"

"That's amazing!" Lupe hugged him and leaned to look for herself into the crystal pyramid. "If you've found a Rosetta Stone—" She hugged him closer. "You're a hero!"

He beamed at her, tears of joy gleaming in his eyes.

She and Derek were instantly ecstatic, the secrets of Omega almost in their grasp. Eagerly, they tried the tetrahedron themselves, but had to give it up.

"We humans are born with a special gift for language that works while we are children," Derek said. "A sort of pattern for grammar, ready for us to fill in the blanks as we learn."

"A gift from the Omegans, I imagine," Lupe said. "And Kenleth still has it."

They began to study with him, copying the glyphs, taking notes, debating rules of Omegan grammar. They kept the robot busy, sending it outside with a sort of video camera to get pictures and collect artifacts. They invented a jargon of their own to discuss every clue to Omegan science and history.

I rejoiced in their delight, but it was hard for me to share. Even coupled together, the two crawlers gave us a very tiny living space. We had room enough to sit, to eat, to sleep, but not much else. I felt shut in, cramped, and useless.

Ram sat alone for hour after hour, brooding, I thought, over all he had lost. Kenleth was restless as a monkey in a cage. He roved every nook of the crawlers and tested every gadget, but always came back to huddle over the tetrahedron, watching the flickering enigmas inside it, listening to the strange heads that sprang out of it, learning alien phonemes.

For me, the confinement became intolerable. I had nothing
at all to do. The effects of the fever were still in me, and I could
never shake off my dread of the eternal bitter night that held us
in prison. I longed for change, for space, sunlight, people, Earth,
my Eastern friends and colleagues, my old house in Portales.

I couldn't help asking when we might go home.

"Don't think about it!" Lupe seemed shocked. "This is too
exciting. We've found a key to dreamland. We can't quit now."

"Look at it, Will." Derek begged me, very soberly. "Of
course we're anxious to get back with all our news, but we
wouldn't be welcome now. What we're finding would upset too
many applecarts. Ten thousand experts in everything from ar-
chaeology to zoology would unite to defend their territories.

"Without evidence they can't deny, they'd laugh us off the
Earth. We'll have to have artifacts, photos. Maybe robots. Or a
giant hopper! One of them ought to persuade anybody." He
grinned at the thought, and grew grave again. "Don't rush us.
Getting solid proof enough together will take time. We can't afford to fail."

I sat there dumb, blinking at them, tears blurring my vision.
I loved them. The Four Horsemen. We'd worked and played together half our lives, even before we found the Sahara gate. I
didn't want to leave them, yet I had to get away.

"You're disappointed, Will?" Lupe gave me a searching look.
"You really want to go?"

My throat aching, I felt more than I could try to say.

"We could send the two of you." Derek turned to Ram. "If
you want to go. If you can learn to work the cybroids and the
trilithons."

"Can I go?" Kenleth appealed eagerly to me. "Will you take
me?"

I'd thought of that. I'd come to love him, the child I'd never had. Life on Earth would be lonely if I did get back alone. Awkward, too, with so much I couldn't try to explain. I would need him, miss him terribly.

I'd weighed the possibilities. He would be illegal, illegal in a way the feds could never figure out, but illegals are common in New Mexico. Perhaps I could adopt him. Put him through school. Watch him play in Little League. Help him find his place on Earth. It could be a great adventure for him, a world as new as his had been for us.

"Of course," I told him. "I'll love to have you with me."

"Thank you!" He came to put his arms around me. "I'd love to see your world."

Lupe looked at Derek and shook her head. Half a minute passed before she caught her breath and spoke.

"Kenleth, we need you here to help us learn the Omegan language. Your tetrahedron is our key to all the mysteries of Omegan science and history. Without it, we could fail. Won't you please stay, long enough at least to put us on the road?"

He wiped his eyes and looked at me. I had to nod.

"If they need you, I think you ought to stay."

"Then I will." His voice was choked, and he had to wipe his eyes again. "But I'll always love you, Ty Will." He put his quivering arm around me and looked at Ram. "I'll miss you, too, Ty Ram, if you go. I hope you'll both be happy back on Earth."

"I've been thinking."

Ram stood up to face us with an expression of austere decision I had never seen before. Muscular and tall, the crown of worlds shining on his forehead, he was suddenly magnificent, a reminder of the colossal figures of Anak we had seen on the Delta.

"Thinking a lot." His voice seemed deeper, and I heard a sudden ring of confidence. "I don't belong here. There's nothing for me on Earth. I had a bad time on Delta. I guess I ran away, but now I see where I belong."

He looked at Derek.

"Can you send me back there?"

Derek frowned and slowly nodded. "If you really want to go."

"My duty." Absently, Ram fingered the glowing crown of worlds. "We left it in a bloody mess. If I can help clean it up, that's what I was meant to do."

"And rebuild the Grand Dominion?" Lupe's voice lifted. "If you can do it."

"A very tall order." Very gravely, he shrugged. "Maybe too tall to talk about. But the killer virus left a vacuum. Chaos will be coming in to fill it, unless—" He stopped to gaze at Kenleth and the tetrahedron. "Perhaps I can begin something better. I've got to do what I can."

CHAPTER
37

Leaving Kenleth and my fellow Horsemen left an ache of loss, but I had to go. I'd suffered too many shocks of strangeness and felt too sick of my own helpless idleness in the cramped little crawler. Too long here beneath Omega's deadly cold and eternal night, I wanted the warm sun of Earth, my quiet home town, the peace of the old book-walled study that had been my father's office.

I had to go alone. Though the weakness of the virus was still in me, my own spirits rose as we planned the trip. Ram helped invent a harmless tale for me to tell. Lupe offered to pack a collection of Omegan artifacts to help me prove my story.

"You'll be getting back with no passport," Derek reminded me. "With no money and nothing to prove who you are."

He found a handful of what he thought were Omegan coins, heavy little metal doughnuts ringed with Omegan script. They looked like gold. In time to come they might be priceless, but not until our story could be revealed. I left them with him.

When I was ready, they gathered at the air lock to say good-bye. Derek and Ram shook my hand. Lupe hugged and kissed me. Kenleth clung a long time to me, and sobbed a promise to come to stay with me down on Earth if ever he was able.

They all stood waving as I hoisted my worn backpack and turned to the air lock. Sudden emotion overwhelmed me. My voice broke as I tried to call a last farewell. My heart was thumping. I felt unsteady on my feet. My vision blurred. Perhaps I stumbled.

"Will?" Lupe looked at me sharply. "You're pale. Do you feel well? Are you really able to go?"

"I'm okay." I had to catch a breath. "Just—just anxious. It's a long way to Earth. I don't know what to expect on the way."

The silent robot stood waiting at the lock, a tall man-shape made of crystal bits. It reached a glittering hand to assist me through the door, but Lupe called me back.

"I'm concerned for you, Will. Don't give us up. We'll be coming. While you wait, there's one thing you can do that ought to keep your hopes up. When you feel able, you might look for influences the Omegan visits may have left on Earth."

"Influences?" That confused me. "What influences could be possible?"

"They are more than possible." Her serious tone surprised me. "The Omegans or their robot proxies were there. They explored the planet and built the trilithon. They abducted prehumans and brought back Homo sapiens. They had to leave traces."

Perhaps I blinked or shook my head.

"There's the Salisbury Stonehenge. Its builders couldn't have known the actual trilithon, but the design must reflect some racial memory. Myth, legend, likely religion. The trilithon can't be mere coincidence. There could be clues in all the other pre-historic megalithic architecture in Europe, Egypt, and Peru. But we carry more convincing evidence in ourselves."

"Our Omegan genes," Derek said. "Don't forget we're part Omegan."

"There's a lot to think about." She spoke faster, conviction in her voice. "That Omegan legacy explains our double nature. Evolution in the jungle selected traits essential for the survival of little family groups. They served our prehuman forebears well enough, but they've become hazards to civilized society. Jealousy, greed, violent aggression. The Omegan genetic engineers overlaid them with the best of themselves. Altruism, love of our fellow beings, love of art and beauty. Our two selves are always in conflict. We enact laws to restrain the primal instincts, teach ethics and follow religious leaders to find and liberate our Omegan selves."

Listening with a puzzled frown, Kenleth had come beside me.

"I'm sorry, Will." She gave me an apologetic shrug. "I didn't mean to preach, but I thought it might keep your spirits up to know the future we hope for. Now with Kenleth's help we can learn Omegan history and rewrite human history. We've suffered too many ages of ignorance and error. It should make a difference to us back on Earth to know who we are. It should transform the world. That's our vision. Don't let yourself forget it."

The robot was waiting. Awed and humbled by the vision, I promised to remember and tried to say good-bye again. My voice broke. Kenleth looked up at me, tears in his eyes. "I love you, Ty Will. You must be brave."

My own eyes blurred, I turned and let the robot help me stumble into the lock. Efficient and well instructed, it drove me back up the corkscrew tunnel, past the glistening mosaics I would never see again, out into Alpha's perpetually frigid night. I had one last glimpse of the cluster's clotted stars rising over that flat white waste of frozen air before the crawler lurched to a different gravity.

And something hit me. The crawler seemed to spin. I remember a flash of blinding sunlight, a pang of sickness at the pit of my stomach, another instant of darkness. I'd hoped to see that hollow in the dune where we had found the buried Sahara trilithon. Instead, I came awake slowly, lying alone on a bed in a small bare room that had high, pale green walls.

At first my mind was empty, without awareness of whom or where I was or any urge to know. Bits of memory came, shadow shapes that took focus: the trilithons, the worlds we'd seen, Lupe's grand vision of a better future for the world, Kenleth, blinking at his tears and calling his quavery farewell.

I had no strength at first, no desire to move, but I turned my head at last to look around the room. I found an open door on one side, a wide window on the other. Beyond a strip of white pavement, a velvet lawn sloped down to an arm of blue water ruffled with whitecaps. Smooth hills rose beyond the water, and far mountains hazed with distance.

All of it looked Earthlike for a moment, until its strangeness struck me. All the land was velvet smooth, velvet green. I saw no trees, no buildings, no creatures, nothing alive. Two bright suns were rising into a clear blue sky. This was nowhere I had ever been.

"Ty Stone?" I'd had too many shocks of wonder, and the strangeness of those words chilled me. "You wake?"

The voice was Derek's, but the speaker was a grotesque caricature, built of little metal and crystal bits. It stood at the foot of the bed, glints of rainbow light pulsing slowly through its thousand facets.

"You are awake." Its tone turned positive. "Tyba Vargas coming."

Mocking Derek's swinging stride, it left the room. Lupe bustled in. The actual human Lupe. I lay blinking at her, my eyes filled with tears of relief. In a neat white jacket, with a stethoscope hung over her shoulder, she might almost have been a physician back at home.

"Will?" She gave me a brown grin. "*Com' está?*

"I don't—don't know." My voice was a rusty whisper. "What happened to me?"

"Heart failure," she said. "A latent effect of the virus. You're a lucky dog that it hit you when it did. Back at home you'd be dead. The robots have had millennia of experience with humans as well as Omegans, and they don't forget."

I lay there trying to digest what she said and finally tried to ask where we were. My voice was only a croak, and she gave me a glass of water.

"We call it Theta," she said. "The eighth Earthlike planet the Omegans reached. We're in a research station they set up here. They never tried to terraform or settle it because they respected its native life. An odd sort of life. I hope we can come back to see more of it when we're through on Alpha."

"You say it's odd?"

"You see that green stuff?" She nodded at the window. "It covers the ground like skin, eats whatever falls on it. Exists only here in the tropics, I think. The survey team left maps and specimens and research reports about the rest of the planet that I hope we'll be able to read."

"Before we go home?" I asked her. "How long will it take?"

Overcome with a tidal wave of sleep, I didn't hear whatever she said.

She must have been impatient to get back to Derek and the mysteries of Omega, but she stayed until she was sure of my recovery. Making the most of her time, she made notes and videos of everything she found at the station and what she could of the world outside.

"Derek will be excited with the double sun," she said. "And Theta itself will be a bonanza for some future science team. I can't read anything, but there are maps and photos and specimens. Other areas must have other sorts of life biologists will have to see."

My strength came back, and a fresh sense of well-being. A day came when she said she had to go.

"Derek needs me more than you do." She kissed me again. "We'll follow you home as soon as we can."

"To remake the world?"

"Our vision." She shrugged. "Sometimes it seems too great to hope for, but we'll do the best we can."

My watch was gone. I don't know how long I was there alone with the robot. Now and then I ventured into other sections of the station, a maze of spaces that I thought were labs or workshops or the quarters of the vanished research team, but there was nothing that made much sense to me.

More often I walked outside, under the double sun. I found the trilithon behind the station, huge square pillars of black granite towering high, looking as new as when it was just erected. I learned to stay on the white pavement. Once when I stepped onto the green velvet land cover, a patch of it turned black and flapped to grip my foot until the robot dragged me free.

The crawler stood near the trilithon. I asked the robot when it could take me on to Earth.

"You wait." It paused, growing taller and more erect, morphing into a grotesque copy of Ram, even to bright sparks for the crown of worlds on the forehead. "Wait for Ty Chenji."

Anxiously, I waited. Next day the robot led me out past our crawler to the trilithon. One moment I saw only the green velvet slope beyond the pillars. Another instant and there was another crawler sliding toward me. The lock opened. Ram climbed out. Kenleth came after him and ran to me.

"Ty Will!" He hugged me. "Are you okay?"

For a moment I wasn't sure. The shock of surprise and delight was nearly too much. With no words to say, I stood blinking at them. Kenleth hugged me. Ram grinned and gripped my hand.

"We've had enough of Alpha." His shoulders hunched to a bitter shrug. "Lupe and Derek love it, but I still get chills when I think about that everlasting darkness and the frozen air. Kenleth had to stay till they learned to operate the tetrahedron, but we left when we could."

"You're coming back to Earth?"

"With a stop on Delta." He nodded, and I saw a shadow on his face. "I want to look up White Water, if we can find him. I'd like to know if Norlan survived the virus, if there's any way to tell."

"But you are coming home?"

His lips set, he took moment to nod.

"Lupe thought I ought to stay on Delta. Derek wanted to send a team of robots to help me try to restore some kind of civilization. They said it's what I was born to do. But now—"

His voice trailed off. I glanced at his forehead. The fine white dots of the crown of worlds still shone faintly, even under the double sun. He saw my glance and shook his head again.

"I can't." He pulled his shoulders straight. "With Celya dead, I've got no place there. I've got to find another life to live. Remember the girl I met at the Leakey Museum, back in Nairobi? We had a great time together. She was fighting AIDS. When Derek and Lupe get back they should bring Omegan science that could wipe it out. We made no commitments, but I know where she's employed. I'll try to look her up."

He shrugged again. I thought he wasn't very happy.

"That's the best thing I can do."

They stayed there an hour, walking around the station and staring off across the green horizons. Ram made a pinhole in a scrap of plastic to show Kenleth an image of the double sun, but he didn't want to go inside the building.

"I've seen too many Omegan mysteries," he said. "They've begun to hurt my head."

We went on to Delta. Climbing after him into the crawler, I asked about our destination there.

"That trilithon above the Blood River? Or the one on Mount Anak?"

"Neither. The robots can open temporary gates anywhere they have good coordinates. They can set us down in Periclaw."

The robot had good coordinates. It set the crawler down and opened the lock. We stepped out on the Fort Blood drill field, black cannon muzzles jutting over our heads. The wind had a chilly bite, and I shivered in the shadow of the huge black blocks in the walls that towered around us. I saw no trilithon.

"They're only markers," Ram said. "The actual gates are magnetic fields that stretch between the planets."

I caught a faint but evil scent on the wind, a thin bitter reek of death and old decay. Ram made a face, and I was glad to follow him back into the crawler. He gave directions and the robot drove us out through the white stone palaces of Periclaw. Still imposing, they were silent, empty, dead. I saw birds in the sky and weeds growing out of mud in the gutters, but nothing else alive.

"It feels haunted." Ram seemed to shiver. "Haunted by all that died here."

He guided the robot to the old Crail mansion. The Blood still flowed wide and brown around it, the far banks dark green with returning jungle, but the mansion had the look of ruin, the lawn grown wild and littered with broken tree limbs, the gate knocked down, perhaps by venturesome vandals. We left the robot in the crawler and walked to the door. Ram rapped with the heavy brass knocker. We waited till I felt sure the house was empty, but at last the door swung open.

I saw a young woman and heard Ram cry out.

"Celya! Celya?"

CHAPTER 38

Of course she was not Celya, but the resemblance startled me. Standing in the open door, she had Celya's fair face and platinum hair. She had the same fluid flow of expression when she peered in a puzzled way at Ram and then at me,

"I had a sister Celya." She had her sister's voice. "I believe she died in the blood pandemic. I am Delya Crail." She looked sharply back at Ram. "You knew Celya?"

Ram nodded and caught his breath to speak, but she had turned away, staring past us in wonder at the crawler and the robot waiting at the lock, the sun glinting on its thousand polished facets.

"What—" She gasped and looked back at me. "What's that?"

"Our vehicle," I said.

"Vehicle?" She gazed at it again. "You came here in that?" She shook her head and turned to blink at me. "Who are you? Where did you come from?"

"From off this planet."

She gaped in disbelief, and I tried to tell our story. Her green-gray eyes narrowed as I spoke. Her expressions changed from scorn to shock and dread. She shrank away from me. I thought for a moment that she was about to go back inside and shut the door. But then she looked past us again, at the crawler and the motionless robot.

"Celya wrote me." She spoke slowly, frowning at Ram and then at me. "She wrote about two strangers who told a ridiculous tale that they had come down out of the sky. A white magician and a black that claimed to be a son of the black god Anak."

"No." Ram's protest was a husky whisper. "Nothing like that."

Lips set tight, she drew farther from us.

"There were stories about them before the ships stopped coming." She seemed not to hear him. "Stories that they had incited the slave rebellion. That they had brought the blood pandemic." Her tone turned bitter. "They killed my sister!"

Glaring at us, she brushed a wisp of that fair hair from her forehead. I saw a mark it had hidden. A little patch of golden freckle had the pattern of the crown of worlds. Ram caught his breath and stood scowling at it.

"Please!" I begged her. "You don't know the facts. If you'll let us explain—"

"I don't know what you are." Her voice turned harsh. "I don't want to know."

She went back in the house and shut the door in our faces. Ram strode grimly back toward the crawler. I followed. The robot stepped aside to let us climb in, but Ram stopped outside and turned to me. He seemed dazed, uncertain of anything.

"You saw that mark?"

"I saw," I said. "I don't know what to make of it."

He glanced back at the house and his face drew harder.

"I—" He caught his breath. "I don't want to be superstitious, but I don't like what I don't understand. Remember the myth? Sheko murdered Anak. You see how this woman hates me. I don't want a replay. Let's get off the planet while we can."

I felt anxious to get back on Earth, but I had seen no real future there for him. And here was Celya's sister, almost her double, with a birthmark almost identical to his! That left me almost as shaken as he seemed to be, but I groped for logic.

"Don't be too hasty," I told him. "Let's take a minute to think about it. Lupe talked to me about the birthmark back at the hospital. She and Derek have a reasonable scenario."

"Reasonable?" He seemed to shiver. "It's too—too uncanny."

"It seems so to me," I said. "But nothing's uncanny to Derek and Lupe. With Kenleth's help, they've begun to decode scraps of Omegan history. Not yet much, but enough to let them guess about the marks."

"So?" He blinked in doubt.

"Here's their guess," I said. "The Omegan engineers must have created several human species that would preserve something of themselves. Sometimes they failed to get the right balance of prehuman and Omegan traits. Lupe thinks they were testing different versions on different planets. That must have taken time. She thinks they died in the middle of the tests, with that terrible war still going on. The work wasn't finished. The people we've met here are some of the survivors. So are we back on Earth, she said, left to make the best of what we are."

"Could be." He shrugged, but still he wore a look of dread. "But what about the marks? On the Hotlan gods. On my Little Mama. On me and now Delya Crail. Birthmarks are not hereditary." He made a bitter face. "I don't like it."

"Lupe said Derek has a notion. He believes the birthmarks were genetic markers, intended to identify one of the experimental strains. We've got no way to know, but that seems possible to me."

"Not to me," he muttered.

Kenleth had been watching from the crawler door.

"Can we go on to see the Earth?" he called. "The robot says it's time to go."

It turned to us, sunlight shimmering on its metal and crystal bits, and spoke in a voice that might have been Kenleth's

"Flight window about to close," it said. "Departure required within twenty-seven minutes, your time."

"I'm ready." Ram seemed relieved. "I want to be human again. Not some weird genetic freak. Not the puppet of any Omegan engineer that died forty thousand years ago."

He was on the folding steps, climbing in, when I heard a shout from the house and saw White Water running toward us.

"Wait a minute!" he yelled. "Tyba Crail didn't know you. She wants you to come inside."

"I don't know." Ram blinked uncertainly at me. "I've had too much of her, but White Water—he's a man I learned to trust."

He turned to ask the robot about the next open window.

"Options are uncertain," it told him. "Planet Earth is remote, the routes seldom tested. Stars drift with time. Unused flight congruences may be lost. Coordinates for another flight must be confirmed."

"Then confirm them."

White Water came on to meet us. In a faded uniform jacket with a gold button on the breast, he looked unchanged—a spry and wiry little man, his weatherbeaten face dark with the black blood that had kept him alive.

"Ty Chenji. Ty Stone." He bowed and moved his hands in the Hotlan greeting. "I am happy to see you back. Tyba Crail will see you if you will come in."

"Maybe." Ram shrugged uncertainly, but he returned the gesture of greeting and asked White Water how he was.

"Riding the waves the way I always did." He waved his arms as if to welcome a brighter future. "Life's coming back to the river. I'm working now for Tyba Crail."

"She was on Norlan?" I asked. "And the plague never got there?"

"Thanks to all the captains who obeyed orders to scuttle the refugee ships." He nodded, with a bleak grimace. "It's just lately that anybody came back to find if anybody survived. She was on the first ship to get here. A lady with guts. You'll like her when you get to know her."

He ignored Ram's scowl of doubt.

"You'll be glad to meet the Norlan officials. They're already negotiating with Toron and the Elders. I think they'll agree to most of what you and Toron were asking for. Equal rights and no more slavery."

"Good," Ram muttered. "Not that it matters to me. Not now."

"It matters to us," he said. "Maybe more to the Norlanders. They did survive, but they were hit hard. Enough to tell them how much they need us. But come on in. Tyba Crail is waiting."

We followed him back to the house and found Delya Crail waiting at the door. Her face pale and set, she stood half a minute peering at Ram and gave him a stiffly formal bow. Silently, she led us down the hall. We sat at a table in a small alcove at the end of the big kitchen.

"Oh!"

I heard Kenleth's soft cry and saw him staring. He had seen

the little ceramic that had been his mother's, sitting on the table. The figures of Anak and Sheko, seated on their golden throne. Ram and Delya peered at it and turned to frown at each other. Half a silent minute passed before she spoke.

"Ty Chenji," she asked, her voice hushed. "Will you take off your cap?"

He was wearing a black beret that he'd found in that octagon on Beta. He shrugged and took it off. The crown of worlds shone with a soft golden glow. Her features hardened.

"So that's who you really are?" The question was quietly accusing. "The son of Anak."

He gave her a quick little grin. "If you are Sheko's daughter."

She stiffened as if in anger, but in a moment she relaxed.

"A Hotman myth. I heard it from a maid when she'd seen this." She gestured at her own golden freckle. "It never bothered me."

The old black cook limped into the room with glasses on a tray and a bottle of Crail's good wine. Delya filled the glasses. Ram took a sip, gave her a grave little smile, and raised his glass in a sort of greeting.

"Ty White Water says you just got here?"

"Two weeks ago. He saw the ship and came down the channel to guide us to the harbor. I had to come!" Her words flowed out in a sudden torrent. "The war killed the colony and left us desperate. A dreadful time. Most of us lost somebody here. Lost investments ruined us all. Food imports were cut off. What was left had to be rationed."

For a moment she had Celya's look of bleak endurance in her last days, but then her face softened and she turned with a pale smile for White Water.

"I was lucky to find him."

"The plague?" Ram asked her. "Are you safe here?"

"I hope we are." She nodded. "The doctors think we are."

"The pathogen must have died out when no more victims were left to carry it," White Water said. "But it left us with trouble enough."

"I'd be lost without him." She nodded at him and made a somber face. "You've seen what's left? The total devastation. When I saw the city, I wanted to get back on the ship, but we're trying to restore what we can."

"It's hard, but we've begun." He nodded soberly. "The Norlanders see how much their lives depended on the colony. Toron and his people know what Norlan can give them. Its civilization, science, technology. The ship's still anchored in the harbor. They're still negotiating. The Norlanders will abolish slavery, promise equal rights for Hotmen."

"Nobody will be coming back without guarantees for us," Delya said. "Security and property rights. We're offering plans."

White Water nodded. "The Crail bank can be reopened. "Maybe as the Hotlan National, if Hotlan becomes a nation. There'll be a new currency, based on labor value. We need it to pay the liberated slaves who are willing to come back out of the jungle. A lot of them should be. They're dislocated by the war, without much food or anything else. With fair pay, I think we can make them happy back at work."

The old cook seemed happy enough. Cheerfully, he made a good dinner for us out of the kitchen garden he had grown in the backyard. White Water had found a few more of the Crail house servants living in the jungle along the riverbank. The mansion was the only home they had known. Seeming glad to be back, paid by scrip to be redeemed when the new bank opened, they were already cleaning the house and clearing fallen branches and rubbish off the neglected lawns.

Kenleth and I were there almost a week, sleeping in the upstairs room that had been our jail. The robot waited in the crawler that still stood in front of the house. Ram spent most of his time with White Water and Delya, involved, in spite of himself, in their plans for the Hotlan future.

One night I heard drum talk, and next day a dugout came down the river carrying Toron in his bright-colored tribal regalia, accompanied by a small black man in the sober garb of the Elderhood. White Water took Ram and Delya down to welcome them aboard his launch and carried them down to confer with the Norlan officials on the steamer.

Kenleth went down to visit the paddlers waiting in the dugout, and came back looking troubled.

"They're from somewhere up the Black River," he told me. "Far up north. They speak a language I couldn't really understand, but they hate Norlanders. They won't come ashore."

He had the cook fill a basket with fruit to give them but failed again to win any friends. The sun had set before the launch came back up the river. Toron and the Elder got in the dugout and it pulled away. I saw Delya smile at Ram when he offered to help her off the launch. They had begun to get along, but he wore a sober expression.

"We've struck a snag." He frowned when I asked how the talks had gone. "The Norlanders want a deal, but the Elders don't trust them."

"Ty Toron wants Ty Chenji to stay." Delya turned to him. "The Elders think you came to liberate the slaves. They do trust you. Everybody needs you here."

"If that's true."

He gave her a long, searching look. The black beret was off, and the crown shone faintly in the dusk. Her eyes fixed on it with a look I couldn't read. They both were silent for a time. He finally nodded. She smiled very gravely and he turned to me.

"Would you mind it, Will? I hate to send you back alone, but I'm really needed here."

"Ty Will, you won't be alone." Kenleth caught my arm. "I'll be with you if you'll take me."

I put my arm around him and told Ram I understood.

Kenleth was eager to see the Earth, yet he and Delya had warmed to each other. Next morning at breakfast she was asking him about his mother and his life at Hake's station. When she saw his solemn glance at the ceramic that had been his mother's, she gave it to him.

"Thank you, Tyba Crail." He gave her a formal bow. "You are very kind to me. But I can't take it." He tried to hand it back her. "It was Tyba Celya's."

"It's yours," she insisted. "Keep it to remember your mother." She turned to Ram and me. "Celya and I kept in touch but we never really knew each other. Our mother came home to visit her people in Glacier Bay before we were born. She took Celya with her back to Periclaw. She left me to be adopted by my aunt, her older sister, who wanted me because she had no children of her own." She smiled at Kenleth. "It means more to you than to me."

"Thank you again, Tyba Crail." Tears in his eyes, he took it and bowed again. "You are very generous and very beautiful. As beautiful as your sister. I love you."

Tears in her own eyes, Delya took him in her arms.

The drums talked again. Toron was coming back. White Water was taking him and Ram upriver to meet with more of the Elders and some other tribal leaders. Before they left, Delya wanted to see the country place where their parents and Celya died. They were in the kitchen that morning, packing a basket of food and wine for the trip.

"Ty Will!" Kenleth burst into the room. "The robot has a flight window open. We can go."

CHAPTER
39

We drove back through the empty avenues of Periclaw to the empty drill field at Fort Blood. I don't know what the robot did, but the ghost of a trilithon towered suddenly across the sky ahead. We went through it. The sky turned black. My ears clicked. The crawler pitched to the different gravity of Earth and slid down the cusp of that long brown dune in the Grand Erg Oriental.

I found a full moon rising over the square black tops of the twin megaliths, still jutting out of the sand a hundred yards behind us. Sandstorms had erased all traces of our camp in the hollow, but the ancient lake bed was still swept bare where Lupe had found that ancient waterhole with its buried bones of early life and those silicon slivers that must have come from some unlucky cybroid.

The crawler was built for all terrains, but slow. We were two nights and a day on our way out of the erg and on to the Gabès road. I had the robot leave us there, standing in the ditch beside it. Kenleth clung to my hand, excited but yet afraid, both of us shivering to a cold desert dawn. Watching the crawler turn and lumber back toward the erg, I felt suddenly a stranger on Earth, unprepared for what might come.

Kenleth seemed eager to know what everything was. Peering around the barren landscape behind us and date palms on the horizon ahead of us, he had a thousand new questions about Earth and my life here, about Tunis, about the roaring machines that ran past us faster than the crawler could move, leaving smoke and a stink in the air.

In spite of our raised arms, none of them stopped. The sun grew hot and I began to sweat, but my poker luck ran right. A tourist van screeched to a halt and backed to where we stood. A window opened. I heard a shout. My name!

A short bald man jumped out and ran grinning to meet me.

"Professor Stone! You are Professor Stone?"

His bare head was pink with·sunburn, but he wore dark glasses. I failed to recognize him till he took them off and reached to take my hand.

"Remember me? Ben Sanders. I was in you're your English 101 a dozen years ago. Somebody told me to inquire about your desert expedition."

He was now teaching history at an Arizona college and here on a field research expedition with a half a dozen students. Astonished to find us, he shaded his eyes for a sharp squint at Kenleth, and asked if we needed help. I told him we'd been waiting for a taxi that had failed to pick us up.

I told him I'd stayed in Tunis to look at the site of ancient Carthage and collect background for a seminar on Flaubert's *Salammbo*. He seemed to accept that, though he took a puzzled look at the odd garments we had found so many light-years away. He grinned at them.

"Dressing in Carthaginian style?"

I shrugged and left him to wonder about it. He turned to

frown at Kenleth, who was keeping very quiet. I said he was a homeless orphan I had found on a Tunis street. With no papers, a history we had to hide, and very little English, he promised to be a problem I hardly knew how to solve.

The van had empty seats. I sat beside Sanders all day, listening to the guide's lectures on Tunisian history. From his vague evasions to Sanders's questions, I suspected that he was inventing most of what he said about the Phoenicians and the Greeks, about Rome and Carthage, the Vandals and Venice, the Arabs and the Prophet, the French and General Rommel. The students took dutiful notes and trooped out with cameras to shoot every bit of ancient stonework where we stopped.

Though my sense of Earth was coming back, I felt that I'd been away for a lifetime. The city of Tunis was a jolt to me at first, almost as alien as Perielaw had been. Without Sanders's aid, we'd have been helpless. I said my pocket had been picked. Back at his hotel, he paid for my dinner and persuaded the clerk to let us register, even with no money and no passport.

Next morning he took us to a barber and then to shops where he put new shoes and clothing for us on his own credit card. Officials at the American embassy were harassed with terrorist threats, security concerns, and the problems of too many tourists, but they helped me get calls through to the university, my lawyer, and my bank.

My identity established and my lost plastic replaced, Kenleth was still a problem. Sanders expected me to abandon him. When I refused, he talked to his tour director. The director called people who had the right connections and an appetite for money. It took another day and a few thousand dollars, but they provided documentation for Kenleth, complete with an American entry visa.

We had a farewell breakfast next morning with Sanders and

his students. They were going on to Egypt to see the pyramids, the Aswan dam, and Luxor. I thanked him, repaid him, and bought air tickets to Lubbock.

Back in Portales without my companions, I had to improvise stories for newspapers, faculty friends, university officials and the campus cops, the state police and the district attorney, and all the anxious relatives. I kept to actual events until we had reached Tunisia and hired the chopper to take us out over the erg.

The chopper landed us, I said, at the site where Derek's radar had located what he thought were half-buried megaliths. I said we'd found no trace of them. A sandstorm caught us before the pilot returned to pick us up. When the winds died down and we could see again, we set out toward a far-off dune where we thought we saw the chopper waiting.

I said we never found it. Never got back to the camp where we had left our food and water. We wandered through the dunes all the burning day and tried to sleep that night. Alone when I woke, I blundered on until heat and thirst overcame me. I said I recalled nothing more until I woke lying in the ditch by the Gabès road and got a ride on a farm truck back into Tunis.

Most people seemed willing to accept the amnesia story. A few were critical. Derek's uncle Daniel was the harshest. He had posted a small fortune in rewards for information and gone twice to Tunis to make his own investigations. He'd looked up our pilot and hired him to fly back over the erg. They found no sign of our camp, located no second Stonehenge.

He'd been fond of Derek, and he suspected foul play. A lawyer himself and once an assistant district attorney, he kept probing like a prosecutor for all I said I had forgotten. Nothing satisfied him. He tried to interrogate Kenleth, who kept a blank face and said he didn't understand the questions. He grew angry and finally concluded, I think, that I'd damaged my mind with drugs.

Kenleth and I are now back in the old house my grandfather built, just a few blocks off the campus. My old faculty friends held a party to welcome me home, with drinks enough and no uncomfortable questions. The university has filled my empty slot with a brilliant young Victorian scholar. I've retired to a part-time position that gives me time to write. Next semester I'll be teaching a graduate seminar on Shakespeare's history plays.

Good neighbors had looked after the house and mowed the lawn. My bank kept the bills paid. The old brown brick is far less imposing than the Crail mansion, but Kenleth is happy in the room that used to be my mother's. He has learned more English, learned to ride a bike, made friends with the neighbor kids.

Some of them tried to torment him at first, for the color of his skin, his odd accent, his silence about where he came from. One day he came home with a black eye. He hadn't hurt anybody, he said, because he didn't want to make trouble for me. I told him to defend himself. He said the kids at Hake's station had taught him how to do it.

I was watching from the car the next day when he walked out to join a baseball game on a vacant lot. Three of the bullies left the game to meet him. I couldn't hear what was said, but the brief encounter left one of them flat on his back and the others in flight. They've since become friends and he's already earning a place on the team.

For his sake as much as my own, I'm still trying to keep the secret of the gate and the far worlds beyond it. The media and scientific skeptics would tear him apart if we tried to tell the truth. I'm going to adopt him. I want him to have a normal boyhood and a chance at a normal life.

I'm glad to have him with me here, the child I never had. Yet our old weekly poker nights have left an aching gap. Sometimes on moonless nights I stand out in my backyard and search the sky, trying to imagine Ram and Delya working to restore the Grand Dominion and Derek and Lupe still busy on that runaway planet out beyond the stardust of the Milky Way, recovering Omegan history.

The adventure is vivid in my memory. I find a kind of comfort in it. When I feel depressed by news of spreading terror here on Earth and the dread of a dark tide rising to overwhelm civilization, it cheers me to recall that we are the new Omegans, with that magnificent legacy waiting for us. We have survived the death of our first sun. Bad times may come, but surely we'll prevail.

I wish I'd brought some relic back. One of those Omegan coins, perhaps, or even a magic tetrahedron like Kenleth's. I spend restless nights dreaming that Derek and Lupe have returned, sometimes bringing a diamond-shining celluform robot to overwhelm the unbelievers. Ram is sometimes with them. Together again, we Four Horsemen could shake up the planet.

That can happen. I don't know when.

ABOUT THE AUTHOR

Hugo and Nebula Award winner Jack Williamson has been in the forefront of science fiction since his first published story appeared in 1928. Now in his seventy-seventh year as a published author, Williamson is the acclaimed author of such trailblazing science fiction as *The Legion of Space*, *The Humanoids*, and *The Legion of Time*. *The Oxford English Dictionary* credits Williamson with inventing the word "terraforming" (in *Seetee Ship*). His novel *Darker Than You Think* was a seminal work of fiction dealing with shape-changing when first published, and still ranks as a great achievement in horror. This and other horror works garnered Williamson a Bram Stoker Award for Lifetime Achievement. He was the second science fiction author (after Robert A. Heinlein) to be named Grand Master by the Science Fiction Writers of America. His recent works include *The Silicon Dagger*, *The Black Sun*, and *Terraforming Earth*. Part of the latter novel, published as "The Ultimate Earth," won both Hugo and Nebula Awards for best novella. His memoir, *Wonder's Child: My Life in Science Fiction*, won a Hugo Award for Best Nonfiction in 1984.

Williamson also has been active academically. One of the pioneers in the field of teaching science fiction as part of a university curriculum, he has taught since the 1950s, and is professor emeritus at Eastern New Mexico University. He lives and works in Portales, New Mexico.